OBJECTS
OF
AFFECTION

BY

Julie Cosgrave

ISBN: 1470164264
ISBN-13: 978-1470164263

The will to become that self which one truly is,
is indeed, the opposite of despair.

Soren Kierkegaard

PROLOGUE

Another polite and polished pair sidled past doing the theatre shuffle, crabwalking their backs and their bums past her nose, squeezing their way to the end of the pew.

Pauline looked down at her purse and then quickly up again as Richard slid in beside her. She shifted slightly to give him room and, rumps shuffled like padded dominoes all along the pew. Brightly dressed wedding guests fluttered a moment, like startled birds murmuring little trills of discomposure, then fell silent.

She closed her eyes. The church was mute, quiet with the sudden stillness of one hundred people momentarily suspended from their Saturday lives. A peaceful heaviness seemed to press down on them; the weight of time and cool cut granite and solid, ancient wood. Traffic whispered by on Burrard Street. Then, scarcely audible at first in the dim and benevolent hush, the organ began to hum. It was a thoughtful sound, which seemed to vibrate gently through them. Here comes the bride.

With a rustling that was like a collective sigh, the newly settled congregation rose up from the polished wood. Purses and little ribbon-tied programs were quickly placed on the floor or on the smooth benches. Expectant faces swiveled to the rear of the church.

Come here, thought Pauline, as this perfectly ordinary event began. All of you. Come, take my hand. Let's fly out the top of the church. Let's form a conga line in the sky and swoop over the crowds of people going about their Saturday business.

We need so very badly to see something marvelous. We need to look up one day and see something so skewed, so out of the ordinary that we stop in our tracks and reconsider everything.

Here comes the bride.

She was decked out in a dressmaker's dream and carrying the weight of a lot of myth. The boy at the front of the church swayed on his feet a little as he beheld this vision. Although he was nearly thirty, like many men, he needed this confirmation – this mythical beginning to his adult life. He needed to see a thousand dollars worth of seed pearls and satin coming toward him – something to remember until he had nothing left to do but remember, on the verandah of a place smelling of age and medi-cines and Pine Sol. A secret memory. His alone. When his bride walked up the aisle to meet him.

The bride, above all, ought to join my conga line in the sky, Pauline thought.

She wondered for a moment, if the God that the minister was about to invoke to bless the proceedings mightn't appear then too, and ask: "Isn't it time you all woke up and got down to the serious tasks I set for you? Instead of inviting me to yet another wedding on yet another Saturday afternoon?"

"Christ."

"Pardon me?" Richard whispered. Trying to look both at Pauline and at the bride as she sailed softly past, his face had the pained look of some-one straining to hear what he knows he heard. Christ? In church?

Pauline smiled and shook her head. She whispered, "Nothing," mak-ing a little swivel movement with her finger which meant: "Turn around, watch the wedding. I didn't say anything."

The bride landed at the altar and the congregation sat down to dream through the ceremony.

"Dearly beloved," said the minister.

⌘ ⌘ ⌘

Pauline's vinyl purse sat on a prettily decorated table among good silver and a nice yellow floral arrangement. The lights were dim and so the purse looked pretty good.

It had been on the floor, hung on the back of Pauline's chair and now the table top. There was a moment there on the floor of the ladies' room that was not pleasant even though they were at a good golf and country club. A lot of cleaning staffs only gave those floors a little swish with a damp string mop, though. Who could blame them? The pee smell on the floor was masked by cleaning compound. Who had time to get down and scrub a pee-splattered floor, even in a tone-y country club? Throw a little bleach in the toilet, swish the floor with a pleasant smelling cleaner and things looked – and smelled – fine.

Just don't set your purse on the floor. Even if you had to balance it on your naked lap or hang onto it with your teeth. Think, after all, where Pauline's purse was sitting now. Right beside Marjorie Trimble's knife and fork. And napkin. Not a pretty thought.

Pauline's vinyl purse sat there though, germ laden but looking surprisingly good in the dim dining room light and the pale glow of a single candle tucked into a centerpiece of boxwood and yellow African daisies and sweet-smelling little bells of Freesia. Setting, it seemed, was everything. Until you picked the purse up, looked closely or opened it, you did not see how cheap and nasty it really was.

Behind her purse, Pauline sat quietly, watching the stragglers smile their way through the receiving line, where the bride's mother, armed with a very good purse and serious gloves, was raising her eyebrows in a high sign to the master of ceremonies. People listened to this woman, even when it was only her eyebrows speaking.

Any minute now the MC would take the mike and tell them all to sit down, to drink, to be happy. Much as the minister earlier had told them to stand, to sit, to bow their heads and to congratulate the newlyweds.

"Ladies and gentlemen," cried a tuxedo-ed uncle of the bride. Armed with the cordless microphone, he strutted the front of the room like a Las Vegas comic. "Let's get seated for just a minute, while our bride and groom take their places."

The crowd applauded and moved toward the tables as he added, "The waiters are bringing out the champagne."

Finally they were seated, all one hundred and fifty of them. A moment later, champagne in hand, they rose as one to toast the happy couple. But while her right arm was swiveling up in salute, glass held high, Marjorie Trimble's vagrant left hand swung out and knocked over a crystal pitcher of Bloody Marys.

What cluck ordered the Bloody Marys? Marjorie. Where did the jug of thick, red, lemon-clotted booze and juice land? In Pauline's open purse.

What would become of Pauline's vinyl job? Its seams began to glow redly as the lining sopped up the viscous, red citrus-y stuff and the outside of the thing was staining, showing its true colors as it were. It began, ever so faintly, to stink.

There was a moment of stunned and paralyzed silence at the table. Then, with surprising dexterity, Marjorie Trimble pulled a narrow Cross pen and a checkbook from her very good leather bag. Swiftly she set them out on a clean spot on the wrecked table and with a trembling hand began to pen a check. Pauline watched, astonished.

What was this? Two hundred and fifty dollars? Marjorie was rich. Not generous. But keen to be known as having done the right thing. But not too expensively. She would not know you could find thirty-dollar purses in discount shoe stores and in department store basements.

Pauline didn't protest as she removed her change purse, lipsticks, embarrassing oddments and spearmint gum from her sopping, former purse.

Instead she thought, "Yahoo."

And then, just as though she had several wonderful purses on the top shelf in her closet – all leather, all cheek by jowl, all happily married to good leather shoes – she whispered, "Marjorie, thanks. Don't worry. That's lovely. I've never been crazy about it anyway."

Ha.

She would get a new purse. A decent one. Not a purse whose picture would appear as a little throw away number in Vogue magazine ("clutch purse by Prada: $1,425.") But a decent leather thing that would hang handsomely from her shoulder and give her secret pleasure. Unless she used the money to pay one of the soggy utility bills she had extracted *from the drowned purse that now lay like a murder victim in a pool of recently spilled blood.*

In fact, the sight of the tomato juice had caused them to recoil, just as though it were blood, puddling indecently on their crisp white cloth. The six at the table stood back a respectful distance, incriminated somehow, and intimidated.

The toast, which had carried on unaware of the death of Pauline's purse, wrapped up and the uncle of the bride invited them all to sit. Which, except for the guilty sextet, they did.

An efficient waiter arrived with a busboy in tow. The floral arrangement and heavy silver were whisked to the side, sponges and dry cloths were deployed. The soggy, crimson mass was shoved quickly into a linen bag and - snap! - a fresh new cloth was laid across the scarred and humble surface of the table.

As the heavy, starched linen fell into place, the table became once more what it was not - elegant. Underneath - and they had all seen this - it was that ancient, cloudy grey Formica. A disguised plywood round that had begun life in the handy man's shop deep in the bowels of the country club. And there it sat, upstairs in the chandeliered dining room, pretending to be something it was not.

The silver was reassembled, the pretty floral arrangement with its yellow candle, was centred and relit and the napkins were replaced. Voila. The six at the table could look at each other again.

It was only spilt tomato juice and vodka for heaven's sake. Who hadn't dropped a fish fillet on a not too clean kitchen floor and then flung it back in the pan? Who hadn't gone out with masking tape or a safety pin holding up her hem?

So, why did they all look so sheepish? The cheap, dead purse? The clutzy, inebriated move of Marjorie Trimble? The sight of the tablecloth covered in thick redness that might have been blood, but wasn't?

Or even the naked table, glaring there; its cheap Formica self momentarily exposed? Who knows, the table had seemed to imply, Marjorie Trimble might be wearing ripped panties or a dirty dime store bra.

⌘ ⌘ ⌘

CHAPTER ONE

Richard cozied up in their bed, arranging a stack of pillows about him and snapping the Saturday paper into a neat rectangle.

"That was quite a wedding," he said.

He didn't think about it long though. Wedding, schmedding. A girl in a long white dress, a guy in a tux. Too much money spent at a country club. Boom. It's over. If you were lucky, you, the guest, had had a good time. A wonderful time if you considered that it only cost you two matching soup plates as indicated by the bride's china list.

Pauline had had a good time but she was listless. Not without a list, but restless, unsure which way to jump. Into bed? Out the window?

She had heard mystery in the trees outside the bedroom window before. If you shut it tight you no longer heard the music from a party that happened in 1942.

Too much weighed her down. How would she get across the room and arrange herself in bed, an activity that required purpose, briskness and a happy sense of having been out, enjoyed yourself like a good citizen and returned, sober to your own bed?

"Christ."

"Pauline." Richard lowered the newspaper and looked up at her over the tops of his drugstore reading glasses. "You said Christ, when we were in the church. What is that all about? What's with this Christ?"

I want to be the young Katherine Hepburn. Swishing down a staircase in a satin gown or slipping elegantly into a barrister's chair in some courtroom. Not someone who brought her things home from a wedding reception in a Safeway bag, because her tatty purse was murdered at the dinner table.

"Nothing," she lied. "I'm just bored."

This was a lethal thing to tell Richard and she knew she had turned on a faucet that might well drip all night. Words, like droplets of water murmuring conversationally in the next room, would now follow one upon the other.

She sighed heavily and turned from the window, dropping the cord of the slatted blind so that it rattled against the sill.

You don't really want to know.

With Richard though, it was a matter of the opportunistic springing of a trap, the way a parent will: *"What did you say young lady?"* the quivering parent asks. *"What did I just hear you say?"*

"How can you say you're bored?" Richard warmed to the task. "You've got lots to do, a nice house, a nice child ..." He paused. "You have work."

Should she hang her head? She imagined it hanging like a yo-yo on the end of its string, over the side of a chair. She made less money than Richard, though, so she would listen to this and buck up. What he told her was true, after all.

Still listless, still restless, she dropped herself into bed and pulled up the quilt. Richard would like to know just what the hell this was all about.

"You should count yourself lucky," he concluded.

So she did.

"I'm lucky," she said and began to imagine the purse she would buy with Marjorie's money.

And in a way, she was lucky. She now had money to buy a good purse and with a good purse a girl never knew what other luck might follow.

Money to fill it; an airline ticket to tuck inside. Keys to an apartment downtown where there were drycleaners and grocers on the corners and Starbuck's Coffee too.

Richard was wrapping things up.

"And I don't think you should have taken Marjorie's check either." He shook the newspaper by way of punctuation. "It looks weird."

Yes, but I'm getting a new purse, thought Pauline. *One that I was meant to have.*

She had wondered since the murder of her purse, if, in fact, *she* tipped over Marjorie's Bloody Marys. Or somehow caused Marjorie's left hand to fling itself out and do the deed.

Nah.

But you didn't know, did you? How you might cause a thing to happen.

On Monday she would look for a tobacco-colored purse of undetermined shape. She knew the color because in her memory she saw Margaret Gage, the mother of Lawrence, her grade ten boyfriend, striding purposefully to her dance studio, a tiny room over the newspaper offices where she had taught four-year-olds how to demi-plie and to dance the Sailor's Hornpipe. Over Margaret's shoulder had hung the most beautiful bag. A seasonless thing, not new or particularly fashionable, it was nevertheless "good." Pauline had yearned toward this purse for nearly twenty years.

Margaret Gage had once painted an oak dining room suite olive green and moved it in front of a living room window. She wore black tights with straight wool skirts and stood with her feet in dancer's positions. She had made Chinese food and kept Life magazines stacked in her pink bathroom. But her husband had died an alcoholic at forty-five and her youngest son drank himself to an early death in which a speeding train was only an accessory after the fact.

Pauline waited for sleep, aware of the curious warmth emitted by Richard's newspaper at her back and of the soft noise of traffic sighing on the Saturday night streets. Then, neither truly awake nor asleep, she saw once again the curious image of someone or some thing beckoning to her from behind her closed eyelids.

In the night, the 1942 party continued, swinging to big band sounds and causing girls in chunky high heels and gabardine skirts to laugh in high-pitched happiness. Pauline heard them vaguely in her sleep and even sat up once when she heard a woman call out, just beneath the window. This had happened before though - a woman calling for help, the sound as clear and ringing and true as the sound of Madeline calling, "Mom!" from the next room. She no longer went to investigate, no longer really wakened.

In the morning a moving truck appeared and someone moved in to Mr. and Mrs. Sheppard's newly empty house on the far side of the next-door duplex. The Sheppards had decamped to Spain and through a complex web of friendship, acquaintance and serendipity it had been arranged that Arthur Dean would live in their house for a year.

⌘ ⌘ ⌘

"There's a moving truck in back of Sheppards," Richard called from the upstairs bathroom. He craned his neck out the open window, balancing a foam-tipped razor in his fist on the sill. His other hand felt along his jaw with the furtive movement that men use when searching for stray whiskers. Like blind Braille readers searching for the next word. It was because he was shaving that he had seen the truck. It appeared in the mirror as he studied his face.

Pauline went to the back deck and looked out to the alley.

Yes indeed. A moving truck.

On the far side of the truck, beyond her line of vision, Arthur Dean stood in the alley rocking back and forth in his new walking shoes. His surprised nose swigged in the scent of ocean and forest and he inhaled deeply, satisfied to be away from Edmonton where his nose would have spent the winter once again smelling city snow and the frozen, hidden river.

From Richard's viewpoint upstairs at the bathroom window, Arthur was an older fellow, a white-haired gent in a nylon golf jacket, busily directing the moving van. No doubt annoying the movers.

If Richard swiveled his neck slightly, he could glance across Burrard Street to the church, scene of the crime, yesterday's wedding. Today, it was a busy place once again. Sunday in the city. Old folks leaning on canes and walkers, trailing their youth behind them, invisible, tottered slowly down Fifteenth Avenue.

It was Richard's turn to say "Christ."

He had swiveled his head, seen the oldsters, and swiftly, unconsciously, lamented the childhood and youth trailing behind him.

The cold breath of some nameless thing fogged up the mirror, but he had finished shaving now. He pulled the plug and began to rinse the sink the way his father had taught him. Doing this, he heard again, the snick-snick of his father's black nylon comb tapping off the excess water on the rim of the bowl. This was the sound Richard Junior had heard each morning of his childhood. The sound he had wakened to.

For just a moment it seemed to him that he was still there, still in that dimension where he was a child waking and stretching in a warm bed. And yet here he was. A grown man, shaving a man's face in the bathroom of an expensive, rented duplex on Fourteenth Avenue.

He did not want to say "Christ," again, but it was in his head, printed across the marquee of his mind, like news in Times Square, before he could stop it. He dried his face and hands and hung the towel in a half-hearted way. He could not think now why he had shaved this morning. It was Sunday.

Oh, the weight of a Sunday, when it caught you unprepared. Downstairs, in the kitchen, a moment of panic seized Pauline, who immediately began to think of what they might do today. Granville Island. The market. Stanley Park. A drive.

This morning, once again, she had been worrying at the question that now seemed to dog her every step. Was it was necessary to create a life from the inside out or could you, by sheer effort, do it the opposite way? Impose a life on yourself?

Richness, events, restaurant lunches, books arriving in the mail, clubs, arcane facts, habits, travel brochures. Might these things layer your life; '*dense-ify*' it into meaning?

Why else had Margaret Gage painted an oak table and chairs olive green twenty years ago and placed them in a way that she must surely have seen in a magazine? Why else the black tights in a town and in a time where stockings came in four or five shades of beige? And the purse?

It seemed on the tip of her tongue – the way one might create a life that was rich (not wealthy), heavy; freighted with color, events, solid furniture, dim sunlight in crowded rooms, invitations tucked in a mirror over the fireplace. She wanted to experiment with creating a life from talismans and trinkets. She wanted to know if being surrounded by muted colors and rich fragments of earthly stuff might draw out the stubborn meaning of her life.

It was not that she wanted to busy herself so she could forget that surely we were here for purpose. She wanted to see if she could call out that purpose by surrounding herself with ... With what?

There were no clues. Or rather, there were clues, but they remained wispy, two-dimensional, like pictures in magazines. She wanted to be like a medieval alchemist, coaxing meaning from the interior by means of crowding an exterior desk. A rock placed here, a flake of mica there, a beaker filled with aromatic oils. Perhaps it was an altar she was after?

She was sick of the thin gruel of meaning to be had by merely being busy, though. While that could crowd a calendar and indeed an entire life, it did not draw out anything. It was make-work – something to fill the time.

The breakfast table set, she carried her mug of coffee out the back door and crossed to the railing. Oldsters made their way up the broad, stone steps of the church. She watched women in woollen suits wearing richly colored hats on their silver hair and old gents sporting suits bought at Edward Chapman twenty-five years ago. Suits which now hung loosely over shoulders thin and bent.

Leaning against the railing she sipped her coffee and invented for the oldsters, dense lives of mahogany bureaus and matching sets of silver brushes; Christmas evenings spent at gatherings of retired UBC professors.

Standing on the deck, her hand visor-ed at her brow against the sharp September light and looking hard out across Burrard Street, she did not see Arthur who still strolled little turns up and down the smoothly paved alley. He too had spotted the elderly churchgoers, but he did not invent meaningful pasts for them. He simply watched and wiggled his toes, admiring his new walking shoes and sniffing the Vancouver Sunday air.

Arthur knew some people who knew some people who knew the Sheppards. The Sheppards, off on their Spanish sabbatical, had needed someone to live in their house. Someone who would not wreck the place or leave before the year was up. Arthur had long harboured a secret yearning to live in Vancouver. Their twin desires, the Sheppards' pragmatic and practical and Arthur's shy and yearning, had collided nicely.

The Sheppards would dance the fandango and drink cheap gin among the British expatriates in Mallorca for a year. But what had Arthur planned for himself?

There was no cheap gin in Vancouver, although there was a government liquor store on Granville Street, just three blocks away. He knew how to mix a martini and a rob-roy. He had invitations to tuck in the mirror over the Sheppards' fireplace. He had books to unpack and exotic rugs from India on which to place the chairs and tables the movers were bringing in the back door even as Pauline measured coffee into the coffee maker in her kitchen just down the street.

⌘ ⌘ ⌘

CHAPTER TWO

The symbol-discerning consumer sidles up to the purse with the miniature, splayed cow-skin dangling from a chain and thinks, "Leather." She even programs her fingertips to feel leather and her nose to smell it. But the tag says, "Pure leather trimmed in man-made fabric."

Pauline's eyes adjusted to calfskin that might not be and to cowhide that might be hiding behind, or framed by, faux leather.

But she could sniff at these poseurs. She had cashed Marjorie's cheque and had two hundred fifty dollars in the wallet she clutched uneasily in her hand, like an absurd, weightless evening bag. No matter, it would soon be hidden in a good bag, slung neatly over her shoulder.

In the elderly Hudson's Bay store, scene of a recent facelift, an entire quadrant of the main floor had been given over to cosmetics and perfumes. A hundred flowery scents drifted richly across to where she stood amid the vinyls and the leathers. Quiet and sober, the handbag section too, gave off a subtle, slightly intoxicating smell. Money. Leather and petroleum-based mystery substances.

She inhaled the rich aromas and prowled on. There it was. Not too hard, not too soft. Not too big, not too small. It was just right. The essence of purses.

A good purse that would see her through five years or more of bill paying and occasional, secret smoking. (*Women who smoke are much harder on their purses,* her mother once observed, apropos of nothing much. *They open them so much more.*) Pauline brushed aside this loopy, stray thought and tried on the purse.

It was difficult to get a real feel for the thing – this purse that looked just right. It was barely weighted; shaped only by some crushed tissue paper, not animated by a wallet and the flotsam and jetsam of a woman's life.

How foolish and insubstantial she felt pirouetting before a mirror in the Bay handbag department, alone, trying on a purse. But there it was. The good purse.

A visceral tug, a surge that was nearly erotic, radiated up from her stomach and spread warmly outward. She smiled at herself in the mirror. The purse hung neatly from her shoulder. There was a subtle, burnished buckle with which to adjust the strap, but it was perfect as it was. The purse was adjusted for a shoulder like Pauline's, for arms the length of hers, for an elbow that crooked just so, like hers. It was made for her.

It was the colour of a bar of MacIntosh's toffee. It was the colour of cigarette tobacco. It was glossy yet subdued, golden-hued where the light hit it. It had the solid earthy lustre of the teacher's library tables that had once existed when oak was spread thickly through the school system.

Did it look like Margaret's purse?

In Pauline's eyes it did.

It was two hundred dollars. Marked down from two hundred and fifty.

The blond sales woman emptied the crushed paper from the bag and patted it in an affectionate way. "A really nice bag," she said.

"A good purse," she added, as though Pauline had just purchased a pet.

She rang the amount in the cash register and smiled. "A real bargain, too."

As she reached for the yellow striped department store bag in which to stow the jewel, Pauline said: "That's all right. I'm going to use it now. Don't wrap it."

A dangerous moment. Too often, she knew, disappointment walked up and took wish-fulfillment by the hand, leaving Cinderella unsure about whether she ought to attend the ball. She looked at the change in her hand for a moment, feeling the weight of the paper bills and the coins, then tucked the change in her wallet and the wallet into the new purse and went out the door.

"Good enough," she thought as she crossed the street to the Four Seasons. A hotel lunch in a window booth would be a good omen.

A small shiver ran up her spine; a frisson of excitement. The purse seemed to make her walk taller; its subtle heft shifted her stride somehow. She had worn her good shoes too, a pair of high-heeled brown oxfords bought at Freedman's annual sale; shoes whose shine and richness never let her down, whose narrow neatness caused her sometimes, to gaze at her feet in distant admiration.

So what if there were women coming out of Holt Renfrew carrying purses that cost easily as much and probably much, much more?

She was swimming, flying, leaping gazelle-like through the on-rush of lunch-hour secretaries and brokerage clerks. Pauline and her purse.

Richard thought it was ill-gotten, she knew. Never mind.

⌘ ⌘ ⌘

"Mommy has a new purse!" Madeline shouted as Richard opened the front door. She ran down the hall, bearing this new thing. "She went to the Bay and bought it."

Madeline, at six, seemed ever ready to squeal on Pauline. Did she know that Pauline occasionally cut corners with the truth? That she sometimes wished to be anywhere but here, slicing carrots and stinking up her sweater with the smell of frying chicken.

Holding the bag, so to speak, Madeline was reverent, impressed. Something important had occurred. She held the bag out for Richard to see and his voice came down the hall to Pauline.

"So I see," he said. "So I see."

And she knew that he saw only a purse, no better or worse than the murder victim dispatched by Marjorie Trimble's inebriated left hand.

Late September sun slanted into the kitchen from the dining room whose swinging door stood open, held against the wall by the stack of cookbooks which she kept there as a doorstop. On top of the pile, *Joy of Cooking's* grubby cover seemed golden, the words illuminated by the handful of autumn sunlight. She forked browned chicken pieces into a casserole dish, carefully crimped foil over it and set the dish in the oven.

She looked down at *Joy of Cooking*.

"Not today," she said closing the oven door with her hip. She turned to set the table.

⌘　⌘　⌘

Down the street, Arthur Dean was admiring his new digs. He rearranged his two good chairs once more. There was a feeling he was searching for and he would know it when he found it.

He sat again. First in the rounded, smoothly upholstered club chair, then in the more upright, but still cozy wing chair. He moved back to the club chair and meditated for a moment on 'club chair.'

What a darling thing for a chair to be called. 'Club chair.' He repeated it; said it out loud, then tried 'chub clair.' A satisfactory sound too. And descriptive since the chair did have a certain chubbiness about it.

He sat silently for a moment, observing the wing chair. No chubbiness or clubbiness there, the wing chair sat up smartly with its hands on its knees. It was kindly and welcoming, even wonderfully comfortable if you got yourself settled in right and the edge of the cushion matched the bend of your knees, neither garrotting a leg, causing it to go numb, nor forcing your legs to stick out straight, making you feel like a small child.

The chair suited Arthur very well. When he felt slouchy and cozy he drew up the small foot stool which matched it. When he felt keen or if he had dress trousers on, he planted his feet firmly on the floor. Either way the chair suited him. He usually offered it to company since it somehow looked down on the club chair, although he had yet to see how this could be since the cushions were the same height from the floor. A matter of perspective, he thought. He shook his head, amused to find himself sitting and communing with furniture.

"Next I will ask the tables how they like the new house," he said aloud. Then because he liked a joke, he did just that. "How do you like the new house?"

Mrs. Sheppard had had all her good things removed to a storage place, leaving behind guest room furniture, the kitchen table and chairs and a massive mahogany sideboard in the dining room, deemed too heavy to move.

Arthur's furniture was spread rather thinly through the duplex. He had decided to buy a desk for the dining room and to create a sort of study there. His bedroom furniture was sensibly deployed upstairs in the large front bedroom, the room that was identical to Pauline's just two doors away.

"Isn't it stupid to take your furniture out there for a year?" his son had asked.

But how are we to respond to a question like this, a question whose true purpose is to expose you as the lesser person, your interrogator as the superior person? What do we say? "Yes, it is stupid. Yes I am stupid. You're right."

Arthur had sailed off the map of the known world as far as Greg was concerned. His father had become strange, odd, different, loony, annoying, embarrassing. Arthur was as happy as a lark.

We are accustomed to rising to the bait, explaining and defending. Arthur had simply stopped. Ask him if it is stupid to do such and such and he would simply give you a polite look. "Hmmm?" his look asked. "Did you say something?"

He had shucked his old self like a wetsuit, a Hallowe'en costume, an itchy pair of long johns.

"I decided to be happy," he explained to his buddy, Beryl.

And he was.

The chairs were satisfactory now, placed just so on the timeworn rug and with a neat little two tiered table placed between them. On the table he had placed his reading glasses, an ashtray, a lidded crystal bowl filled with humbugs, (those sensible little amber sweets from England,) two books - a novel and a Canadian history - and news magazines. The cord of a slender brass pillar lamp snaked behind the table. The lamp's old-fashioned tasselled pull dangled beneath a black shade that was lined in gold.

What a lamp. Arthur eyed it with affection. He had conjured that lamp. It appeared not long after he clipped a picture of one just like it from an airline magazine his sister had brought home from her trip to England.

⌘　⌘　⌘

"Two hundred dollars? For a purse?" Richard could not believe his ears. "I can see fifty, or maybe even a hundred. But two hundred bucks?" He shook his head. "What did you do with the change?"

Pauline turned from admiring the new purse, which was beaming gently from the dresser and looked at Richard, who was struggling with a sweatshirt.

His face, his entire head, was hidden by dark green fleece. He was a man without a head. And yet he had spoken. Sharp, accusing words, like the piercing whistle of a locomotive pulling a long train of cars that were the various grievances of their lives. You heard the whistle blow on that engine and even if you couldn't yet see it, you knew it was pulling something.

"I had lunch," she said.

And what a lunch. Extravagant, yet not too extravagant. Silken fish chowder, an asparagus omelette, a tiny raspberry tart. Entirely satisfactory.

So you see, there was a free lunch. But did Richard congratulate her? Cheer along with her at this satisfactory turn of events? He did not.

"You had lunch?" He snorted with a quick huff of air as he pushed up the sleeves of the green shirt. He turned toward the mirror and using his hand began to smooth down his hair which remained thick, lank and still the sunny blond of his childhood. She was dismissed.

Like many people, Richard didn't really think about what he said. A nice man, a kind man,- he said things because they were pretty much what someone like him would say. If he really thought about what he said, his vocal output would be halved, Pauline thought. Just for starters.

"I haven't eaten at the Four Seasons for ages and so I just thought, well why not?" Pauline said.

She bent to pick up a tea towel. "I will not get mad," she told herself. "I will count to ten."

She was folding laundry. The basket and the neatly folded towels were balanced on her side of the bed and a white cloud of shirts, panties and pillow slips lay piled on the brown and ancient wicker chair which she had pulled over from beneath the window.

Standing there in a flannel nightie that had seen too many winters she felt tired and she looked tired too. Without makeup, her eyes looked myopic, stunned, although this was partly the effect of mashing at her eyes with cold cream. Still, she didn't look so hot.

"I bought the goddamn purse because I wanted it," she said to his reflection. To his back. Her jaw had tightened and there was a queer strangled feeling in her throat. "Okay?"

Shocked by the sudden twitch of facial muscles, by the rising heat that caused the tops of her ears to sting and her scalp to prickle, she found herself taking sharp little sips of air.

She looked down at the tea towel and saw it coiling into a thick white rope as it twisted in her hands. What was she going to do with this noose? Hang someone? She flung it toward the pile of laundry and it drifted softly, insubstantially, onto the carpet.

She felt cheated now. A lunch. A purse. So what? She wanted suddenly to have only her own business to mind, and to have no one mind hers. Talking, watching, commenting on each other. It was all suddenly too much. She wished to go mute. Deaf might be nice too. Her heart was racing.

"Mom!" Madeline called from the next room.

Heart pounding, fists tightly clenched and with a new headache beginning to pulse at her temples, she crossed the room, her bare feet stinging with the furious weight of her movement.

"Why aren't you asleep?" she whispered as she crossed to the little white bed.

Madeline looked little and good. She looked like goodness itself in the meager light shining in from the hall.

"Lay down with me, mummy" she said and her voice was good too. She had none of the petulance her voice sometimes took on in the day; none of the modulations of manipulation that caused Pauline to wonder sometimes if she hadn't got a changeling in her house.

"Please mummy."

They settled in, each in a warm spot beneath the duvet. Not too close, not too far away. Like her mother, Madeline liked room. Soon they were off. Sound asleep together in the white metal bed.

They traveled safely through the night, their synapses firing gently, pulling them through memory's chambers and on through their heart's desires. During the night their hearts beat in perfect synchrony. They slept unafraid and Pauline heard nothing in the September streets but the sighing of cars pushing swiftly through the moisture-filled air.

Later, when he saw that Pauline was not coming back, Richard fell asleep with the neatly folded towels for company. In the morning they were still there, forming a wall of soft geometry that Pauline saw when she went in for her robe.

Another wall had gone up in the night too. Richard was not speaking.

The purse. The lunch. Scarcity of sex. Scarcity of money. The electroplating business he had inherited by default from his father. It was too much. He too, sometimes wished that he were deaf. This morning though, he was simply mute.

⌘   ⌘   ⌘

During the night Arthur had heard strange sounds on fourteenth avenue, but he had rather enjoyed them, drifting in a kind of half sleep, believing at first that he was remembering a party he and Joan had attended in 1947 and then realizing no, the sounds were from another place, another time. He slept and listened now; listened and slept.

He no longer flung himself at the night, furious if sleep eluded him. He had learned to meet it halfway and so, if the night brought up sounds, well he was there to hear them. Even the strange ones.

In the morning he wakened in his new bedroom with the newly familiar little feeling of happiness pinching his heart. He began to hum.

⌘   ⌘   ⌘

Pauline was downstairs in her kitchen measuring coffee into the coffee maker. Madeline was sitting at the counter on a stool, humming and spooning cereal and milk into her mouth.

About them there still clung a dense quiet. It was a small dividend, brought back from their shared sleep. They were awake but had not yet been assaulted by the day. They drifted in a modest puddle of happiness, composed of simple things like quiet, warmth and good will.

Later in the day, their hearts might break, but just now they were still beating in synchrony.

Could flannel sheets in the little white bed do this? Wrap up the heart like cotton wool?

Thinking of the flannel sheets, Pauline smiled at the memory of making up the crib when Madeline was small. Who knew that tucking in the corners of soft yellow flannel could yield such momentary happiness?

She wondered fleetingly, if piling up memories of happiness helped to create a happy life or if one needed to keep creating them, moment by moment, from this instant to the next.

Time to drive Madeline to school.

"Just a minute Maddy. Mummy has to get her purse." And she and her purse were off on one of the prosaic chores that made up her life. Yet, driving the same streets in the same car with Madeline reading out loud the same signs, was different today. Her purse was beside her. A totem. Life would not be the same.

⌘　⌘　⌘

"I'm writing menu copy," Pauline said into the phone. She was at her desk, leaning back in a creaky secretary's chair purloined from Richard's factory, and talking to Ellen. Ellen wanted to know about the wedding.

"And you took the cheque?" Ellen laughed, astonished .

How unlike Pauline to accept the cheque; to take the money and run. And not just run, but spend it. Every penny.

"What did Richard say?"

The $64,000 question. What did Richard say?

He was miffed, he was pouty. And just now, he was not speaking. He created a wake, in which Pauline had floated, half asleep, until now. She could not decide whose fault this was but she was awake now with the feeling that the house was on fire. Or that a speeding train was bearing down on her with an unbearable noise. To complete the analogy, she was stuck on the tracks with her foot on the gas in a car that would not move.

Why, it's the Perils of Pauline!

Ellen was still talking.

Pauline listened and looked out her window at the street where the chestnut trees waved in a last September hurrah. Her little office, still pale green with a deep border of soft pink clouds where the walls and the ceiling met, was the former nursery, the room where Madeline spent her baby years, waving back at the trees.

⌘ ⌘ ⌘

Two doors down Arthur was looking out the window of the same room in his house, thinking about the sounds he had heard in the night. In his new and temporary home, this was the room where the Sheppards had stored decades of boxes and old furniture. No babies slept here, ever. It was a room which puzzled him in a gentle way.

⌘ ⌘ ⌘

Ellen clucked. "What did Marjorie say? Did she try to give you more money? Or did she just pen a cheque on the spot for $250?"

"She just wrote it out and I just took it," Pauline said. How to explain simply taking the money?

Perhaps it was meant to be. How often we walked by the meant to be, the opportunities that were spread before us. No, we told ourselves. No, it's not for me. I'm dreaming. I must stick to this path. Walk on this sidewalk. This is me. This is the way I have always done things. These are the possibilities in my life. We walk and sleep. Sleepwalking.

She had shocked Richard. Ellen was shocked.

During the night, while they were sleeping, did Madeline accept that things had changed? That while she slept, Pauline was changing; waking up even as she was asleep?

Pauline felt baby Madeline, still in this room, still ten months old and standing in her crib, right here, where Pauline's desk now sat. Could time collide like that? Be then and now at the same time? It seemed that it must. Here was her desk, her computer. And yet. For a moment, it seemed, she inhaled the fragile fragrance of baby powder. Then, like a sigh, it was gone.

"Marjorie Trimble's a nitwit," said Ellen. They agreed to meet for lunch. Tomorrow. Ellen wanted to see the purse. But did Pauline want it to be seen? All this sharing of her talisman seemed to be taking something away from it. Ah well.

Pauline hung up the phone and went back to her menu copy. Was this fit work for a grownup? Writing a menu for a fish and chip restaurant in Horseshoe Bay? She began again, to string together marine words.

She was creating a picture of crispness, freshness and goodness. Day trippers who drove to Horseshoe Bay on Sunday afternoons wanted to feel they had done a wonderful thing. Eating fish and chips at the seashore was part magic, as Pauline knew.

When next she looked out the open window at the chestnut trees it was afternoon. No voices sang in the trees at this time of day. How foolish the idea seemed in the autumn light. The trees were prosaic, still. An occasional nut fell earthward with a furtive, rustling sound.

She spell checked and then began to print the pages of her menu copy. While her copy printed, she drifted.

⌘　⌘　⌘

While she drifted, Arthur checked his list of chores. This was another thing he had only recently learned to take pleasure from. The making of lists.

Today he would buy food and gin and bread. He would mail a note to Greg and a post card to Beryl and walk among the flowers in a greengrocer's on Granville Street. He would buy a roll of postage stamps. All these errands were on his list which he tucked neatly into his trouser pocket.

He got his light canvas jacket and his new walking shoes from the hall closet.

⌘　⌘　⌘

Pauline packed the pages of copy in her canvas brief case and took down her brown linen blazer from its hanger in the hall closet.

She picked up her purse. It looked ordinary today. A place to put her brush and her wallet. It seemed to have forgotten that just yesterday it was lunching at the Four Seasons Hotel.

⌘　⌘　⌘

Arthur tied his shoes and stepped out the door. He pulled the heavy wooden door behind him and heard the satisfying thub, as it closed and locked. He pocketed the key on its ring with the oval brass tag. The key tag was shaped like the label on a bottle of expensive champagne and he liked to rub his thumb along the smooth brass, trying to read the engraved words with the soft pad of his thumb. Like reading Braille.

He stood a moment on the sidewalk, listening. The trees were still. Where had the wind gone? The street was silent.

Pauline stepped out the door and saw Arthur, a man of seventy or so, standing on the sidewalk, one hand in his jacket pocket, staring up into the trees. Around him, covering the sidewalk, were the polished wooden chestnuts, a mad comedy of round, shiny conkers.

Was this what went bump in the night, Arthur wondered? Is this what caused such curious night sounds?

And so Arthur and Pauline met. On the sidewalk, among the nuts.

They smiled and shook hands and politely exchanged the formal currency of civility. "How do you do?" "Welcome to the neighbourhood." "Anything I can do to help." Yes our houses are identical" "Just for a year."

And so on.

Pauline got into her car and Arthur turned his steps toward Granville Street. They had met.

⌘　⌘　⌘

CHAPTER THREE

The purse looked better now. It sat neatly on the seat beside her and next to the battered canvas case which held the menu copy. Something fishy.

At Pick-a-Peach Promotions, Pauline spread the pages of menu copy on the table in Karen's office.

"Ummhmm. Ummhmm." Karen nodded with quick, brisk, little noises and movements meant to convey assent, approval.

"Great," she said finally. "Good work."

She picked up a folder from the corner of her desk and opened it using a pencil tip as a sort of pointer. She handed Pauline a page of notes for a new job. A newsletter for "What To Where."

"Fabulous purse," said Karen, laying heavy emphasis on the first syllable. "New?"

Pauline nodded. She was brisk too. She was being her modern self. Awake, alert, on the prowl for the next thing. They stood beside the work table in Karen's gray office; a cool room, self-conscious and sniffy. Could one stand in it and be other than brisk? Did Karen create the room or did the room create Karen?

Here, Pauline was arch, ironic. Cool. Was her purse to be a prop for more of this? Ironic detachment? She didn't think so. Still, it was only a talisman. It was up to her what she used it for. It could be just a thing for others to admire. It could be a prop to prop her up. If that was all she asked of it. The purse was a mystery now and she felt suddenly weary of it.

Is this what she wanted it for? This is not what Margaret Gage was reaching for, Pauline knew.

They talked about the winter clothes at What To Where and Pauline agreed to meet the manager to discuss the newsletter.

Karen's purse sat on her desk, blinking a Morse code. It spoke the language of expensive resorts and matching luggage. Its sisters and brothers were on airplanes taking Japanese tourists to Hawaii and bringing them here to Vancouver to ski and to shop.

Pauline's aged, canvas briefcase wanted to cry for the stuff it was forced to carry and the purse was stoic. She gathered them and tucked the What To Where memo inside the briefcase.

Karen's purse, all hieroglyphics and glitter issued a siren song. Did Pauline want a desk like Karen's, in an office like Karen's? This can be yours, sang the initialed purse. All that's required is that you become quick, angular, modern. Pauline sold words that sell this, after all. Had even worked in places like this. She could do this thing. It beat frying chicken that made your sweater smell.

"Gotta run," she told Karen, looking pointedly at her watch. This was a signal Karen understood. Watches are watching us. But was Pauline running to her next appointment? Was she off to a meeting? No.

"I have to pick up Maddy."

But Karen had dismissed her. "Ciao," she said and waved her fingers. The telephone rang as Karen moved toward it.

⌘ ⌘ ⌘

Arthur enjoyed irony. He liked the well-crafted bon-mot. He could parry and thrust. But having decided to be happy, he had jettisoned much of it. He was lighter now, no longer anchored. He was free, for instance to simply roam among the flowers in the Asian market. If people thought him an odd old fellow humming and wandering about, well excellent!

If, like Richard, when he spied Arthur in the back alley, bouncing up and down on the balls of his feet in his wonderful new walking shoes, they thought he was probably an annoying old chap adrift in memory, that was fine too.

He plucked a bouquet of astrolomeria from the galvanized bucket and they emerged dripping and shining, their slender green stems bound tightly by flesh-colored elastics.

While their stems appeared wounded, the flowers looked joyous, bountiful. Tall flowers, not posies, that's what he was after. He pictured them in one of Doris Sheppard's tasteful vases. Excellent.

Pink flowers with little brush strokes the color of red wine and fine narrow leaves, where had these wonders come from? A field in Chile or Colombia, the product of a laboring agrarian family? Or had they grown ten miles away in crystalline greenhouses on the banks of the Fraser River?

Next he chose an anonymous but pretty bunch of baby carnations. No, two bunches. And autumn gladiolas, which made him think of his mother. Curious how much happier these glads looked than the ones which had marched past the fence in his childhood yard. These were glad glads.

The Korean shop keeper was happy now that Arthur had bought something. He was real now, no longer a retired and doddering time-waster. Arthur could be brisk too.

She had taken off her rubber gloves and was ringing up Arthur's purchases. They had met across the flowers. Not because she was sentimental about her product; she was not. But she and Arthur had agreed on the most satisfactory way to bundle the flowers and were both pleased with the neatness of the result.

"Thank you," he said and reached out to shake the woman's hand.

Startled, she quickly pushed up her damp sweater sleeve and offered her hand in return.

They both smiled. What calm satisfaction they had gotten from this domestic transaction, so neatly carried out.

⌘　⌘　⌘

Pauline was driving and her face felt as though she had been crying. It was not wet, but felt wounded. As if the skin had shrunk and pulled against the bone somehow. The fragile skin near her eyes seemed taut and tender. She wriggled her jaw and wondered about this as she pulled her car to the curb across from Madeline's school.

In the rear view mirror, she saw her anxious face. Her brown eyes, clear and tearless (but sad?) looked back at her. The line neatly cleft between her eyebrows seemed permanent now.

That will make you cry for sure.

She moved the mirror back on its pivot and saw more mothers in Volvos and minivans lining up behind her.

Here came the children, flowing in a choppy, colored wave. One dot, just one dot in this riot was Pauline's. This was what she had added.

If before birth we're all souls circling the earth like anxious shoppers circling the good parking spaces, do we sometimes end up with second string parents? Like shoppers parked too far from the mall? And like those shoppers with the less than perfect parking space, do souls who end up with their second or third choice parents, have too much to carry? Too far to walk? Do their dreams ask them why they bothered?

Here was Pauline's dot. She had navigated safely across the playground and the crosswalk, carrying her backpack in one hand, a large paper in the other. The large paper was like a mast, a sail, carrying Madeline across the sidewalk to her mother's car.

What on earth?

"We made pictures of ourself," said Madeline, her voice rich with pride and pleasure as she flung back the passenger door. Brown-eyed, like Pauline, Madeline was blond, like Richard and tall. Fine boned, yet with an athlete's rooted stance, she moved with a quick, innocent happiness.

Pauline leaned across the seat to receive the day's treasures. The backpack, a sweater, discarded when the morning fog blew away, revealing the surprise of more summer. A pink notice sheet telling parents about a field trip, causing fleeting anxiousness to flutter the chests of the connected.

Your child, this paper said to those who read with their hearts, *is going on a big yellow bus across the city, through enraged and murderous traffic to some place where strangers will have charge of her. Trust that her anonymity on this field trip is not a dangerous thing, that spirits watch over children and that most people are kind. Please sign and return.*

An instant, tiny movie unreeled in Pauline's head, in which she saw herself frantically searching the school bus for Madeline. She felt the visceral terror. As though from a memory retrieved, she had the urge to reach out and smack the teacher, the bus driver ... the world

She wondered if she was losing her grip. Here was Madeline. Safe. Beside her. They flowed into the not-yet-murderous traffic. Day care children rode home in the murderous rush hour traffic, but here they were in their car in the middle of the afternoon, perfectly safe.

Madeline was buckled up. The doors were locked. In the rear window there was a fading "Baby on Board" sticker. Pauline had her purse. Perfectly safe.

"We laid down on the floor and drew a picture around each other," Madeline explained. "Then we colored it. It's as big as me. But wearing my red dress. I changed that. The teacher said we could."

I need a friend.

Someone to take her hand and guide her across the vast space of the unconnected dots of her life. She needed a friend. Indeed. We all do. But how seldom we get a true one.

We're all like children, tugging at each other's hem. Listen to me. Listen to me. Watch me. And we know this and we tell ourselves to buck up. What

a lonely business. And what a miracle that we can parent someone newly arrived when we are trying to grow ourselves. Trying to be born.

⌘   ⌘   ⌘

There were flowers on Pauline's doorstep. Was there a note?

Madeline rushed up the walk, kicking aside chestnuts, her small feet making scritch-scritch noises on the fallen leaves which lay drying in the September sunlight. Someone had left flowers on the doorstep! This was so extraordinary, so out of the usual flow of things that she was momentarily speechless.

But then.

"There's a letter too!" she cried, waving a small flag of paper.

"Dear Pauline," read the note that Madeline finally gave up. *"I hope you won't think me too forward, but I would very much like to meet you again and to meet your family. You were kind to direct me to the shops on Granville, where I found a shop filled with buckets of flowers. I wanted to share my bounty - I hope you will accept them as a sort of thank you. Can you come for tea? Or a glass of something? My telephone is not installed yet, but you would be most welcome any afternoon around four o'clock."* He had signed his name to this block-printed message in an English public school sort of writing. *"Arthur Dean."*

She had drawn a protective veil between her and the secrets that life had been trying to whisper in her ear. Life, so prosaic, so predictable in its flat non-loopiness had stolen her wishes and turned them in her mind into something less. But here was Arthur, quite concrete, sending her flowers and notes.

She sank down on the wide top stair of the wooden porch with Madeline's backpack still clutched in her hand. Her purse was beside her and Madeline was running in the small, formal square of green that was their lawn. The sun was behind the house now and so they were in the protective shadow of the lovely duplex in which they had lived since Madeline was an infant.

The twin shadow outlines of the roof, the pair of chimney stacks, were etched in stark clarity on the sidewalk. It was an easy house for Madeline to draw. It was simply a conjoined twins version of the house that every child in North America is born knowing.

The archetypal house times two. The pitched roof a mere triangle, the tall body of the house, a simple rectangle. Did Pauline conjure this too?

Don't laugh. Philosophers argue, you know, or rather they used to, about whether we and everything else, are drawn toward the future or whether everything is pushed from behind. Is the future there, tapping its toe, waiting for us to arrive? Or is it an inert block, against which we must heave and shove?

Arthur was just down the street now. In a house identical to Pauline's except for some unfortunate modern touches that Mr. Sheppard had seen fit to add to the front.

"Unlock the door, Mommy. I have to go pee," said Madeline, who had grown bored with running on the grass.

Pauline gathered her purse and the backpack and Madeline's artwork and they went inside. She tucked Arthur's note in her purse. Madeline carried the flowers, but they no longer interested her. They had served their purpose; another of life's daily surprises.

For Pauline they had just begun their work. She felt oddly embarrassed by the flowers. As though someone were courting her, causing her to feel shy, but secretly pleased.

"I'm going to get the vase for you," said Madeline as she emerged from the bathroom, tugging at her skirt. It had hitched up into her panties. Again. But she didn't appear to notice; simply reached down and flipped the pleats out.

Something had occurred which Pauline did not yet see. Listen to Madeline. Pauline heard her say "vase" rhyming it with gauze, the way her Grandmother did. But she didn't hear Madeline's voice, hadn't noticed that the whiney, complaining tone of just yesterday was gone.

She was going to wrestle happiness to the ground yet, if she just paid attention. Life wasn't going to grab her by the lapels though, and give her a slap like the hero in a thirties movie trying to get the heroine to pull herself together, pull her back from the brink of hysteria.

But she was waking up. The just-cried feeling which caused her alarm earlier this afternoon? If she thought about it a moment longer, she might recognize it as the just-woke-up feeling instead.

Meanwhile there was the mystery of the flowers. Madeline had brought the crystal vase and Pauline began to unbundle them, pushing aside the rustling, marbled paper in which they were wrapped. She snipped the cruel-looking elastic bands with the stubby school scissors she had taken from Madeline's crayon bucket.

Freed, the flowers lay there, moist and delicate looking on the pebbled white surface of the kitchen counter. Arthur had given her the astrolomerias, the ones he meant to arrange in Mrs. Sheppard's snazzy art deco vase. Had he known they would look better in crystal?

"We got flowers!" Madeline shouted to Richard two hours later.

He stepped almost furtively into the hall and bent his large body to her for a hug, gathering her against the hot cotton of his shirt. He was a decent man, a good man trying always to balance things, trying to account for goodness received and given. He believed that he gave out more than came to him, that his books were never quite balanced.

Except with Madeline. It would be several more years before he began a trial balance of the ledger which was splayed open when first he saw her on a fine summer morning at the Grace Hospital.

The crystal vase on the dining room table was radiant in the six o' clock sun which slanted now through the west facing window. The window, high and ornate with leading which suggested the shape of a lily, was very old, its glass brittle and wavy looking. The light falling through it looked old too, like light streaming peacefully through a church window. The window, the vase, the tall and elegant flowers contrived to present a silent tableau that was vaguely religious. Even the shining wood of the table, which caused Richard to think fleetingly of the polished chestnuts lying on the front sidewalk, looked church-like, hallowed. He paused in the arched doorway and simply looked.

⌘　⌘　⌘

Arthur had arranged the gladiolas in the art deco vase and they looked spectacular. Daring even. The carnations, pink, prosaic and a little too perfect looked perfectly nice in their little glass jug. They added a note of cheer to Mrs. Sheppard's utilitarian kitchen with its spare, dull counter tops and ancient sink.

Had Arthur been with Pauline at the wedding three days ago, when her purse met its fate, he would recognize the counter top as the same gray stuff which lay hidden beneath the elegant table cloth at the golf and country club.

And what would he have thought of that?

He had grown to expect these connections, become accustomed to life's shorthand. He had learned to decode meaning. You didn't need to slap Arthur Dean in the face. But was this construct? Had he simply changed from a blind, lock-step, non-seeing to a nutty kind of animism which saw messages everywhere, read signs in the everyday? There were those who would think so but that way of thinking had a far shorter pedigree than the kind of thought which Arthur had adopted.

Not modern? He was post-modern. No. He was post-post-modern. Not for him the deconstructed bafflegab of modern literature and economics. He was heading for the source of things. Arthur - it was not to be forgotten - was a happy man. He had neither created a construct nor deconstructed all that he saw. He had decided to be happy, not stupid.

⌘　⌘　⌘

CHAPTER FOUR

Pauline was in her kitchen. The dishwasher was full, the counters were wiped, the placemats folded and put away. Two shining pots dripped cleanly in the green wire rack.

She loved this room; loved this moment when all was tidy and squared away. She would like to take this room, this feeling and this late evening warmth and set sail on a dark sea. Alone, and with everything in good order.

What called to us in this tidiness? What part of the soul answered with a solitary cup of tea in a darkened kitchen, content to just sit?

She sat at her kitchen table and saw her reflection in the black window. Behind the cool and dreamlike version of herself in the glass was her neat and orderly kitchen. There were her baskets, her two prized Italian fruit bowls, the green lattice wall paper which she had hung last winter. She stared out the window but saw only herself and her kitchen.

Richard was upstairs, flopped on the couch which turned Pauline's office into a guest room and TV room. She resented this without acknowledging it and pictured him now with the telephone wedged between his shoulder and his cocked head. He would have the remote control in his hand. Tomorrow, before she began work on the What To Where newsletter, she would fluff the cushions on the little couch and straighten the woolen throw. She would return the remote to the top of the tv. Why not just acknowledge that she felt invaded? Made small?

She wondered if she would go to Arthur Dean's for tea tomorrow. Or a drink. Where was her damn purse?

⌘ ⌘ ⌘

Arthur was listening to CBC Radio and snooping through Doris Sheppard's cupboards.

"We're not gossiping maliciously," Beryl told him once when he wondered whether they had stooped to a new low. "We're trying to figure out humanity. That's all it is."

Arthur was trying to figure out humanity this evening. Doris Sheppard, specifically. What a nut bar.

She had every plastic bag ever created, all stuffed into a tall utility cupboard in the little mudroom off her dreary kitchen. He had not really meant to snoop, but was drawn by the mudroom cupboards with their small, neat, spring-loaded latches and their trim vertical slats.

They don't make cupboards like that anymore, he told himself, admiring the row of four narrow doors and neatly latched overhead bins, all tucked smartly into the end of the mudroom.

But look at these plastic bags. Arthur imagined Doris unloading groceries she had trundled in from the back lane. He pictured her stuffing the bags in this cupboard, in the mudroom off the kitchen of her house that had remained the same since it was built fifty years ago. Imagine

Arthur shook his head at the sheer marvel of it.

And yet. And yet. She and her husband - a sixty-five-year-old man who must be content to boil his Sunday egg in a kitchen which looked the same as it had when he was a newlywed - had taken themselves off to Spain.

In a curious way, Arthur admired the fact that Doris had left behind her plastic bags. Did she think: "Oh, what the hell. That's the way I keep house." Or did she fly across the Atlantic firm in her belief that someone would live in her house for a year and not look in the mudroom cupboards? Did she know why she kept those plastic bags? Did Doris ever feel invaded?

Arthur shut the cupboard and ran his hand down the smooth surface. He snicked the neat little lock into place.

The mudroom had small-paned windows along the back and on the side where the back door stood. There were no curtains. He opened the door and breathed deeply. There was salt in the air. Could this be? He looked up at the sky then stood at the open door looking out into the black September night. He saw the dim, pale light shining out from Pauline's back porch.

⌘ ⌘ ⌘

Here was the damn purse. Pauline yanked it up by the strap. It had been sitting patiently on the floor, just inside the dining room doorway. The room was dark now but she could see the vase and the astrolomeria, shining on the table. There were the flowers and the purse together in her dining room.

Don't leave your purse where a prowler or burglar will see it as an invitation to your locked house; take it upstairs when you go to bed. Also, tuck it in the freezer if you run out to the garbage or downstairs to throw a load of wash in the dryer. And when you try on a coat in a department store, for heaven's sake hold on to your purse. Don't prop it on top of the rack and go off to look in a mirror.

Her head was filled with practical advice.

So, was the purse an albatross or a convenience? She hefted it over her shoulder and considered its weight. Perhaps she was wrong to think that this was the purse for her. Maybe she ought to have gotten a small one whose diminutive proportions would impose order rather than invite the chaos that a roomy purse does.

She went through the kitchen, stopping to push against the door of the dishwasher and spin the rasping dial to normal wash. Normal. In the morning her dishes would be clean. All would be normal. She flipped the light switch and the tiny halogen beam over the sink went instantly, silently, black. As the kitchen fell into darkness the dishwasher began to hum.

Before going silently up the carpeted stairs, she checked the lock on the front door, thumbing down the brass lever and pulling at the handle.

Upstairs, she crossed Madeline's room to twirl the plastic wand of the slatted blinds, shutting out thin stripes of pale light that shone in from the Burrard Street lamps across the park. She pulled the thin cotton curtains over the blinds.

Cars moved steadily through the night, their sounds mixing with the purposeful humming and sloshing of the dishwasher below. All was peaceful and ordinary. Normal.

Look how long Madeline was! She had grown angular over the summer, her baby roundness had gone. Or nearly gone. Brushing her lips against Madeline's forehead, Pauline felt again the downiness she was sure that only she knew. She could read them still, these tiny whorls of fine hair that connected to Madeline's smooth and perfectly shaped eyebrows. She could read this fine, invisible hair with her fingertips, with her lips; just as she could the day Madeline was born. She waited a moment, then traced again the tiny, warm forehead. Surely, she conjured Madeline too? Dreamt her into being, long before she arrived.

⌘　⌘　⌘

Arthur was on the phone with Greg. He sat in the wing chair with the phone cradled in his lap.

"Just this evening," he said into the phone. "I wasn't sure that it had been connected, but just checked it a minute ago."

They agreed that it was wonderful that you could bring your phone along and plug it into a wall jack. Greg wanted to fit his father's journey, his decampment, into some sort of framework. And so they had settled into a pedestrian chat about the nuts and bolts of moving. Just as though

Arthur had needed to move to Vancouver and was setting up house-keeping there for good.

They discussed the street. Arthur told Greg there were chestnut trees on the boulevard. He could see them now, waving darkly in the September wind. There would be lots of chestnuts on the ground in the morning. There were shops nearby, Arthur said. He did not tell Greg that he had bought a half dozen bouquets of flowers. And gin.

They hung up and Arthur sat a moment longer in his wing chair, in the dark.

The Sheppards had left no ghosts behind. The house was silent. Yet just on the other side of the wall, a thick, soundproof thing of old-fashioned plaster and lathe, there was a neighbor. A silent woman called Isobel, who left very early in the morning and returned at dusk.

Arthur had not given her flowers. She had not come to say hello. If you were to stand on the street, beneath the chestnut trees and look at this duplex, you might see Arthur sitting in the darkened living room to the far left of the building and Isobel sitting to the far right. Bookends, propping up a vast space.

Arthur pulled the cord on his brass lamp and warm golden light illuminated the center of the room. He looked at the lamp for a moment and wondered anew that he had not known about this kind of lampshade before. A black lampshade, lined with dull gold paper. Arthur found it almost magical, the way this shade changed light from ordinary incandescent illumination - something to read the paper by - to something truly luminous. Magical.

There was no one beneath the chestnut tree to watch him lift the lid on the candy dish and pluck up a humbug and pop it in his mouth. No one beneath the trees to see Isobel in the flickering anonymous light cast by her TV.

The building next door - Pauline's house - the house which Madeline could draw before she went to nursery school, was in darkness. The shade was pulled tight in Pauline's office; no light escaped that room where Richard sprawled uneasily asleep before the muttering television set.

The Poulos, Pauline's neighbors and landlords had gone to bed early; their teenage children were hunkered down in the basement watching TV. They heard nothing from Pauline's side of the building except the muffled whoosh of water coursing through communal pipes as the dishwasher began to rinse and wash.

Arthur took up another candy from the glass dish and thought about Pauline.

⌘　⌘　⌘

Pauline, who did not know that she was being thought about, was in the bathroom examining her face. Small lines radiated up from her eyes. There were vertical lines bracketing the mouth too. Beneath it all, the soft tissue at the junction of her neck and chin had begun to droop ever so slightly. Recently, she could feel the tiny resistance at the top of a turtleneck sweater.

We grew up. We sent our roots down. We tried to grow into ourselves. Into our skin. And through it all, the body was constantly loosing its grip. You needed this as a child, said the collagen slipping quietly away, leaving the skin to fend for itself. You needed your beauty and plumpness to tether yourself here, to become fair and rooted. You are to let go now, move out of the stuff of ego that once bought your ticket to the dance. Let it go. You are to go inside and bring out the heart stuff, the soul stuff. Cobble together an airier self, propped up by wisdom.

Love your body, look after it, but remember it is not the only you, the real you. And in case you don't get the message, watch as it begins taking its leave. The corporeal you, this said, is not the real you.

Pauline traced a finger across her forehead and frowned. Her fingers remembered Madeline's warm skin, covered in the down that was still so like the invisible fur that covers the waxy newborn. Was it called lanugo? Let it go.

She washed her face; patted it dry. Should the lunch at the Four Seasons have been instead a jar of fruit acid cream for her rapidly aging skin?

The bathroom was pink. Pink tiles, pink walls, a candy stripe shower curtain. All this pinkness reflected well on Pauline's skin. She was a picture of radiant health.

⌘　⌘　⌘

"I really don't feel well," she told Richard in the morning. Her voice was weak and breathy, as though the vocal cords had exhausted themselves in the night. It was an effort to speak.

She felt jumpy, clammy and hot. Her skin prickled and seemed to hear the fibres of the cotton sheets as she fell back against the pillow. She felt a jerkiness in her movements, as though information were being relayed back to her senses with a time delay.

Richard reached across and laid his hand against her forehead. It felt unbearably hot and dry. Heavy against her skull, his hand was meant as a kind gesture, but Pauline wanted to fling it off. She could not move.

"I'll get Maddie up," he said and pulled back the quilt. Cold air rushed in and she shivered. He tucked it gently, around her.

"Do you have appointments or anything you want me to cancel?"

"Ellen," she said slowly. "I'm supposed to meet Ellen for lunch. Will you phone her?"

"I'll call her," he said on his way out of the room.

Their silence of the past twenty four hours was forgotten. Richard was kind and concerned. Solicitous.

He returned to the room and she heard him set something on the night table beside her.

"Paul," he said softly. "There's water here and aspirin."

He left and she heard the shower begin. She wakened shortly and heard him moving quietly about the room; dressing, closing the louvered closet doors slowly, taking elaborate care not to squeak the elderly hinges. A coat hanger rang dully against the wooden pole in the closet, then there was silence.

Next she heard the house shudder as the heavy front door was pulled shut. They were gone. She had slept through the dressing and the lunch packing and the breakfast; had not heard Maddie come in and stand beside the bed.

Pauline opened her eyes and slowly pulled her self upright. She fumbled for the cool pillows from Richard's side of the bed and arranged them against the hot one on which she had been sleeping. Leaning back, she assessed her weak and damaged feeling body.

Heat and a prickly coolness arced across her back and shoulders. The flannel nightgown felt soiled and damp against her legs and chest. The duvet comforter was heavy upon her but seemed to give no warmth. Her hands felt useless and dull, as though they would flap if she attempted to use them.

Like any adult on waking to find themselves truly sick, she was going over in her mind, just how she felt yesterday. Were there any warning signals? Had her body sent her messages which she had neglected to heed? And had she heeded them would she be up and about today? She had no answer.

Just how long, she wondered, could an adult sit in bed like this, doing nothing, thinking no coherent thoughts? Ten minutes passed while she stared at the drawn shades, at the gray shadows. The house went about its business, humming, ticking and occasionally creaking. Water rushed through the communal pipes as Mrs. Poulos ran her washer or flushed a toilet. How long could Pauline just sit there?

What was going on? Had a virus got hold of her? Or was she just sick and tired?

She stared some more and finally turned her head to observe the aspirin bottle and the glass of water which Richard had left. The white plastic bottle looked dull and dusty, an elongated marshmallow with a red cap.

Waiting for strength, desire - will - to move her hands forward, she sat. Nothing happened. That part of her brain seemed to have moved on and so she was left to simply stare. But it was not unpleasant, this unfocused staring, this lack of effort. It was strangely soothing to simply watch the aspirin bottle. Perhaps this was even better than actually taking the aspirin? She was detached watchfulness; no trains to catch, no meals to cook, nothing to write, no one to speak to. Her brain was empty, it seemed. The smooth whiteness of the little bottle, with its gentle sloping shoulders was hypnotic.

When finally her eyes blurred, she blinked and moved her head slightly. Ah, Madeline had left her a note. A picture really. She still communicated with hieroglyphics.

Time passed. Chestnuts fell from the trees onto the sidewalk and the lawn. Pauline heard them land, but the sound was cushioned and pleasant. Far away.

She remembered briefly, lying in the bath tub as a little girl, feeling her hair stream and wave in the warm water and playing with the sound of nothing, her ears sealed shut by the weight of water. That was what she felt now. Cocooned by the weight of the air.

Strange that we did not notice how heavy it was. And yet we said that things were light as air. How could it press down like this? How could it be so dense? She could not imagine the strength it would take to rise, to put her feet on the floor, to walk.

What if everything is truly absurd? What if there is only construct and consensual reality. If everyone wakes up one day feeling like this, just what will happen? Will we drift off? Will the show be well and truly over?

Thinking about this, she wondered if everyone carried the weight of the world on their shoulders. Quite literally. Poor Madeline.

And thinking this, she turned her eyes once more to the little night table. She stared at the folded square of paper on which Madeline had drawn and colored a heart and a bouquet of balloons. Strings really, with balls on the ends, but they had drawn these often and it was their particular and agreed reality that this represented balloons.

Was it that the novelty seeking mechanism shut down when we were unwell? The brain, like a dog at a fair or a flea on a skillet, hopped around constantly, running this way and that, looking for stimulation, but when we were sick, all that seemed to disappear. And it felt restful.

She rubbed at her eyes. Was dying like this for some people? Not boredom, not pain. Just fading of attention? So that we might say of someone who died, that they simply stopped paying attention and drifted off? Like one of Madeline's balloons?

What a lot of effort everything seemed from this semi-horizontal position. Food and a trip to the toilet were in order. Another half hour passed.

She was upright, tall and airy, a different person from the one who had lain in the rumpled sheets, wrapped up in the duvet which now looked creased and unclean.

Pauline lifted her tired arms and pulled the flannel nightie up and over her head. This exhausted her and she sat again. She had misplaced some necessary thing. She had misplaced her will or her force. She lacked that essential thing that sees us move quickly and surely through our days, driving through traffic, making meals, talking on the telephone. She was inert.

"Go pee, Pauline," she said out loud. "Get your robe from the hook and walk to the bathroom."

Finally in her robe, she shuffled to the pink bathroom, which felt awfully bright. South facing, it was a room filled with and suffused by sunlight. Ordinarily, this made her glad.

Today, she felt like the guilty, self-loathing, morning-after-drunk and the brilliant light in the pink tiled room did not make her glad. She had no hangover, she was sick, but like the repentant inebriate, she could not bear to look at her image in the mirror. She was fragile, stooped. Her feet made old-lady scuffing noises on the tiled floor. The coldness of the smooth tiles felt remote, like a description of cold.

Washed, dried and unevenly combed, she took herself slowly down the stairs. A delicious silence greeted her. The living room was still and dim, a room which existed mostly in shadow. The hallway was brighter, illuminated by borrowed sunlight from the wide kitchen windows.

Unlike Doris Sheppard's shadowy kitchen where Arthur was sitting at the table reading the morning paper and drinking orange juice, Pauline's kitchen was renovated, bright and modern, filled with light.

The Poulos had removed the ancient mudrooms from the back of this duplex many years before and added wide porches for children to play on. Nothing blocked the southern sun here. Through the windows, Pauline could see her flower boxes, the geraniums gone leggy and burnt looking in the fading days of Indian summer.

"They need water," she said out loud. "Poor things."

She measured coffee into the coffee maker while thinking that she should have tea.

⌘   ⌘   ⌘

Arthur had considered tea this morning. He had bought several kinds because the tins amused him. They added color to Doris's kitchen. They looked happy, somehow, these little brass tins with their colorful labels and elegant script. Mint. Almond. Chamomile

He had another list going. This one was fastened to the door of the ancient General Electric refrigerator, a fridge which reminded him of a Buick he had owned in the 1950s. On his list, held there on the scarred white surface by an incongruously frivolous looking ladybug magnet, he had noted things to buy today. And not just gin and bread either.

Was this how he created happiness? By shopping?

In a way. Gathering small, colorful tokens to brighten rooms, tables and walls gave him enormous satisfaction, now. He was sorry to have missed years of doing this and years of doing it for others.

Bright, shiny objects! He sometimes laughed at himself, that he had become like a magpie, gathering bits to himself.

Think how happy Joan might have been with a little desk in their house and small things for it. A lamp! Like his brass one with the black and gold shade. And paper weights. A beautiful pen. Books. But he had not known then, the secret he now possessed.

When he was a younger man, he had believed there was wisdom in attaching no meaning, no importance to things. If a plate broke, for heaven's sake it was a plate. If Joan lost a favorite earring, it was of no consequence. An earring. If Greg broke a treasured trinket, he told him - kindly, he had once prided himself - that it was only a thing. Nothing of consequence. Now he saw that it was he who had been the materialist. He was the one who had held fast to the rationalist point of view which said that objects imbued with meaning were meaningless. This, he now saw, was a mistake.

It was another false idea he had let go of since deciding to be happy. Things were important. Be careful how you chose them. They had power.

⌘　⌘　⌘

Pauline poured coffee into the flowered mug she had taken from the dishwasher, and carried it to the breakfast counter. She sat heavily down on the narrow stool.

Madeline had eaten her breakfast here as she always did. Pauline could see the ring of dried milk where the little cereal bowl had sat, the streaks of dribbled orange juice drying on the counter. Richard had swept the toast crumbs away with modest success, only a few remained scattered across the counter's cool, dimpled surface.

The coffee tasted and felt wonderful. She had decided to drink it black and its thin, hot perfection warmed her instantly. She recoiled briefly, thinking of the cream that she would ordinarily add to her cup. This was perfect. Hot, thin, strong. And it smelled wonderful, too.

What a satisfying thing. Tea would not have done the trick, she decided, although it might have been kinder to her stomach.

"I have a cast-iron stomach," she often said. "I can eat anything."

This was how Pauline thought of herself. Very medium. No sensitivities. Nothing hurts. *I am bothered by nothing. I can wash my face with dish liquid, scrub bath tubs with caustic cleansers and no rubber gloves. My skin doesn't react.*

"Oh, for Christ's sake," was how she often responded to sensitivities in others. Except small children. Especially Maddie.

Was this sudden sickness a whack across the head with a two by four? Something to get her attention? Draw her away from mediumness.

Sitting at the counter, in her silent house, she was feeling better and better. A piece of toast sounded good. The crumbs Richard left behind had been emitting something like pheremones. Eat toast, eat toast, they cried.

A little dizzy upon standing, but otherwise quite, quite good. In fact, Pauline now felt as though she had been left with only the pleasant slightly out-of-focus part of a hang-over. And none of the bad stuff. The aches and pains; the headache; the fever, they had all receded.

She dropped a slice of bread in the toaster and thought about the poor leggy geraniums on her porch.

"That's next," she said as she buttered the toast.

Revived by toast and coffee, she wiped the counters carefully and considered the day, the state of her health. She reminded herself once more about the flowers.

Then she remembered the other flowers. The ones which Arthur Dean sent. She had not thanked him for the flowers.

Charming.

She stepped out the French doors and crossed to the railing with a jug of tap water for the geraniums and there he was. Arthur was standing on the Sheppards' back step, breathing deeply.

⌘ ⌘ ⌘

CHAPTER FIVE

He could not get enough of this Vancouver air. Its novelty. Air suffused with droplets of water, which he could feel travel through his nose and his mouth. He fancied that he felt the moisture settle peacefully in his lungs.

The dampness, even on these hot autumn days, felt invigorating.

He was intrigued with the mystery of things holding together while they were damp through and through. Wood, concrete, trees, houses, even people, Arthur imagined them just slightly soggy. Steam, like an aura must emanate from them. Having known prairie dryness and sensible high, blue skies all of his life, he was enjoying the sense of enclosure, of living within moisture almost surrounded by sea and mountains. He liked the night sounds of traffic, moving through moistness, of the rustling trees, sighing as though inhaling the wet air.

He couldn't just hang around and breathe, though. And he had seen Pauline, in her flowery robe, step out onto her back porch

"Hello," he called out.

He had a gentle voice, just slightly gravelled by the passage of time and nicely modulated. The sound of it didn't startle. Hearing it, people often felt they had been in conversation with him before. Intimate, it was the voice of a friend happy to see you again.

Shielding her eyes from the morning sun, Pauline lifted the glass pitcher with her other hand in a sort of awkward salute. "Hello," she called back and she sounded a little scratchy, her voice still unsure of itself, a bit weak.

"Thank you for the lovely flowers." She increased the volume and her voice sounded firmer, carried a little better. "I love Alstromeria."

"I'm just about to put on some coffee," Arthur called. "Would you like to come over?"

This courteous yelling across the back of the Poulos' kitchen, over the fence and past Isobel's mudroom and back stoop seemed a little silly and she felt she owed Arthur more than just a thank you flung across the backyard, so she called out,

"I'll have to dress. Twenty minutes?"

"Lovely," he said and with a little wave, he went inside, pulling the glass paned mudroom door shut behind him.

What about the fever, the trembling illness of only an hour ago? Where had it gone? Pauline was puzzled by how well she felt. Clean and clearheaded, as though something had lifted or broken.

Like most, she was accustomed to the modern division of the body, the spirit and the brain, and even though medicine had begun to grudgingly accept the ancient wisdom, that what we felt affected how we felt, still the individual hadn't truly enfolded the information into everyday reality.

Stress, oh yes. That might set you up for the flu or a cold. But, actual fall back on your pillow illness as part of a sort of spirit longing? How could that be?

She stepped up on to the Sheppard's front porch, where Mr. Sheppard and neighbor Isobel had ruined the proportions of the house's front by adding black wrought iron curlicues and concrete slab steps in place of the broad wooden porch boards and stairs which the Poulos' had retained on their duplex and faithfully painted battleship gray each year.

The wrought iron was firmly anchored in the concrete and bolted to the house, so that the effect was one of paradoxical firm flimsiness. Pauline felt exposed there, on stage.

What were they thinking when they tore off the old damp and weathered boards and affixed this monstrous cement thing? Did anyone stand back and truly look at the house, wonder about proportion and human scale?

In truth, the Sheppards and Isobel usually used the back door and had ceased to care about such things as the pleasure of entering their homes.

Arthur answered her ring immediately and drew her inside with an outstretched hand, which she shook and returned.

"Come in. Come in." He smiled broadly. He wore his walking shoes and bounced on the soft soles, ever so slightly. "I'm so happy you came over. This is so nice."

Pauline stepped into the hallway, which was just like her own and yet not like it all. The oak floor was the same, the stairs curved off to the right, a mirror image of hers which curved left. The angled closet, like hers, was tucked behind the front door which Arthur still held open. But it was dark; here; no light issued from the hallway, from the kitchen at the end.

Arthur closed the heavy door and then led her through a louvered door into the living room, not down the hall toward the kitchen as Pauline did with most guests.

He led the way with springy, soundless steps and Pauline followed with her hands behind her back

"After you," Arthur said, sweeping out his arm in a mock, old-fashioned, courtly gesture.

"I like this," Pauline said, reaching out a hand to touch the club chair.

She was enchanted with the two chairs on their elderly British India rug. The room, in truth was rather bare, but Arthur's arrangement of the chairs and the shining walnut step table with its lamp and books and neat little candy dish, looked inviting. He had stacked books on the floor along the wall.

The dining room, visible through an archway framed in dark oak, just like the one in Pauline's house, was still quite bare. Arthur had yet to search for the desk and the bookcase he had planned for that room. Still, the whole effect was one of welcome and coziness.

"Sit down," he said. "Take the wing chair."

A little pale looking after her mystery illness of the morning, Pauline was just about her old self. Her thick brown hair was pulled smoothly back, unparted and clasped at the nape of her neck in a flat mock tortoise shell barrette which belonged to Maddie. Her eyes were not made up, but looked alert and shiny. She had put on her bright lipstick and dusted brown powder blusher on her cheeks.

The blusher and the small scattering of amber freckles, left over from the recently faded summer, made her look almost burnished and robustly healthy. The memory of this morning had made her want coolness, crispness next to her skin, and she had put on one of Richard's navy blue striped office shirts over her jeans. She looked and felt fresh and restored. Someone recently recovered from an illness.

She sat back in the wing chair and her feet, in flat slip-on sandals, touched the floor, her knees bent comfortably. She leaned back in gratitude, into one of those rare chairs that made you sigh with pleasure.

Why is this a difficult thing in a chair? And more mysterious, why don't we notice the absence of comfort? Instead we're surprised, nearly stunned when we happen by accident to settle into a truly comfortable chair. Are we in a constant state of discomfort? Or are we just numb?

She was enveloped in such a feeling of well-being, sitting in Arthur's wing chair, that for just an instant, she was gone. Lost in the bliss of perfectly supported relaxation, she closed her eyes.

"What a comfortable chair," she said and opened them. "It's wonderful."

"I know," Arthur said happily. "Isn't it remarkable? It took quite a long time to find it, though. Had to sit in a lot of chairs."

They smiled. Quite at ease.

"I'll go get the coffee," he said.. And then as he rose from the club chair he looked around, bemused: "Do you want to sit somewhere else? It's a bit dark in here, but I haven't created a bright spot yet. Or found one."

"It is a bit dark." She looked around the room, which was in fact dim and shadowy. "I was only here once when the Sheppards had a little neighborhood confab about the apartment building across the street. Do you know them well? The Sheppards?"

"I met them only once in person." Arthur said beginning to move across the room. "At a party in Edmonton. They're very good friends of friends of mine. We made the house sitting arrangements by phone, actually."

He stopped at the archway. "Excuse me for just a minute. I'll get our coffee."

Pauline heard him whistling and moving about in the kitchen, setting out cups, opening the fridge.

He called out: "I bought scones at the English Bakery on Granville Street. Will you have one?"

Pauline rose, about to go to the kitchen to tell him she would have the scone but suddenly it seemed ridiculously familiar to simply follow him into the kitchen. She stopped and called out "Yes, please," then moved across the shadowy room to study the books which were propped against the wall in neat stacks.

"We're doing a lot of yelling again," Arthur called out. "Do you want to just sit in the kitchen?"

They settled in at Doris Sheppard's scarred wooden table. Arthur had pushed up the elderly double hung window and drawn the curtains back as far as they would go. The back door was open, letting in the filtered sunlight from the mudroom.

They sat down in the little spot of autumn warmth and light with the plate of toasted scones between them on the table.

Their coffee cups were simple mugs, white and tall. On the table with them was a little cream and sugar set, old and heavy and plain;

stoneware, which he had set out on a little ceramic tray. The scones were on a cake plate he had found in Doris' cupboards. There was a basket weave design along the perimeter of the plate and bright painted hollyhocks which Pauline saw when she lifted a scone. The plate was meant for fancier company than the homely toasted scones which look lumpy and not delicate at all. She was charmed.

"It's an evening place, I think," he said. "The living room. It doesn't work that well yet, for daytime."

"I think they are always on the go. Doris and Edward." She looked around the kitchen. "I doubt they notice their house very much. This kitchen can't have changed since 1955."

Of course she saw the gray formica countertops and thought instantly of the table at the country club last Saturday night. But, unlike Arthur, she didn't allow herself to read meaning into the events of her life. Yet. She was still putting one foot in front of the other; toeing the linear line.

"Butter and jam." Arthur stood suddenly. He had been about to pour the coffee. "I've forgotten."

She watched him take a jar of berry jam from the ancient refrigerator and carefully transfer two thick spoonfuls to a little tulip-shaped egg cup. It was pink, balanced on a chubby green stem. He placed it on a clear glass saucer and laid a tiny spoon across that. The butter was a neat stick set out on a cut glass plate.

He had given them flat white salad plates for their scones. Beside the plates were green fringed napkins and small knives with bone colored handles and oval spatulate blades.

Where would she put this new hit of caffeine? And the enormous toasted, buttered and jammed scone? The seductive lure of fat and sugar along with Arthur's pretty table had ambushed her.

All her senses felt primed, on alert. She heard the ticking of the chromed and enamelled clock on Doris Sheppard's stove, felt the surprisingly cool breeze that lifted the dusty ancient curtains and saw with acute clarity the little dust particles as they rose in the light, riding the upward gust of September air, then drifted downward toward the flecked amber linoleum.

She felt restful, suspended in time, chewing her floury scone, sipping her coffee and listening to Arthur.

"The little egg cup I found in the junk store near the bakery," he said. "The knives I got at the antique shop, near the little pizza place there. The Blue Pig or the Blue Whale?"

"Whale." She was amazed. He had gathered all these little comforts to him in less than a week.

"That's a handsome bag you have," Arthur said. "I like it."

She wiped her fingers on the little fringed napkin and bent over to pick up her purse which had been sitting beside her chair, on the floor, like an obedient pup. She handed it to Arthur who took it carefully, like someone set to examine a Ming vase or a piece of pre-Colombian pottery.

After he had examined it and remarked on the color and the suppleness of the leather, she told him the story of the purse. He laughed, flinging back his head and removing his glasses to dab at the corners of his eyes with the green napkin, when she described Marjorie Trimble and the accidental left hook that knocked over the bloody marys and killed her vinyl purse.

"I was surprised at myself for taking the check," she concluded. "It isn't the kind of thing I would usually do."

She pushed at a crumb on the thick white plate. "My husband thinks I'm daft."

They drifted a little more, sipping their coffee, thinking about the sound of the word "daft," as it echoed in the room.

They might have been in a house in a forest where tree silence and the cushion of fallen cedar branches quiets everything to a still, fragile immediacy which can be broken by the small sound of a twig snapping nearby or by the far away rip of a chain saw suddenly tearing through the absence of sound.

They could have been in a walkup flat over a grocery store in a city where afternoon traffic had descended to perfect pitch and beat, canceling itself out, leaving two coffee drinkers sitting at an oil-cloth covered, wooden table in a smooth, hopeless silence punctuated only by the sound of a tin of milk being pushed across the table. A movie scene.

But they were in Doris Sheppard's silent kitchen; a place where time seemed not to exist and where you half expected a shirt-waisted house-wife to carry in her paper-bagged groceries with cotton gloved hands, a sturdy leather purse dangling from her wrist. A dutiful husband in a fedora might appear too and say something like "Gosh, honey..."

"Daft?" Arthur said after a moment. "For taking the money? But didn't this Marjorie owe you something?"

He was puzzled. The outsider male who could see that somebody in this equation was not acting rationally. And it didn't appear to be the wife. In this drama, it looked like the husband was the one not dealing from the top of the deck. If her husband thought she was daft - it wasn't for taking Marjorie Trimble's money.

"Well, she may have owed me something," Pauline said. "But not two hundred and fifty dollars."

"But if that's what a good purse costs?" Arthur persisted.

"But mine wasn't a good purse. It was a piece of junk," she said. "I hated it."

"Ah," he said. "I used to make do with things that I didn't like. I stopped."

"Well, maybe I have too," Pauline said. "Which I suppose is why I took the money."

Arthur nodded and raised the white mug to his mouth.

Pauline looked out the window. She could see her spindly, yellow-ing geraniums from here, perched on the railing of the back deck of her house. She was embarrassed at this turn of conversation. The meaning of the purse lay humming just beneath her consciousness.

She felt like the child with a special object which upon being admired by an adult suddenly loses its power. She was balanced on a precipice just now, and a pinched and burning feeling encircled her head. The memory of shame. Or yearning.

She wanted to fling the purse away, like the confused and seemingly petulant child who sees her object lose its mystery, become ordinary. And she wanted to draw the purse nearer. Hide it, store its power away.

A feeling like grief and loss was down there with the humming. She blinked and turned away from the window.

Oh, what's the use?

And what after all, was the use? Was the purpose of ordinary, everyday life to simply survive and pass on a child or two to the next generation, trusting all the while that we were here to gather some agreeable trinkets to divert our attention and perhaps a little admiration to round things out?

"Are you allergic to cigarette smoke?" Arthur asked.

"No. No, I'm not. Please smoke," she said quickly.

"It's something I do rarely, now," he said. "Sometimes it seems like a certain cup of coffee just cries out for one. I don't know why that is."

He pushed his chair back with a brisk little movement and crossed to the mudroom.

"I guess I'm sort of hiding them from myself," he called back to Pauline, his voice muffled. He had his head inside of one of the neat little cupboards.

He returned bearing a small tin ash tray and a package of cigarettes.

"I've been keeping them out there in a cupboard with Doris's plastic bags," he said. "When I have to ferret around in there for my smokes, it reminds me of our various and strange human compulsions."

He withdrew a cigarette. "Kind of satisfying really."

"May I?" said Pauline raising her eyebrows in the direction of the package.

"Indeed."

Quickly he handed her the cigarette he had just withdrawn and took another from the pack for himself. He picked up an old fashioned kitchen match from a small box and drew it across the pebbled edge. It made a dry, scratching sound. When the sulfur had burned away he presented the match to her and then lit his own.

They smoked in silence for a moment, watching the smoke rise and fall and then drift toward the window.

"If you ever need a plastic bag, Doris Sheppard is your gal," he said, reaching to refill her cup.

Pauline was grateful for this ease, the way he had of drifting along with time, not pushing at it, punching it, wondering what the next minute would hold, what it ought to be filled with. Or asking you to fill it up, either.

This was the same peace that she and Madeline had drifted back from sleep on, yesterday morning. Time was passing gently, with a rhythm like the little wavelets which plop daintily at the lakeshore on a summer evening. Nothing pulled at them, nothing demanded their attention. They sat.

"Does she have a lot of plastic bags?" asked Pauline when several quiet minutes had drifted away. She turned to look at the mudroom.

"Two of those cupboards. Crammed to the gunwales." He leaned forward to stub his cigarette in the little tin ashtray then brushed at his kahki slacks, flicking aside invisible ash and scone crumbs.

Doris's clock ticked on in measured little chrome beats.

"Hmmph," said Pauline. "Funny the stuff we keep."

She stubbed her cigarette.

"And the stuff we're drawn to," said Arthur.

"True," she said. She could almost feel her purse there beside her.

What a strange conversation for them to be having. They might have been expected to gossip about Isobel; about the Poulos family; about Doris Sheppard and her husband. They might have expected to find themselves talking about the weather, the sights ... But they were not.

"I have a beautiful lamp I brought with me," Arthur said. "Something that I was drawn to. In a magazine."

"The one in the living room?" she said. "With your chairs? It's beautiful."

"I had never seen a lamp like that before I saw the one in the magazine. With a shade like that. Lined in gold paper or some kind of heavy material." He shook his head, smiling at the recollection of holding the magazine up close to his face, carefully studying the lamp.

I didn't know I was searching for you until I saw you, says the lover to the beloved.

That's what Arthur felt about the lamp. There it was. Gold, luminous, imbued with magic; created, in existence already, somewhere deep in his soul. It had been with him always and he had not known it.

"A few days later," he said. "I was walking with a friend of mine, near her apartment, and I saw it. The very lamp. In a store window. At night. The next day I went back and bought it."

When he and Beryl stopped that night in front of the furniture shop window, he did not tell her that he had clipped a picture of the very lamp from his sister's airline magazine. He did not tell Pauline now, how he had cut out the picture, feeling furtive and silly, yet compelled.

Pauline smiled and looked down at the toffee colored purse, still leaning neatly against her chair.

"I really should go," she said. "I'm sort of playing hooky. In fact, I'm having a sick day."

"You're not well?" Arthur asked. "A flu or something?"

"I don't know," she said, pushing back the chair and rising. She felt so very well now, not even dizzy from the cigarette. It was hard to recall.

"I just felt dreadful earlier. My husband had to dress Madeline, my little girl, and take her to school," She stopped. "I'm fine now. Thank you for a wonderful coffee break."

CHAPTER SIX

She stood in her silent kitchen listening to the telephone message from Richard. His mother would pick Madeline up at school.

"Mother will keep her until dinnertime, then drop her home. Are you feeling any better? You looked really wiped this morning. Call the office if you need anything, Okay? See you later. Oh, yeah, I called Ellen. She said she'll give you a ring later on. I've gotta run. By."

The machine beeped and began to rewind itself. It chuffed swiftly backward then clicked and the kitchen was perfectly silent again.

Pauline sat down on Madeline's stool and folded her arms across the cool white counter top. Then, laying her cheek against her arm, on the cotton sleeve of Richard's striped shirt, she began to weep.

⌘ ⌘ ⌘

In Doris's kitchen, Arthur was washing the dishes - the washing up, as Joan had called it.

He plunged the sturdy, white plates into sudsy water in the deep and ancient enamelled sink. No dishwasher for Doris. No normal wash for her.

When the plates and cups were rinsed and neatly stowed in the draining rack he dried his hands and took down his new list. He placed a new slip of paper under the lady bug magnet. There was a book he meant to get, a bottle of wine to pick up to take to dinner at the home of retired friends. He was being wined and dined these first weeks in Vancouver.

We had forgotten the power - unless we were deeply religious or spent time in a monastery, Arthur thought - of ritual and repetition. It called to us, it offered us power, but we had turned away from it; seen it as primitive, mindless.

But he had listened intently and heard the call. He was careful to observe himself though, on guard against fussiness disguised as ritual and soulfulness. He was vigilant but open hearted.

Pauline was being called, but she had grown accustomed to the casually brutalizing forces of modern life. She thought she was a doing and not a being. Her circuits were jangled, her brain was frantic with grief and longing, but she had come to believe that what Peggy Lee sang long ago, must be true. That's all there is.

Nothing to mark the seasons but back to school sales and Christmas frenzy. Nothing to celebrate but brittle wedding ceremonies like the one last Saturday where everyone donned costumes and no one remembered the meaning of any of it. No wonder she had her head down on the counter weeping. Her heart was breaking. And what did she see as solace? Nothing.

For a few moments on Saturday afternoon, at the wedding, she had thought that exquisite clothes might do it; might impart some purpose, but she hadn't the energy to chase them. And now the bloody purse and its apparent importance. She was hobbled by the paradox of important objects. Should we want stuff or want nothing? Did stuff have meaning? Or not? It was a delicate question.

But Arthur? Arthur was happy. A suspect state in Western culture, he knew. Sneered at by nihilists and doubted by intellectuals; deemed dubious by Freud who thought the best we might expect was a sort of mitigated misery. Nevertheless, there he was.

At Joan's funeral service and again at the burial, he had felt calm and detached, unmoved. Later, packing up her things, he had worried about this lack of feeling. Joan had left the house, left the planet, left him and there was nothing to be done. Neither happy nor unhappy, she had died much as she had lived; quietly and unobtrusively. A sudden heart attack while watering plants in her austere living room. Gone. The door had slammed shut after her, leaving Arthur with rather than grief, a sense of puzzlement.

Tidy, tidy, tidy. Joan had lived not lightly on the earth, but dutifully. The kitchen, the laundry room, she'd left them clean all right, but curiously untouched.

As was Arthur then. Clean but untouched.

"When did you start going to church?" Greg asked him on a Sunday afternoon when Joan had been dead for a year.

"I'm curious," Arthur said.

Out of curiosity had grown conviction; the conviction that he was being followed or shadowed by possibility. By the possibility of his own life. He had to slow down and pay close attention if he was to apprehend it. And it was a shy thing too. It couldn't be called out by simple busyness and the ritual round of doing. But it could be apprehended by attention.

So, he began to pay attention. And he decided to be happy. Not foolishly happy or happy in spite of. Happy. He stopped, saw where he was and decided to be happy.

What gives me joy, he asked himself each morning of that second year. And he began to gather things to him that he had not known for sixty years.

The sound of small, moving water made him glad, he discovered. Or rather, he remembered. So he began to take walks beside the little stream which coursed behind the recreation center, a startling modern building where someone had had the wit to leave a brave little forest of shivering aspen and birch and stoic stunted pines. The stream ran through the forest and out into the hummocky prairie grasses, turning marshy at the edge of a new subdivision. He walked the length of it through three seasons, until it froze then disappeared. He began to look at water in a new way.

Smooth stones called to him and he began to gather them up, sorting the truly numinous ones from the ordinary and placing them about the house in jars and on saucers.

He studied the dishes in the kitchen that was now his alone and discovered that they meant nothing. He boxed them up for the Salvation Army and replaced them with plates and mugs in a brilliant blue which reminded him of marbles he'd had as a boy.

Figurines and ornaments which had sat in a pale oak curio cabinet went next. And then the whole house was gone. Sold. A house which he had built.

"Dad sold the house," he heard Greg tell a neighbor. "Sad, I guess."

And he was sad in a way. But he thought too, "This is my real life."

Joan was slipping, slipping away, until looking at her photographs he could not recall the sound of her voice or remember the way she moved.

He learned to cook pieces of halibut and chicken breasts and realized that all his life he had eaten food that he really hadn't liked. English food. And in his new apartment he read late into the night. He was burning away a former self. Burning until being with Greg or with his sister was like being in a play.

"You've hardly kept anything of Joan's," his sister said. "Those beautiful Royal Doulton figurines she had all those years. The lovely furniture."

What he had kept, what had seemed to him to be truly his wife, was a small, oval gift shop picture. A black palm tree silhouetted against a fiery tropical sky. It was a cheap thing, but Joan had kept it tucked among her stockings, a private memento which Arthur's sister had discovered as she emptied the bureau.

"It's a tchochke, a piece of junk," Lillian clucked when Arthur said he would keep the little picture.

Ah, he thought, then why has she kept it all these years, tucked like a forbidden secret, among her stockings?

Then he felt grief. Not for his loss of Joan but for her; for the loss of her life, the life she had never truly claimed even while she lived it. Could we help each other to do this, he wondered. Truly claim our lives? Or was it strictly a solitary pursuit?

So his grief then too, was like a burning thing. He kept Joan's palm tree picture and an old childhood photograph of her on his bureau. He was trying to know her now, as he had never known her through nearly forty years of marriage.

He wasn't becoming a daffy old widower though, surrounded by mementos and balls of string. He was open to possibilities. He said the Lord's Prayer in the morning and at night; devoted himself to quiet listening several times a day and turned the phone off when he listened to opera tapes or to the CBC.

"I tried to call you, last night," Greg would complain. "Were you out?"

Poor Greg. His father was daft. The circle of his life now had an enormous wow in it. Arthur would not be circumscribed and his defection had left Greg feeling fierce. For this too Arthur felt something like grief.

Hadn't he and Joan tricked Greg into believing that this sleepwalk was the real thing. Arthur didn't know how to shake him to wake him up. He kept a childhood picture of Greg on his bureau too, and one of Galen, the baby boy who died when polio swept into Edmonton in 1954.

Is this kind of creepy, Arthur wondered? Morbid? Yet, those photographs seemed right. He decided to keep them there, on his bureau and just wait and see.

Was Joan giving him his life? Greater love hath no man than this; that he lay down his life for another. Was that what Joan had done? Unwittingly? A grim thought that occupied him all one winter two years after she died.

Still, he was happy. A sense of joyous aliveness accompanied him even as he chewed over the slightly ominous idea that perhaps she had laid down her life in order that he would have his. After all, what would they have done, had she lived? Continued their lives, each unwillingly to jar the other awake? What of Joan and her funny, little tropical picture?

Its lurid colors were not something you saw in her life, certainly. What called to her in that scene he wondered, picking it up, dusting it, polishing it absently on his hip.

They had travelled to Hawaii and to Antigua; had seen sunsets on the flat, even Pacific and on the curve of the Caribbean Sea, but he had never seen her swoon in the face of one. What a strange thing to be trying to know someone backward, as it were.

"Joan didn't want that ravine lot, you know," his sister confided when Joan had been dead three years. "She wanted a house downtown."

By then he was living downtown, near the river, in an old building where the ceilings were high and the baseboards came up to a man's shin. He had spent forty five years building houses, entire suburbs and there he was in an apartment building quite as old as he was, with windows that creaked when you pushed them up and an uneven bathroom floor tiled in tiny mosaics which felt fiercely cold to the foot all winter long

Joan hadn't wanted the ravine lot.

Could you blame her? On the other hand, in 1956, when your husband built a new housing development and built you a nice, modern suburban house on the best lot, who said no thanks? But think what she must have felt, leaving the leafy confines of the streets where she had pushed both prams, walked both babies to the grocery and to the bakery. Where she stood on the corner to watch Greg walk home from church basement kindergarten. The house where Galen died.

But she was being called on to be modern, to move with the times and she went too, berating herself for silliness when her chest grew tight and achy as she packed up the old house.

Being young she convinced herself she was mistaken in what she felt; indeed wrong. When people said she was a lucky girl, she smiled and smiled.

Why was Arthur not surprised when he really looked at his house, to discover that Joan had never truly moved in? Selling it had been a piece of cake. He never looked back.

But he had her little gift shop picture and the photograph of her in a smocked cotton summer dress, taken in 1930 on the back porch of her grandmother's farmhouse near High River.

"Joanie, five years old. Summer '30 at Mother's," her mother had written on the back of the fading black and white photo.

Arthur studied the picture often, looking at the smiling little face before the screen door, trying to imagine what she had been doing just before the photo was snapped. What she went on to do, just afterward.

This little girl had not wanted the ravine lot. She hadn't wanted the modern house.

Looking at the photo, Arthur sometimes fancied he could hear the screen door slam.

"Is this a shrine?" Greg had asked.

He was looking at Arthur's photographs and his stones set so neatly there on the bureau top.

"In a way," Arthur had answered.

After all, he even had a candle there at that point. It was a rolled beeswax one from the summer market and the smell of it kept calling him toward a memory. But of what? It was just out of reach.

"Poor bastards," he said to Beryl when he was mulling over the meaning of the candle with her one evening and they had wandered quite naturally to the topic of Alzheimer's.

As moderns do when they misplace their keys, or forget the name of the insurance agent.

Imagine, having everything, the whole universe, on the tip of your tongue and not being able to name it. Or claim it. And you would know it in some part of your brain or mind, Arthur thought. You would know that you had once possessed words for it all. But that they were beyond reach now. Speechless. And yet there must be a cacophony, a buzz, a swarm of knowing, in the mind of the senile, the Alzheimer's patient.

"You're not old, Dad," said Greg, when Arthur sold the building company he had begun with Gene Clarence in 1950, the year Greg was born.

"Maybe not," Arthur had said. "But I'm awful tired of building houses."

In truth, he had only begun to really think about houses, about homes. When he learned that Joan had never wanted the modern house on the ravine lot, in his heart he was unsurprised. Prepared.

"Do you think it's a good idea to sell your business so soon after selling the house?" asked Greg. "Just selling everything doesn't seem that wise, to me."

"I know it seems odd to you," said Arthur. "And I know you didn't think I should sell the house so soon after your mother died."

How to explain it all?

"The house was too big," he offered. "Clarence and Dean mightn't be worth so much down the road. Building is changing. I'm tired of it."

Let me get this straight, Greg had telegraphed to Arthur in his annoyed huffs, his furious controlled movements. You sell the house we lived in nearly all my life, most of your married life. You sell the company you've always owned. And you move to a drafty apartment downtown. And you start collecting rocks and old furniture.

"Sixty-three is pretty young to retire you know," said Greg. "A guy like you. Always on the job. I can't see it, Dad."

What would he do with his time? Shuffle off to play checkers down by the river?

No. He rose early, made lists, haunted bookstores, looked through magazines he'd never heard of and attended every lecture that piqued his curiosity. Bulletin boards at the university library and at rundown bookstores seemed like signposts to an unknowable future.

He sold his car and one spring morning met Beryl at a bus stop around the corner from his apartment building.

"She's not my girlfriend," he told Greg.

Beryl too was busy refining herself, a divorcee with no need for a permanent partner. She would snort at being called a girlfriend.

"Your lady friend, then," said Greg. "Invite her with you some Sunday."

Was he ashamed of being a grandfather, of having a son whose voice boomed and who wore golf shirts so smooth and neat they must have come from the drycleaner's on hangers and covered in polythene film?

"He's very yuppie," he told Beryl.

"Oh, I'll meet him some day," she said.

Arthur admired her gravity, her quickness, the folded-in smoothness of her. What a pleasure to admire a woman, see her nose turn red in the winter cold, watch her laugh at the theater and yet have no hold on her.

"Oh, we're a pair!" she laughed once when they were walking in the mauve light of a spring evening that was heavy with the scent of newborn lilacs.

They had been talking about irritation. People grew annoyed with one another over time. What was it? And how did some manage to stay comfortable? Unannoyed.

"I think it's when they fold together into one person," said Beryl. "When they agree at some point in the marriage or whatever that they won't change."

She was as tall as Arthur, walking neatly there beside him, her hair piled up on top of her head in a precise ash-colored twist, her arms swinging smoothly.

"Like one person?" Arthur asked. "Interesting thought. Did you try to do that? Be that way when you were married?"

"In a way," said Beryl. "And I'm not sure how you can be one person and live easily with another. Unless one person agrees to not take up space. Which I think I tried to do for years."

"I cannot imagine you not taking up space," said Arthur. "You're too much yourself."

"You didn't know me before," said Beryl.

They had walked in silence for a while until she suddenly laughed and said they were a pair.

⌘ ⌘ ⌘

"Grandma says we need a real house," said Madeline.

She was at the counter, the plastic pail of crayons at her elbow, an old coloring book and sheets of paper spread around her. She turned the coloring book this way and that, working hard at the new skill of staying within the lines. Of not scribbling

"One where there aren't cars all over," she said. "That's by itself. And a yard too."

"We have a yard," said Pauline. She picked up her wine glass and took a sip.

The back door was open onto the deck. Across the park, she could see the steady stream of home bound traffic. Bumper to bumper. A conga line of cars threading anxiously toward the suburbs. The noise of them hummed through the kitchen.

"Not a big one, we don't. Like Leslie has," said Madeline as she searched the crayon bucket, her little pink fingers picking neatly through the felt pens, the Crayola stubs and the broken pencil crayons. Searching for the right color.

This new compulsion to use the correct color, to stay within the lines of her artwork, to stick with a picture even when she had grown tired of it, squeezed Pauline's heart. It was as though Madeline was waving good-bye; no longer the anarchist who took no notice of convention, who lay down on the floor when she felt tired and who gently broke wind when her bowels said to and not just when she was alone.

And now, a Trojan Horse, an emissary from Richard's mother, Madeline was bearing the news that they should move to a real house. Buy a house. Since they could not afford a house in this part of the city it meant the suburbs. Madeline was the well-aimed arrow, the heat-seeking missile aimed at Pauline's heart.

"I love Grandma's house," said Madeline. "I love this house too. I'll draw you a picture of Grandma's house."

Of course, it was time to move. Literally and figuratively. It was absurd to continue to pay rent. It was absurd that she was still piddling around at freelance copywriting now that Madeline was in school most of the day. It was time. It was time.

She needed to make real money, she needed to get some ambition. They needed a real house.

These things seemed to be floating on the wind; a force gathering around Pauline's duplex on fourteenth avenue. There was a storm gathering strength and it was going to blow them all about. For her part Pauline felt she ought to dig her nails into the palms of her hands and wake up for Christ's sake! Do something!

There wasn't a crisis, though. Yet. She didn't need to get a passport, grab her child and flee. They weren't being pursued by invading armies or even by a psycho husband. Things were prosaic, still and calm. The gale though was gathering strength about them. Pauline could hear the howling, but she wasn't sure whether the sound was inside her head or out there in the streets.

"You need a real job," Ellen told her.

"Get a nice house in the suburbs," said Daphne. "Someplace where Madeline can ride her bike."

And that was what was on offer. Stop stalling. Get a house, get a job, jump into the river with the rest of us. And by the way, if you're thinking of having another baby you better do it but quick sister, because time is wasting.

Time. Time. It was ticking away.

"I'm going to take Maddie out to my folks place this weekend," Pauline said.

They were in a truce, an uneasy state of non-war that was not peace and carried little goodwill on the part of the temporary noncombatants.

"Good," said Richard as he placed dripping plates in the bottom rack of the dishwasher. "That'll be good. We'll be doing the inventory all weekend."

"Ellen was here," Pauline offered. "She stopped by on her way to an appointment up on forty first."

"What did she have to say?"

"Not much. More business. More money. The usual. No new men in her life and her mother is coming out from Toronto," Pauline said. She paused at the counter across from him. "Want some tea? A cup of coffee?"

"No, I drank too many today. I'm coffee-ed out." This was said with elaborate politeness. Then, an added dollop of civility. "Thanks."

Would a director yell, "Cut! You people are sleepwalking through this. Let's have a little emotion!" Or would they drift through this scene and a thousand others until they were called on to take a final bow for this insipid little domestic drama?

"Ellen say who her new clients are?" Richard asked.

He liked to hear about Ellen, was in fact fascinated by her. She was a woman who careened about on too high heels and drank too much on weekends. She was rigidly compartmentalized though and could narrow her eyes and her mental focus like a little hyena. She got in there and got the good stuff, Monday through Friday and got fluffy on weekends.

She was a freelance purchasing agent.

"It's perfect work for me," she fluttered at men. "I love to shop."

What she really loved to do, though was rip through men who tried to dismiss her ferocious pit-bull intelligence. She negotiated for, on an ordinary week, refrigerator parts from Italy for a manufacturer of restaurant appliances, switches and dials from Germany for a shipbuilder on the north shore and cool Ontario slate and used Chicago brick for architects. She lived on the phone and drove a sports car. She was tightly wound and acquisitive. Ellen saw Pauline as a responsibility and a challenge. Pauline needed to be brought up to speed.

Pauline often thought how well it would work if she could give Richard and Ellen to each other. That would tie the ends up neatly.

"I should talk to her about chrome," said Richard. "She probably has a line on overseas clients."

Richard, former broker and bon vivant and now manager and nominal owner of a dreary business his father acquired some years before, seemed bowed under by the enormity of the thing he had taken on. This huge task, this business, employed nearly one hundred people and they all depended on him to stay interested in the matter of chroming and plating all manner of shiny commercial goods from automobile bumpers to marine parts. He was heartily sick of it, but could not imagine what might be better or what he might do with his life.

And that was it. He could not imagine.

But who taught us this? Who suggested it might be a good and necessary thing to imagine. To learn to read our singular imaginings.

What, instead did we learn to imagine? Stuff. Give me stuff. Lots of it, which would be replaced in short order by other stuff. We needn't even imagine the stuff. Its images were conjured twenty-four hours a day on screens and on every printable surface.

Richard wouldn't laugh at bright, shiny stuff though, because that was what the poor bugger was manufacturing. It lay glittering in his factory; reflecting in curious wows and elongations; concave and convex. The people who worked there had grown accustomed to seeing themselves reflected back as though in a fun house mirror. Richard, though, was still disconcerted, when he was on the factory floor, to see himself comically stretched and shining there, while he talked about shipping dates with over-alled men with clipboards.

Standing on the catwalk, high above the shop floor he could see these parts of things just shining and shining. He could not imagine what he was doing there.

He wanted Pauline to share this puzzle, to bear with him the weight of this dull business of shiny objects. "We are doing inventory all weekend," he said and she was meant to say: "But, I'll help."

⌘　⌘　⌘

CHAPTER SEVEN

"He's doing inventory," Pauline said..

"What? Counting all that stuff? It's not all on computer by now?" Paul Davies shook his head.

Pauline was at the counter in her mother's kitchen, buttering bread for a sandwich for Madeline who was in the backyard. Pauline could see her mother, Grace, sitting on the step of the laundry stand, one arm raised to shield her eyes from the sun, the other resting easily in her lap. She watched Madeline run in circles on the uneven lawn, a soft smile on her tanned and gentle face. Madeline was chasing bubbles, made from dish soap and cooking oil and blown through an old pipe from the toy box Grace kept in the covered porch.

Pauline's father, fiddled with the coffee maker. He could not see whether the water measurement was indicated on the inside or the outside of the machine. Even so, even as he was nearly defeated by this domestic contraption, he was absurdly cross with Richard for not having all the bits of his business, numbered and inventoried on the computer. This from a man who still went into his millyard and counted the shake blocks piled there and the bound pallets of split shakes ready for loading, using an arcane and personal multiplication method he had developed three decades ago.

The numbers are in the computer, Corinne told him, when he stalked past her desk, pushing the hard hat well back on his head so he could scratch at his forehead. Ha. He kept a flat lumber pencil and creased bits of paper in his shirt pocket.

Had Pauline run home to Cedar Mills? Why would she not? It was where she had grown up, looking out a kitchen window that gave immediately onto a field ringed with blackberry bushes as large as Volkswagens. She could see the bushes now as she reached for a plate above the sink.

You dropped a plank into one of those thorny bushes, then simply walked in and filled your pail with the enormous, elegant berries whose perfume would haunt your days and whose flavour remained a persistent puzzle. Blackberries, Pauline had decided when she was young, tasted like the scent of the cologne her grade two teacher, Mrs. Reid, had worn. Small explosions of aroma in your mouth that were read first by your nose, then by your tongue. Some people wouldn't eat them though, because the seeds were heavy going. Grace Davies sieved these seeds out when she boiled the berries up to make jelly each fall.

Dripping in purple-stained cheesecloth set in an old aluminum colander suspended over Grace's stainless steel mixing bowl, the cooked berries were also the smell of new clothes and of back to school.

Peaches sent down from the Okanagan by relatives and kept under newspaper in cardboard boxes out in the closed porch added their sharp yellow scent, in counterpoint, so that Pauline and her sisters reeled off to school, drunk on the smells of their mother's kitchen and forever after unable to separate the smell of new books from the textured aromas of gold and purple fruit and heavy autumn air.

September was golden in this little village tucked in the folds of the Fraser River as it spilled smoothly toward the Pacific. Here, in the house where Pauline grew up and all the way down the hill to her father's mill, the air stayed heavy this time of year, dense with the moisture that the earth and the river traded back and forth by way of the high and urgent sun which seemed to burn hotter in the autumn, even as it moved slowly, slowly southerly and away.

She had not wanted him to come. Was glad that Richard was counting metal objects in a Richmond warehouse.

I'm a selfish and secretive person who needs to learn how to share, she told herself as she lay next to Madeline on the fold out sofa in her old room. It was now her mother's "spare" room, a small space piled high with rows of books on sagging shelves and curtain fabrics folded and stacked on a brown cane chair and boxes of canning jars recently brought up from the basement and smelling slightly of damp and mold.

Even here there were late-ripening peaches, set out in a cut down cardboard box and covered in dry and yellowing news paper. It had not occurred to her or to Grace to move the peaches which lay on top of the old mirrored bureau, snug in their box, like fuzzy rose and amber colored eggs in a flat.

It was these singular smells which called and called to her. The fruit scents which she gently inhaled as she drifted off, were a mere overlay to the more essential smell of her parents' house, the smell which caused guests to feel oddly comforted and good, should they enter through the covered back porch. Cedar and sweat. This was Cedar Mills, don't forget.

The smell of Western Red Cedar. It was not the antiseptic smell of Tennessee cedar, meant to keep moths from your woolens over the hot months of summer storage. A more esthetically pleasing moth ball as it were. No. This was a wild rain forest smell. There were locked-up giant ferns and moss and smooth stones in the smell. Rushing water and damp earth.

The nose swooned to inhale it, saying more, more. And in this cedar's scent was the memory of something primordial or perhaps it followed us from heaven. It was clean and homely; both warm and cool at once. An essential smell. It was a key fitting smoothly into a lock inside the brain. It opened a little box of yearning which might be deep in some recess of the amygdala or in Broca's brain. Somewhere, both ancient and very new.

Pauline was sound asleep in it with Madeline tucked up there beside her.

They were breathing deeply and soundly in the silent house in Cedar Mills, a small village flung across both sides of the Lougheed Highway, tipping over that old road's embankments and so down to the mills and fishing boats on the Fraser River. The cafe and service station was shut up and asleep. On the other side of the highway, Mr. Delmonico's General Store was shut too and he was asleep upstairs dreaming his widower's dreams.

Subdivisions were marching toward them though. Even now, commuters lived among them. Mr. Delmonico stocked Dijon mustard now. And bagels. But for now they were a village asleep on the edge of the Fraser River.

Forty five miles away in Vancouver, Arthur was tucked up for the night too, gently asleep to the sound of the chestnut trees swaying smoothly in the September gusts which played in the night time streets.

Richard had fallen asleep in front of the TV set again. As the little room grew cooler and cooler he shifted in his sleep, pulling into himself for warmth. He tucked both hands between his legs like a child, as he folded uneasily into the little sofa in Pauline's office.

A short drive from Richard's chilly sleep and Arthur's gentle snoozing, over in Kerrisdale, Daphne was up for the third time. Dick snored and Daphne wore earplugs, a mask and several pillows over her face, but she was still summonsed from sleep by demons and once awake held hostage by the steady roar issuing from Dick's face. Perhaps the pillows should be over Dick's face? Rather firmly? The thought had occurred to her.

⌘ ⌘ ⌘

The peaches were piled high beside the sink. Next to them, the jars, clean now and no longer smelling of damp earth and mildew, stood steaming. Freshly washed and still hot, the jars were ready to be filled with the smooth yellow crescents Grace was neatly sectioning from the fruit.

"Pauline?" she called, then paused to listen. She used the back of her wrist to push up a stray curl, the sharp little knife still in her damp hand, its curved blade resting neatly against her thumb.

"I'm awake, Gramma."

Grace heard Madeline pad across the kitchen, her bare feet making little splatting sounds on the tile floor.

"Mommy is in the bathroom," Madeline said as she stooped to pull at the door beneath the sink. She pulled out the little wooden step stool and Grace stepped aside to let her push the cupboard door closed.

"Mind your fingers," she said, absently.

"I've got it." Madeline climbed up to stand beside her. "There's a lot," she said. "Who eats all the peaches?"

"Well, some go to your house. Some go to Auntie Dee's and some are for Grampa to have at breakfast time in the winter. They all get eaten up."

Grace bent to kiss the top of Madeline's head, a sort of punctuation. "They all get eaten," she murmured.

"Well, it's a lot," said Madeline, trailing her fingers in the warm water where peaches bobbed, their peculiar, gritty fur gathering in a fuzzy scum at the rim of the sink.

This peach muck reminded Grace of the backwash of cedar bark and mill junk that gathered on the river at Paul's mill. There was the mechanical busyness of the brain, going about it's business. This is like that, it said. This incessant brain chatter, this comparing of pictures was like the boring relative who could be counted on to say, "That reminds me…"

Grace did not think all this, but simply smiled at this busywork of her brain as the image appeared, was acknowledged and then drifted off, to appear again next year, when she once again stood there at her sink full of peaches.

"I'll just put these on to process, Missy, then I'll get you some breakfast. How 'bout that?"

When she had settled the rack of jars into the ancient speckled canning kettle and set the lid, she drew paper towel smoothly from the roll above the sink and dried her hands. They were sore from the acid of the fruit; dry and wounded feeling. Later there would be brown stains beneath her nails and fine cracks in the delicate pads of her fingers. This too happened on a yearly basis.

She reached up for the small plunger bottle of lotion that she kept on a little pie-shaped shelf meant for plants or some sort of kitchen ornament. On the shelf were her rings too, her car keys, a stray earring, pins, a paper clip or two, coins - the personal miscellany of tiny things a woman piled up in her daily round in the kitchen.

"Why do you always look out the window, Gramma?" asked Madeline.

Grace rubbed the lotion in delicate circles on the backs of her hands.

"Ha. I don't know." She quickly wiped the dampness of her palms across her apron. "Do I?"

She settled Madeline with cereal and juice at the wooden table, then went to the window in the little breakfast area to push back the striped curtains.

"Rain," she said peering out. "Looks like rain's coming, Maddie."

She carried the coffee pot to the sink. While the water ran, she looked out the window. She didn't know why.

"I didn't even hear you come in for those jars." Pauline stretched deeply as she entered the kitchen, raising her arms over her head and pulling her shoulders back. Like someone rowing backwards.

"I slept like I'd been shot."

"You were always a good sleeper, hon," said Grace.

What was this balm in hearing about yourself? As though one were still a child overhearing a parent talk about you with another adult?

Pauline gathered the comment into herself like a lush compliment. See? My mom observes me, notices me. Has always noticed me. I am special.

Did she come here for this? A deliberate step back in time? To wiggle in the comfort of being known? To be cosseted by the familiar smell of her mother's kitchen, the cedar scent of the covered porch? Had she quite literally been led here by the nose? By her nose's longing for the familiar?

"I was admiring your new purse," said Grace, setting out coffee cups. "I've always like that color, but, you know me. I always got a black one for winter and a white one for spring and summer. I like that. Like toffee."

"No one can look in Mommy's purse," said Madeline. "You always have to ask."

"I was always like that too," Grace said, with a little laugh. "That's probably where your mother gets it."

"I was going to help you can those, Mom." Pauline nodded toward the rows of amber jars near the utility sink.

And that was part of what had brought her. She liked canning peaches. She liked the orderly neatness of the jars; the pleasure of seeing them fill up with slices of fruit. She liked the bountiful, sustaining feel of it. The filled jars, left out to be admired by anyone who came through the kitchen. She liked to see them lined up on a clean dish towel.

"Well you still can. There's another dozen jars, I'll bet."

"Good."

"I don't want to can peaches," said Madeline. "I'm going to catch a cat, I think."

"You watch out, Maddie," said Grace. "Those kittens were born out there in a tree stump. They don't know about little girls chasing after them."

The kittens, born early in the summer, to a feral cat who had wandered in from the woods, played hide and seek with Grace when she went outside to leave them milk or bits of ground meat.

"I should call the SPCA."

"Don't Gramma. I'm going to get one. For me."

Pauline swirled the coffee in her cup and smiled across at Maddie as she took a sip.

"Maddie, your dad doesn't like kitties. And he certainly wouldn't like a wild country cat."

Madeline picked up her cereal bowl and drank from it.

"If I just brought it home?" she said placing the bowl on the table. "Couldn't he like it then? Leslie has a cat."

Was this a sly reference to the suburban house they ought to have? Like Leslie's. And once there would they then not have the right to a cat?

Where was all this leading? Pauline was wasting time or marking time and there was a roaring noise in her head which said, hurry up, hurry up. To where? For what?

⌘　⌘　⌘

The kitten sat neatly on Madeline's lap, undisturbed by the movement of the car, the heat of Maddie's small hand on its back. It did not purr, but simply sat.

The Sunday evening traffic moved smoothly along, carrying them back to the city, back to fourteenth avenue, back to Richard. The cat, the girl and the woman.

There were six jars of peaches on the back seat, boxed neatly by Grace, small pieces of paper tucked between the jars. Their perfume filled the car.

"I'm not worried about what Richard will say," Pauline told herself. But she was. Did she have the energy to defend the acquisition of a cat?

"I'm going to name the cat Mutter," said Maddie. "Like in the story."

"That's Murmmel," said Pauline.

"I like Mutter. It's like a noise," said Maddie. "Mutter, Mutter."

"Maddie and Mutter," said Pauline. "That sounds good together."

"She can be Mutt for short," said Maddie. "Like a dog. I'll keep her in a box in my room."

They were in cahoots.

It was a subtle form of undermining Richard, Pauline knew and she felt alarmed at the small thrill this seemed to be giving her.

Madeline was asleep when she nosed the car in beside the back fence, tucking it into the alley after circling the block in vain. In the suburbs she would be pulling neatly into her own driveway and sliding smoothly into a double garage.

Instead she was sneaking in the back door with a cat.

She took the warm and moist feeling kitten from Madeline's lap and set it gingerly on the back seat. The cat shook itself, then settled against Madeline's book bag and closed its eyes. Why was it not alarmed?

"I could be taking you to your death." She rubbed the mottled little head.

She reached across and unbuckled Madeline, whose head tilted at an alarming angle, her limbs sprawled and limp-seeming.

"Played out," Pauline's father would say about a child sleeping this way. "All played out."

And Madeline was.

Pauline stepped out of the car, closing her door softly. Already, the darkness was closing in on them; the great Canadian darkness stealing down from the north as they tilted away from the sun.

She pulled her denim jacket against her and looked up into the sky. Fewer stars to see here than in Cedar Mills. The sound of the city, even on a Sunday night, was dense about her. Tonight, though, there were few cars on Burrard and this absence of automobile noise nearby allowed her to hear the small domestic sounds of her street. Standing alone in the alley, while her daughter dreamed on, she listened in the gathering dark.

Richard answered the bell in his green sweatshirt and running shorts. He stepped onto the dimly lighted back porch and she handed Maddie to him.

"I've got stuff out in the car," she whispered, disentangling herself from the loose arms and the damp warmth of the sleeping child. "I'll be back in a sec."

"Christ, Pauline, you know I don't like cats."

We were always and ever trying to defend ourselves and to preserve our sense of "me." I'm a person who likes their eggs over easy, who likes summer evenings on a porch, who goes to family gatherings only on sufferance. As though we thought these might keep us anchored here. Tethered. What if you simply gave that stuff up? Stopped defining your-self by what you liked or did not like? By what you approved or disap-proved of? What then? Anarchy?

What was Richard basing this on? This dislike of cats?

The tiring thing was, it left others like supplicants. Deeking and weaving; wheedling and cajoling. Some people drawing lines and others trying to scamper over them or under them.

"I realize you aren't fond of them, Richard. But Madeline really enjoyed the cats at Mom's. She seemed genuinely attached to this one."

What was she going to do? Beg?

"Please Richard. I think she's one of those little girls who will really look after a pet."

They were sitting at the kitchen table. Perched really. Each of them signaling by their posture: *I'm not really settling in for this.*

Madeline had been tucked up in the little white bed, still in her tee shirt and panties, her jeans in a little blue pile on the braided mat beside the bed.

What if we let go of wanting to be right? But how would we get our way? How would we overcome?

"Come on honey," said Pauline. "It can't be that awful. It's just a little cat."

She settled back in her chair, telegraphing to Richard that she was willing to be sweet about this.

"They kill birds," he said.

"We'll keep it in the house. Maybe get it declawed?"

"That's creepy," said Richard. "It seems brutal."

"Ummhmm. I know."

Richard leaned back in the chair. "How are your folks? Your dad still the same?"

It was their joke. That Paul was ever the blustering woodsman, a man who wore a hard hat until his wife reminded him to take it off.

"Still the same. The mill is busy."

Pauline got up and turned on the hanging lamp over the table. She hung her denim jacket on the chair back and went to the counter.

"Mom sent you peaches. Six quarts," she said carrying the coffee pot to the sink. She turned on the water and held up the pot. "Want some?"

"You drink too much coffee, Paul," said Richard.

"You can't call the stuff at my parents' house, coffee."

"True," he said with a small laugh.

The mood was lighter now. They were on familiar ground, with their familiar banter. This might be going on up and down the street. People acting out their familiar parts. And the awful thing was that it was not so awful. This predictability. They had safely portaged the rapids, were heading into safer water now.

"Okay," said Richard. "I'll have a small cup." He stretched and peered around the room. "Where is the little bird-killer?"

⌘   ⌘   ⌘

CHAPTER EIGHT

Arthur let himself in through the mudroom door, stopping to take off his walking shoes and set them on the rubber mat. Quite unaware of doing so, he ran his hand absently along the storage cupboards, admiring anew their soundness, then pulled open the kitchen door. He had come in through the back way because he liked the alley. He liked to walk down it, with the duplexes on one side, the flat expanse of the park on the other. A paved alley! And yet it was not totally civilized, he could see. Withered morning glory vines wound up the power poles and guerrilla weeds split the concrete near the garages and garbage cans. He liked the sense of it.

He had been to dinner this Sunday evening. Again. Ever short of novelty, the retired friends of friends, in an ever-widening circle, were inviting him to dine. He was meant, he could see, to be a source of entertainment. And he could do it. Up to a point. Part of the discipline of being happy, he had found, was in telling himself "Don't take that train." This meant, when his mind wanted to wander off criticizing or blaming, he reined it in. "Don't take that train," had become his mantra. A small prayer. Thus, when his mind, admittedly tired this evening, wanted to begin a dissection of this evening's hostess, he had reminded himself; "Don't take that train."

His equilibrium thus regained, he filled Doris' ancient electric kettle and made himself a cup of mint tea. He carried it through to the living room where he stooped to turn on his golden light and set his cup on a small coaster.

"September," he said out loud. "September."

He was curious to know how long this golden season might last, here on the coast. This mellowing down, this sense that blackberry bushes and laurel hedges could overtake the place by morning, made autumn a very different animal in Vancouver than it was in Alberta. Here, things were moody, brooding; there was an undercurrent. In Alberta, the harvest was brought in, the sky got brighter in a false way and next thing you knew, you were knee deep in snow. The prairies, he thought, were rational and linear. Things followed in lock-step. You knew where you were because things were just as they appeared on the surface. Colder than a whore's heart or hotter than a forty-four. There were no currents, no mystery. Even swishing through thigh-high prairie grasses, listening to the satin-sounding rustle you made as you passed; even that, though it might make you glad, give you a little shiver of delight, even that you could easily toss off. Tell yourself you were just enjoying the fresh air.

Vancouver was different. As though it might evaporate over night. He drew a box of note paper from beneath the walnut step table. Setting it on the table top, he then arranged a makeshift desk on his lap, using a device he had discovered under Doris Shepperd's mahogany sideboard.

It was a table protector, he had finally discerned, folded up and stored with three identical pieces, meant apparently, to protect the mahogany table that Doris had shipped off to storage. While one side of the ancient and stained thing was covered in dull greenish felt, meant to sit gently on the fine wood during holiday and company meals which Arthur could not quite imagine Doris hosting, the other side was smooth and firm, Perfect for writing on and a nifty little lap desk, which fit comfortably across his knees as he sat in the wing chair. Curious, he thought, how things sometimes fit so well, for some unintended purpose.

With a sheet of the ivory note paper positioned on his little desk and the tea comfortably at his elbow on the walnut table, he began his letter.

Sunday, September 18, 1995

Dearest Beryl,

You won't be surprised to know that I'm being wined and dined by your friends. Perhaps you've already heard? What may surprise you is that the circle keeps widening out, with friends of friends inviting me along to their tables! I don't know that I'm any good for these kinds of things any longer, the smile on my face begins to feel like a death-mask, a rictus that is bound to begin frightening hostesses. Nevertheless I sail on, doing my duty and receiving several decent meals in return. I shouldn't complain.

Are you well? I'm settled in here, very neatly and am enjoying the sensation of being an anthropologist, digging about in Casa Shepperd (not actually and not too deeply at any rate.) Did you know he was an engineer? I found that a bit of a shock, because there is the most unusual porch clamped on to the front of this house. Not something I would have expected an engineer to do. But maybe it's a case of the "shoemaker's children going barefoot?" It's a beautiful old place though. About fifty years old I suspect. Have you been here? I don't remember your mentioning it. There are four identical duplexes on the street, each with a different exterior, this one a sort of clapboard, the one beside me in English shingles and the one on the other side in nice grey stucco - the old-fashioned kind. Very pretty and very Vancouver. The furthest one is a little rundown, badly in need of paint. Still recognizable as one of the "quartet."

Did I tell you about the girl - "girl" to me, though she is probably closer to thirty-five - who lives in the grey stucco? She came for coffee the end of last week. I had bumped into her in the street and she'd given me the low-down on shops etc. I took her a bouquet of the wonderful flowers I found at the Korean greengrocers. Now that I think of it, it seems a bit forward. What do you think? It's hard to know how to be 70. And a man. At any rate, they were nice flowers and I left some on her step. We had a nice visit when she came for coffee. A bit sad, I thought.

Are you taking your courses as planned? And your book club? Everything on the go, as usual? I think of you often. Will you come to Vancouver this winter? I hope you will.

I'm sitting at my "desk" a little shelf affair I've rigged from one of Doris Sheppard's table pads. It fits neatly on my lap in the green wing chair and makes a cozy spot to write. I'm off tomorrow though, to scrounge the second hand shops and antique stores on Main Street, looking for a real desk to tuck in the dining room. I'll write you longer letters from there!

I'll close this little ramble now by sending my fondest thoughts,
Arthur.

He folded the note paper and tucked it in the envelope which he drew from the box. He addressed it in the firm draftsman's block printing that architects had often admired during his house building years. Stamps were on the list for tomorrow. He would get them during his desk-finding mission.

The letter written and set aside and the house in darkness but for the pool of light from his golden lamp, Arthur sat. The house was growing cool, the dampness that intrigued him so, seeping in through the ancient single pane windows. He stretched out his writing hand and flexed it. Arthritis. Especially in the joints that had gripped a hammer; balanced a long, heavy level; held down the metal measuring tape in the sharp, prairie cold.

Had he been awake all those years? Measuring, cutting, hammering, seeing houses grow under his hand? He flexed his hand again, then reached for the mint tea. It had grown cool in the cup, while he wrote, and now tasted faintly bitter. He set the cup aside and reached instead for a humbug, holding the glass lid of the candy dish in his cramped hand, while he reached for the candy with the other.

What would it be like to have a manicure, he wondered as he watched his hands go about this business. To have your hands gentled and smoothed by another pair of hands; to have the nails clipped gently while you sat pinned in your seat. Think of it! You would not be able to move because someone had got hold of your hands.

He had been conscious of his hands all his life; careful to scrub beneath the nails when he returned from work, using a mixture of sugar and dish liquid to clean them. And later, when he no longer hammered very much or used the saws, but more often pushed a pencil, still he had seen his hands. Caught sight of them from the corner of his eye as they gripped a steering wheel or brought a bite of food to his mouth. More disquieting than the aging of your face, he thought, the drooping and wrinkling written there for all to see, was the strange intimacy of watching your hands grow old.

He folded the table pad and set it beside the chair, then gathered up the letter and his tea cup and went to the kitchen, where Doris' old fridge and stove were humming their appliance duet in the dark.

It would be very easy, he realized, to settle into melancholy. Easy to shuffle from one lonely thought to another. Less easy, but still seductive, would be denying the darkness that comes in these quiet moments and forcing oneself instead grimly along the path of forced light-heartedness. Or settling simply for distraction. Television, for instance.

There wasn't one here, he realized with a start. Had Doris and Edward worried that he'd make off with the twenty-one inch screen, which surely must have been in the living room? Or maybe upstairs in the back bedroom?

The back bedroom. Madeline's bedroom in Pauline's house. The third bedroom, tucked at the back of the house, near the top of the stairs and closest to the bathroom. A child's bedroom, surely? That's what a housebuilder's mind would think. That's what Arthur's mind thought.

⌘ ⌘ ⌘

As Arthur was shutting off lights and locking doors, still thinking about that third bedroom, Madeline was turning softly in the white bed in her blue bedroom, sleeping easily and soundly, her small round hands tucked beneath her delicate chin. As though in prayer.

Pauline tiptoed across the room. Always a warm blooded child and a sound sleeper, Madeline often ended up with her quilt thrown back and her nightie rucked up about her. Tonight though, in her T shirt and her cotton panties, she slept covered and tranquil. Played out.

There was Mutter, no doubt flea-ridden and harboring ticks, curled up at the foot of the little white bed. Also sound asleep.

Fourteenth Avenue went to bed.

⌘ ⌘ ⌘

Pauline was on the phone in the kitchen. Madeline and the cat were on the floor near her feet.

"I'm off to the vet, then What to Where. But I can meet you for lunch."

There were strange things going on at Pauline's house, Ellen thought. Last week an ill-gotten purse, this week, a cat.

"I'll meet you at Quarter Past Moon," said Ellen. "We need a spinach salad hit, don't you think?"

Pauline laughed. "I'll meet you at, say, close to one o'clock? Does that work?"

"It works. I'll see you then."

They hung up and Pauline began to clear the kitchen, setting her coffee cup and Madeline's bowl in the sink and wiping down the counter. She picked up Richard's solitary juice glass and rinsed it, feeling for a moment, something of the sad puzzlement with which she knew he now lived his days. Juice, vitamins, push-ups, a coat and tie, a striped shirt, coffee in a commuter mug, then a cat and mouse commute to the Richmond factory. All before eight o'clock. Was his heart breaking too?

"Maddie, I'm going to get that old picnic basket. The one with the lids. We can take Mutter in that," Pauline said, opening the basement door. "Put you lunch bag in your pack, okay?"

Cat, kid, coat, purse, briefcase. They were in the car. Mutter sat mutely in the picnic basket on Madeline's lap. Was it brain-damaged, Pauline wondered. It was a wild cat, born in a tree stump in Grace's garden, yet here it was, day two in captivity and acting as though it was born to be a domestic creature.

"I love you Maddie."

"Me too," said Madeline. "I love you. I love you and Daddy for saying I can have a cat."

They stood at the curb, particles in the Monday morning wave of mothers and children sweeping toward the school.

Pauline bent for a kiss. "Have a good day, Sweetie."

"Look after Mutter, Mother," said Maddie. Then in a little sing song. "Mutter and Mother, Mother and Mutter. Mommy and Maddie and Mutter!"

Pauline laughed "I'll look after Mutter. Bye bye."

She watched Madeline run toward her classroom, backpack and ponytail flapping

She had finished filling in the forms, where she was required to list the cat as Mutter Thorne. She set the pen down and pushed the form across the counter. Richard would puke.

"You can pick her up at two or so, Mrs. Thorne," said the vet. "You're a good little kitty," she said as she withdrew the cat from the picnic basket.

"Why is this cat so passive?" Pauline asked. "It seems strange for a kitten born in the wild to act like that."

"Hmmph." The vet shrugged.

Who knew? She seemed to say. Life is filled with mysteries. This isn't a big one.

A young woman in blue jeans and black turtleneck sweater, the vet wore a long white lab coat which swished as she moved. Hair like Orphan Annie, a halo of coppery curls, surrounded her small, serene face. There were three tiny turquoise studs in one ear, marching up the fragile translucent cartilage. She wore rimless glasses which flashed little prisms of light as she nodded her head up and down, reassuring the cat.

Pauline was mesmerized.

"I'll be back about three then," she said. bending to gather up the picnic basket and her purse.

The vet looked up from the cat. "Great purse," she said. "Magical color."

We are always ready to disregard possibility. To throw away magic. Fire? Seen it before. Yes, but look. Flames, churning up nothing out of something and leaving, what? Heat and light, a small bit of ash. But then? Gone. It's magic. But we are ever prepared to disregard it. It's everyday stuff. What about the cat which acted as though it has always lived with Maddie? Had the child conjured the cat?

Pauline left the parking lot, easing the Toyota past the sign where "The Cat Vet" was written out in sinuous letters across the black silhouette of an elongated Siamese Cat. A sensuous kind of sign for a vet's clinic, she had thought passing the sign before.

Life was indeed mysterious.

"Pauline Thorne to see Deborah Kee," she said to the girl behind the counter at What To Where. "Is she in?"

She handed over her business card and the blonde girl received it in a long, manicured hand.

"I'll check," she said. "Is she expecting you?"

She held the card between two pointed fingers and regarded Pauline with a small formal smile. Her lips, like her long nails, were polished a glossy mahogany and her face was taut and blemish-free. Pauline could see where matte powder had been smoothed across her skin, erasing errors on the girl's bland face.

"Yes."

With Pauline's business card held out at her side like a smoldering cigarette she tottered off on short, patent boots whose chunky little heels clicked importantly across the pale wood.

Pauline watched her retreat to the back of the store, then set her canvas case on the counter and looked about. No mystery here at What To Where, although the name tried to insinuate that there might be. Here was the dark heart of fashion, spread out for maximum stimulation of the acquisitive gene. Sleek trousers suits of trim shoulders and narrow legs were lined up just so, their padded ecru hangers at precise Monday-morning angles. Pale sweaters rested on shelves of bleached wood. Shirts, tissue-thin and light as air and neat black sweaters were precision stacked on a marble-topped sideboard near the window. On the counter, near her canvas case stood a rectangular vase filled with angular white Cala lilies. A holy place, clean and antiseptic, the store seemed to offer the redemption by good taste which Pauline had wondered about in church two weeks ago.

⌘   ⌘   ⌘

She smelled cat clinic on her clothes.

"You do not," said Ellen.

They sat in a booth at Quarter Past Moon, a fourth avenue restaurant whose gypsy excess settled around Pauline like a soothing antidote to the clothing shop's exquisite purity.

Ellen leaned across and sniffed.

"You don't smell like cats." Case closed. "Let's have a glass of something. Not Chardonnay."

"When I drink wine at lunch, I want to lay down and sleep," said Pauline. "It feels like paralysis."

"Mix a little water in it," said Ellen. "That's what I do. Put some ice in it."

They ordered the wine, then spinach salads and cheese bread from the dark eyed waiter.

Was he wearing eyeliner? A flamenco dancer come to serve them salads, bring them wine?

Pauline watched his slim-hipped walk as he moved away from the table.

"Eyeing up young waiters, now, Paul?"

"No." She swivelled back toward Ellen. "No. I'm just intrigued by people today."

She told Ellen about the vet with the copper curls and the turquoise earrings and about the chic young thing on the desk at What To Where and finally about Deborah Kee.

"She's perfect," Pauline said. "She had on this expensive taupe-y gabardine suit, with those slim trousers. With little nicks at the ankles? Spiky heels. And perfect hair."

The waiter returned and poured wine from a small green carafe that sparkled in the dim light. He seemed to click his heels as he withdrew.

"Isn't this a vase?" Ellen picked up the little flask and held it to the light. "It looks like a vase."

She set it down and picked up her glass. "Cheers."

"Cheers." Pauline scooped ice from her water glass and dropped the tiny cubes into her wine. "This is tacky, I know."

"Don't worry about women like Deborah Kee," Ellen smoothed at her hair, then tucked a neat chunk of it behind her ear. There. "They make me sick."

"Well, yes, but how do they do it?" said Pauline. "Is it just extra energy, or what? Do they wake up looking like the rest of us?"

"You look great," said Ellen.

She leaned across the table and rubbed the fabric of Pauline's blazer between her fingers. "It's a great jacket. You look nice." She let go of the cuff and gave the sleeve a little pat.

Their salads arrived. The waiter set the green lacquered bowls before them and drew a long and shining black pepper grinder from beneath his arm.

"Shall I?" he asked.

They nodded.

"Did you see his hands?" Ellen whispered when he had turned away to the next table. She picked up her knife and fork and began to assemble a mouthful of salad. "They must be acrylic nails."

The perfect baby leaves of spinach and the finely grated egg were topped with small, diced bits of Italian bacon and pale flakes of Asiago cheese. The rims of the pale green bowls were dusted lightly with finely chopped parsley. A tiny bundle of chives, like a miniature wheat sheaf was laid across the lip of the plate that held it all. It was exquisite.

The waiter returned with a wicker basket of cheese toast and set it between them with a ceremonial flourish. He peeled back the white napkin, folded it and patted the edge of the basket then nodded his head slightly and retreated.

In his wake was just a hint of gardenia or freesia. Something fragile and fragrant. The air around their table seemed clean and refined, like the fleeting scent of negative ions which she sometimes thought she could smell at the edge of the small creek in the forest near her parents' house.

Pauline watched him leave.

"Very chic," she said. "Where do these people get the energy to be works of art? It's depressing."

"Don't be depressed." Ellen pulled a piece of grilled bread from the basket. "Tell me about the clothes we're going to want this winter. Then I'll get depressed." She laughed. "How are you going to write about this stuff? Is it all in the store now? Tell."

⌘　⌘　⌘

Pauline sat in Quarter Past Moon telling Ellen about the sweaters, scarves and trousers which would soon make everything they now owned seem shabby while Arthur sat comfortably on the Main Street bus, enjoying the ride.

He had found a desk. It would be delivered tomorrow. As for bookshelves, he would take the bus to Richmond on Wednesday or Thursday and get inexpensive ones at Ikea. He was very satisfied.

The desk was walnut, stained to look like mahogany, spied behind some tables in a warehouse-like antiques store on Main Street. A butler's table, cut down at some point, the dealer had told him. It had been pressed into service as a desk, when it became clear that very little but-tling would be going on in the future. It was going to look just fine with Doris' sideboard and would turn the dining room into a very handsome study, Arthur thought.

This is a constant, in life, he reflected, as he rode along on the bus. Things began as one thing and became something else. A new use was found for them. People rethought the purpose of a thing and reinvented it. He had done this with himself, in a way.

He had begun as an ordinary man from Alberta, a successful builder of suburbs, and recreated himself. And it had begun with the decision to be happy. No, perhaps a step back, with Joan's death.

He could look back now, like someone observing a brother, or per-haps his father. He could see who he had been, the outside shape of that person, but he could not see his motivations, nor his perceptions.

How had he felt for instance, when Galen died? Sad, indeed. An infant, after all, only just becoming real, only just untethering itself from the ether; only just becoming a part of them, of their family, and then he was gone. But Arthur hadn't thought all those things.

He couldn't remember now, what he felt when the baby died. It was a sad occasion, but what had he felt?

It was Joan's pain which had lain so heavily upon him. He would build her a new house! Remove her from the site of her suffering. Fix things! The very wrong thing to do. And it had only taken thirty-five years for that to become clear. Galen and Joan, removed now, to another plane. Together?

What if he had decided to be happy then? Perhaps they would have stayed in her little house downtown? No doubt. But if he had done that, seen that she was embedded in her little neighborhood and with good reason, could he have gone on building the kind of suburbs that he had? It was a circle. There was no point at which he could intercede in the past. He had been who he was, a man created by the time in which he lived, as had she been a woman created by the time.

It was a very rare individual who could step outside the centrifugal pull of their times. But he felt he had done it now. He lived on the perimeter of things and knew freedom. Had, he thought, become his real self.

He held the bus transfer in his hand and bounced his heels gently on the floor of the bus. A steady rain fell and Vancouver became the whispering, wet sound which reassured city natives that they were home. The driver increased the speed of the wipers and they whacked like a metronome, a sharp, dry counterpoint to the wetness as the bus travelled downtown on streets stained the color of midnight.

⌘   ⌘   ⌘

"Did I tell you about my new neighbor?" Pauline asked. "He sent me flowers."

Ellen looked up from the table where she had been scanning the bill.

"No. Really?" She set the bill on the little plate and placed the twenty dollar bill which Pauline handed her on top of it. "Who is he?" She peered into her wallet and pulled out two tens and set them on the plate. "Why'd he send you flowers?"

"He's an older fellow," said Pauline as they gathered their purses. "He's staying in the Sheppard's house for a year. The next duplex over? They went to Spain."

"The flowers?" Ellen pushed open the door of the restaurant. "Rain! I forgot my umbrella. Damn."

Pauline pulled up her collar and pressed against the side of the building, dodging the rain which had begun to fall up from the sidewalk, splashing their ankles and causing trouser legs all over the city to begin to droop.

"Oh, he was just saying thanks for telling him about the shops on Granville. The bakery and so on."

"Hmmph. That was thoughtful." Ellen was already elsewhere, Pauline could tell. Already on to the next thing.

They hugged and said goodbye. Ellen pulled up the collar of her navy silk trench coat and gathered it around her, hugging herself. Then, holding her purse over her head as a sort of shield, she ran toward her little car, parked, as ever, where it should not be. In a loading zone snug against the drugstore across the street.

Pauline considered her purse, then tucked it awkwardly inside her blazer, safe from the increasing drizzle. She had left her car a block away in the What To Where lot.

⌘　⌘　⌘

"You're all wet!" said Maddie. "Didn't you have an umbrella? Bad Mommy."

She piled into the Toyota, trailing a damp backpack, limp artwork, another notice, her cardigan, a small umbrella printed with stars and moons. A volume of sheer stuff encircled her, as it does all children. An orbiting chaos of things for mothers to organize. They flung it in the backseat and Madeline buckled herself in.

"Where's Mutter?" she asked, suddenly remembering. She tugged at the hood of the plastic rain poncho and craned her neck, peering into the back seat.

"We have to pick her up," said Pauline. "She's still at the vet's."

"Awww. You were supposed to bring her."

"This way you can meet the vet, a really cute and smart lady, okay? And she can tell you how to look after Mutter."

Mollifying Maddy. What a tiresome task of mothering that was. Essential, yet the adult wanted to say, *"Ah, knock it off. Grow up."*

Indeed, that's what the child was trying to do. Pauline could see Madeline wrestling with the desire to pout. Her arms were folded across her chest and her ankles worked furiously against each other, crossing and re-crossing. She was holding herself in, working this out.

Disappointment caused her little chin to jut out, her eyes to narrow. She looked out the window, watching the rain, watching traffic.

"We'll be there in a minute, Mad," said Pauline, easing the car into the convoy of minivans and station wagons. She stopped to let the school bus lumber out of the school's driveway.

Madeline's attention was suddenly focused on the big yellow bus. "Kristen takes the bus," she said. "She's my new friend."

This was the olive branch of childhood. *Here's something interesting from my day. All is forgiven.* The adult chose whether to accept it or to hang on to the dubious task of showing the child the error of her ways. Pauline accepted the branch and jumped to higher ground.

"Do you get to sit together?" she asked.

And they were off. Kristen, artwork, her teacher, Mrs. Lewis, lunch, recess, the length of the grade one school day versus kindergarten, and finally:

"What a funny sign."

They were at The Cat Vet.

Mutter had no ticks, no lice, no fleas. And yes she was a she. All in all a satisfactory cat, said the vet as she crouched down beside Madeline to tuck the kitten into the picnic basket. Madeline reached out to touch the copper curls.

"I like your hair," she said.

"Well thank you," said Dr. Drew reaching up to touch it herself. "I hated it when I was your age, but I like it very much now. It's springy, isn't it?"

She and Madeline regarded each other. Smiling.

The cat sat in the picnic basket. Waiting.

The rain continued.

"I'll carry the picnic basket," said Madeline. "You carry my stuff. Please?"

They were in the back alley again, the car tucked up against the back fence. How long, Pauline wondered, until she got to park out front again? Who owned all those bloody cars?

They would have to run through the downpour which sounded now like gravel being poured onto the roof of the car. It had become torrential while they circled their neighborhood.

⌘ ⌘ ⌘

CHAPTER NINE

"**M**utter hasn't got fleas or anything!" Madeline shouted when Richard stepped through the back door at six o'clock. He had been in traffic since five fifteen. He too was parked in the back lane.

"And I'm going against the tide, when I drive home," he marveled later in the evening. "Those poor bastards driving out to Surrey." The real commuters. He shook his head.

The doorbell rang as Pauline came downstairs from Madeline's room at seven thirty. She looked the question - *"Who?"* - at Richard as he went down the hall toward the door.

"Mom and Dad," he mouthed, stopping to shut the closet door. Then in a whisper, "Sorry, I forgot to tell you they were going to drop in."

Christ. The Dick and Daphne Show. She went to the kitchen to make coffee.

And there they were, resplendent on the living room sofa, when she entered the room.

Dick jumped up. "Darling Girl!"

She stepped into his hug, then bent to peck Daphne on the cheek.

They were both highly colored, partly the effect of a lifetime of daily cocktail hours and partly of golf and gardening.

Daphne settled herself smoothly into the sofa, neatly tucking her woolen skirt beneath her broad hips and giving herself a little shake to adjust her sweaters. It was fascinating to watch this settling process, Pauline thought. Like watching a large dog shake off water after a swim. Finally, she was set.

"We were just telling Richard about Catherine and Tink's boat," said Daphne happily. She pushed up a sweater sleeve and paused momentarily to admire her silver bracelets. "They want to have both of you and Madeline out for a trip before the weather gets awful."

"It's getting pretty bloody awful already," said Richard. "It took me forty five minutes to drive in, tonight. The rain just buggers things up royally."

"Well, of course that's not just rain, Richard," said Dick. "It's all the commuter traffic."

He pronounced this with the air of someone delivering sound and reasoned information which might throw light on a subject, heretofore obscured by ignorance.

Oh, yes, I see," the audience was meant to think, rather than "No kidding," or "Duhhh." Which was what Pauline thought.

Having delivered this nut of wisdom, Dick settled his bottom comfortably and looked around with a sort of beaming self-satisfaction.

Daphne nodded.

"Catherine and Tink are about a ten minute drive from the office," she offered pleasantly.

And they were off. Pauline went to get the coffee.

Catherine, Richard's sister and Tink - Timothy - her husband, had lived in Richmond for several years, in a new and affluent neighborhood, where the trees were planted fully grown and then cared for by hired gardeners. The lush and exclusive nature of this preserve was what Daphne had in mind for her Richard. Maybe right next door to Catherine.

And who really, could blame her? She wanted the satisfaction of knowing that her two children, good productive products of her womb, were well and truly settled in material comfort and on their way to increasing prosperity and further comfort.

Lesley, child of Catherine and Tink, and the cousin to whom Madeline compared herself, was nicely settled in The Keatly Day School and took Suzuki violin lessons. She could ride her bike among the leafy safety of those prepackaged trees, while Tink hosed down the driveway on weekends. She was two years older than Madeline and possessed of a superior and knowing nature which Pauline found spooky.

There was subtext afoot, she could tell when she returned with the coffee tray. She had set out her bone china mugs and the embossed coffee pot her Grandma Davies had given her. There were packaged cookies for Dick's sweet tooth.

"English Bakery?" he asked hopefully, choosing one from the tray while Pauline fussed with the coffee, pouring Daphne's mug only half full, the way she like it.

"No, just store-bought," she said, handing him a mug.

Dick bit into the cookie.

"Pretty good," he said, crumbs of disappointment in his voice. He studied the smooth, white biscuit. "Coconut," he pronounced.

"Maddie likes them in her lunch," Pauline said. She sat down in the upright side chair that Richard had drawn up for her. Quite suddenly she remembered the exquisite comfort of the wing chair at Arthur's house.

⌘　⌘　⌘

Arthur sat in that chair, beneath his golden lamp, studying the Ikea catalogue. On the little walnut table lay his mystery novel and his Canadian history, both open. He had set them aside for the cheap thrill of leafing through the Ikea book, deciding which shelves he would look for on Wednesday or Thursday.

A bookcase. A bookcase. What a wonderful thing is a bookcase, he thought. A shelf of books over a desk, a small case in a child's bedroom filled with nursery rhymes and picture books, a glass fronted cabinet filled with elderly, leather bound tomes. Any kind of bookcase offered such comfort, he decided. The pictures in the catalogue bore him out. When the designers wanted to suggest coziness, what did they tuck into a room setting? A bookcase.

He meditated on this. Why had he not fitted the little bungalows he first built, with built-in bookcases? Not expensive ones, he thought dreamily. Just bookcases. Imagine building them into a child's bedroom too. In his mind, he constructed just such a bookcase, choosing the wood, adding a filigreed molding across the top, and fitting the case snugly into a corner, near a window, so that a child could draw up a chair or flop on a bed nearby, and read in the sunlight. He thought of an illustration from one of Greg's childhood books, of a child reading in a window-seat which had bookshelves tucked beneath it. Imagine.

Imagine the private world you could create for someone simply by offering them a bookcase. And you needn't fill it with only books. A toy, a vase, a plant, a collection of stones, a cigar box filled with private treasures, a candle. A bookcase.

"Hmmph," He shook his head. He had been staring off, building bookcases in small houses, which had long since, no doubt, grown shabby and derelict. If he could build houses now, he would put built-in bookcases in the bedrooms and in the living rooms too.

He closed the catalogue and picked up "Rumors of Civilization." He ran his hand along the raised title. Like reading Braille, he thought, feeling the letters with the callused edge of his thumb. Like reading his key chain. He closed the book and set it aside.

"Think I'll have a smoke," he said. He went through the kitchen and into the mudroom. His cigarettes and the small tin ashtray were now on narrow shelf at the sill of the window. No longer stashed beneath Doris' plastic bags. He took the package and stepped outside. The rain had stopped and high silver clouds were racing inland, as though recently freed from some pull over Vancouver Island and set in motion. What did these clouds do when they got to Edmonton? Drop snow on Beryl? On Greg? Too soon. Too soon for snow.

He struck the wooden match on the door sill and straightened up, lighting his cigarette. The smoke and the sharp smell of sulfur drifted toward the door which stood ajar, tugged inward by the warmth, the vacuum, of the little porch. He stepped out onto the concrete stoop, drawing the door shut behind him, still thinking about bookcases.

⌘　⌘　⌘

"What was all the kerfuffle at the wedding by the way?" Daphne set her mug on a coaster which she had lined up at a precise angle to the edge of the coffee table. "When they were doing the champagne toast?"

"Marj Trimble whacked over a jug of bloody marys," said Richard. "What a mess. Paul's purse was on the table and got the worst of it. Ruined it."

Daphne looked at Pauline with a little moue of sympathy pursing her lips.

"Oh, no!" she said, leaning forward for details.

"Marjorie Trimble's a nitwit," said Dick.

"That's exactly what Richard said," Pauline said. "Exactly. Ellen said it too."

"Well she is," Daphne concurred. "What did you do? About your purse?"

Pauline sketched the story of her wretched purse's demise, how Marjorie had given her money for a new one and how the table had been rescued and reset so neatly by the country club staff.

"They're top cabin," said Dick nodding sagely.

Pauline picked up the coffee pot. "More coffee, Dick?" *Speaking of nitwits.*

"And you got a new one, Pauline?" asked Daphne, keen to know more.

"*How much?*" hung in the air. Unasked.

"At the Bay," Pauline said, deflecting her. "Quite a nice one."

Daphne resettled in small waves. *Well. A department store purse. Okay.*

⌘ ⌘ ⌘

"Why were they here?" Pauline called.

She was in the tiny walk-in closet, a modern convenience created by the theft of a roomy linen cupboard which had once existed in the hallway and by the annexing of space from the third bedroom where Madeline and Mutter were sleeping silently in the little white bed.

She opened the louvered door.

"Did you hear me?"

Richard looked up, withdrawing the fake tortoise shell reading glasses and rubbing the bridge of his nose. His eyes looked fragile.

"To visit," he said, setting aside an investment magazine. He was propped against the headboard, pillows tucked about him. Like a hospital patient, Pauline thought.

"Richard."

"What?"

"No, really." She crossed to the bureau and picked up her brush. "Why were they here?"

"Come here Pauline." He patted the bed beside him. "I feel like I haven't hugged you or touched you in months." There were little catches in his voice. Burrs or thistles. He sounded parched, like a man who cannot swallow. "Paul?"

The street was silent. The quartet of duplexes behind their sentry of giant chestnut trees was at peace in the damp night. Overhead, the high silver clouds moved quickly, silently inland. Windows were shuttered, curtained, closed against the dark and the coming cold. The street was turned inward, dreaming. No light issued from the houses.

Nearly asleep, Pauline and Richard lay twined, each feeling the familiar flesh of the other, each sensing that they were growing cooler, that their skin, even as it lost its firmness was somehow losing warmth too.

This thinner wrapper made them perceive each other as somehow more dear, more poignant, more human. Transient, somehow. But wordlessly.

She ran the palm of her right hand down his thigh. He shivered.

Were they being made privy to some secret? That firmness and thickness of skin leaves and we are left with more essential selves? And if we could somehow read this with our finger tips, feel each other without the transit of words, without wanting the transit of words would this tell us some new and deeper thing about our selves, about the other?

How fragile they seemed to one another, lying naked beneath the duvet, in the dark bedroom. They were not back yet. Not back to fear, to the place where they had positions to defend, points to make, tiny selves to prop up. They were still splayed, vulnerable and thin; their bones, their ankles and elbows and wrists, barely contained, scarcely wrapped in flesh.

Pauline wakened in the night shivering, and caught up her discarded nightgown from the bottom of the bed. It had entangled her feet causing a moment of panic which pushed her, startled, from sleep. She pulled gently away from Richard and drew it over her head in the dark, then fell instantly, deeply asleep.

In the night, the wind came up again and the rest of the chestnuts rained down from the trees. With no one to see, no one to hear, they unloosed themselves and fell simply to the ground. In the morning, there was no wind, no rain, but instead bright, hot sunshine shining and shining on the fallen chestnuts which lay glistening there, damp and polished on the fading lawns.

⌘ ⌘ ⌘

"Beautiful day," called Arthur with a little wave. He stood on the sidewalk watching the delivery man peel a quilted cotton wrapper from his new walnut/mahogany desk.

Pauline walked toward him on the littered sidewalk, stepping carefully around and between the chestnuts.

She smiled as she drew near. "Fabulous," she agreed. "How are you, Arthur? What have you got there?"

"A desk," he said. "I'm tucking it into Doris' dining room. To create a little den."

They turned to admire the desk, now fully freed from the bulky quilt and shining there on the lowered tailgate of the delivery truck. Like Venus Rising.

"It's lovely," said Pauline. She waved to the delivery man, who was relaxing in the sunshine, quite unhurried. "Hi."

He waved, a little salute, and jumped down from the metal platform. "Where to?" he said, pulling the desk toward him.

"Would you like to come inside for coffee?" Arthur asked her. "This will only take a minute to get organized."

"I'm off to the bank and the bakery," she said. "But, I'll only be an hour. Probably less. Can I stop by on my way back?"

"Perfect." Arthur moved toward the truck. "I'll see you then."

She left them, a curious and awkward little parade with Arthur holding one end of the desk and shuffling slowly backwards and the lanky young delivery man holding the other end of the gleaming desk, his long legs stepping gingerly among the chestnuts.

At the bakery she chose cookies for Madeline's lunch box and some meringues that Richard liked, then added crisp apricot squares whose fruit centers lay like golden egg yolks in a puddle of thick custard. The elderly woman behind the counter ran two loaves of whole grain bread through the electric slicer for her.

"Mind you don't store these near heat, now."

The soft roundness of her brogue lilted across the glass pastry cases. It drew customers back again and again in much the same way as the warm and yeasty smells which went out the doors to lay heavily on the senses of passersby and of commuters waiting for the next bus on Granville Street. Both hinted at some lost thing; offered a salve to unknown wounds.

"You'll want to tuck one in the freezer, I should think." She slipped the loaves neatly into plastic bags and flicked the twist ties sharply.

"There, deary," she said, wiping her hands on the white bib front of her apron. "D'ye need a bag, then?"

At the bank, Pauline deposited the check which had arrived in the morning mail from Pick A Peach.

"What a dippy name," Richard had observed when she had written her first project for Karen. "No wonder she pays so lousy."

There was a little gold peach imprinted on the corner of the pale orange envelope which held her check. *It was a dippy name.*

She thought of the peaches she had recently canned with Grace. She smelled the warm, sharp scent of hot fruit for a moment and wondered if Karen had recently bought scented stationery. She sniffed the envelope. No. Only a memory of a scent.

⌘ ⌘ ⌘

"Oh, yes," said Arthur. "I find smells very evocative. The dirt smell of beets? I feel like I'm back on the farm immediately. And certain talcum or bath powders. The old fashioned ones? When I smell those, I'm in church when I was a boy."

They were at Doris' table, the golden apricot squares reduced to crumbs and stickiness on their plates. Sitting on the gray formica of the kitchen counter, Pauline's bakery bag exhaled, filling the little room with aromatic joy

"Have you smelled western red cedar?" she asked suddenly.

"I believe I must have," Arthur said. "I used to build houses. Though not many of them had cedar shake roofs. Too expensive on the prairies. It isn't like Tennessee cedar, is it?"

"Do you know," said Pauline. "I think the air here ... at the coast, is filled with it.. It's not just the ocean we're smelling."

He nodded. They were off on some fanciful stuff, sitting in Doris' kitchen, once again drinking coffee and gathering stray thoughts, quite at ease.

They had admired Arthur's desk, newly settled across from the mahogany sideboard and looking very good, indeed.

Did Pauline think the bookcase he was going to get, should go in here with the desk? Or in the living room with the chairs?

"With the desk," she said. "That way you'll have a cozy little writing area with your books all tucked in beside you."

But what was he going to write? They did not stray down that street, but rather stayed on the pathway they had already paved with their fragile new knowledge of each other. Like nascent lovers.

"My desk is crowded into an office that is also a den slash guest room," she said. "It's that little bedroom at the front?"

"Bookcases?" he asked, still meditating on their importance.

"Two," she said. "And a shelf over the desk."

"Ah." He nodded. "I'm off to Richmond, to the Ikea store, in the morning to get mine. Maybe two of them. The simple kind. Inexpensive."

When they had finished their coffee and she was helping him to gather the plates and cups to set in Doris' antique sink, she said,

"I grew up in a little place out in the Valley called Cedar Mills. My dad has a mill there. Our house always smelled of cedar. Dad's clothes, the porch ... I sort of grew up inside the smell."

⌘   ⌘   ⌘

In her kitchen she pressed the button on the answering machine and listened as she unpacked the bakery bag.

"Pauline, it's Karen. Listen, I've just got a rush job for a brochure thing for a developer out in Richmond. They're doing a new subdivision called The Counties? Can you do a sort of drive-by, tomorrow? Get a feel for it? Don't rush on the newsletter for Deb Kee. No panic. Give me a call. Thanks. Ciao"

Without stopping to consider what it might mean, she went out the door and across the nut-strewn lawns to Arthur's. She mounted Mr. Sheppard's weird porch and rang the bell.

"Would you like a ride to Richmond in the morning?" she asked when he appeared at the door.

Arthur was waiting on the stoop the next morning. He sat on the top step, leaning against the wrought iron railing, like a teenager waiting for a friend on Saturday morning. When he saw her, he stood up and dusted the seat of his pants.

They were shy in the car. This was a different intimacy than Doris' kitchen table and it bound them up, causing Arthur to look out the window as they drove south on Granville Street, heading toward the broad sky of the delta, where the Fraser River poured wide and brown into the ocean.

Pauline turned on the radio. On CBC, Gzowski was talking about egg salad.

"It's funny to have the mountains behind you," Arthur said after a while. "I've grown used to them being right there. Right up against me."

This seemed too intimate.

"Very different from Edmonton."

"What am I doing here?" Pauline thought.

She had hurried through the morning. Getting Madeline ready for school a little too quickly, causing her to get balky.

"My red shoes are gone!"

Depositing her there before their usual time.

"Kristen's not here yet."

"We'll find her!"

And so on. Until there they were, she and Arthur, snug in the front seat of the Toyota on their way to exotic Richmond.

She felt a little embarrassed. As though he (or someone!) would know that she had felt something like excitement about this little trip. That she had rushed through the morning.

"It was all farms not too long ago," she offered as they neared the airport.

They were at a delicate stage in the negotiations of this new romance - for what is friendship but a sort of romance? They had performed some of the first steps of courtship. He had brought her flowers. She had brought him sweets from the English Bakery. They had fed one another.

They had spent time in private establishing the dance and now they were on their first public outing. It was going to need careful choreography if they were to continue this sweet waltz. Things were tentative, just now. There was the possibility that one or both of them would suddenly see themselves not as the delicate, hesitant souls they were. They might at any moment see themselves not through their own eyes, but through the cool, measuring gaze of the world.

A retiree and a thirty-five year old woman. What was *that* about?

They were momentarily outside chronos. They were in mythos, the time that will not be measured, that does not march lockstep out of the past and into the future - but it was dicey.

Why had she not taken the other bridge? Now she would need to double back to drop Arthur at Ikea. Why, in fact, had she brought him?

"What is that?" asked Arthur as she negotiated through the airport-bound taxis and delivery trucks, seeking the turn lane she now needed.

"Burkeville," she said eyeing the traffic in her rear view mirror. "Wartime houses."

"It's a little village," he said. "How wonderful."

He leaned forward in the seat, to better see this tiny town which rose apparition-like, beside them.

"Amazing!" he laughed. He slapped his knee softly.

And it was amazing. Tucked there, where it ought not to be, a little neighborhood, built in the 1940s. With back alleys and front porches, maple trees and garages.

Pauline relaxed. Her hands rearranged themselves on the wheel and her spine softened. She felt her shoulders lower themselves inside her jacket. She sighed, a little exhalation of breath she had not known she was holding.

She glanced over at Arthur.

"Would you like to come see this new subdivision with me?" Arthur was still straining to see more of this unlikely sight. "I can take you to Ikea afterwards. I can browse around while you get your bookcases."

"I'd like that very much," he said. He settled back in his seat and smiled. Burkeville went past them and they crossed the small arm of the river where sailboats and houseboats rocked gently in the wake of a passing barge.

They were back in sync, safely over the small and delicate hurdle where they had almost begun to see themselves as foolish and transparent. Pauline leaned forward to turn off the radio

"I have to find their office first," she said. "Find out exactly where it is we're going."

Arthur marveled at the dikes whose delicate rise he could see across the barren field beside the construction site. Beyond the dike, across the river, was the airport.

She had found the offices on Three Road and been given notes and a map by the blond receptionist who presided there. Near her vast marble-topped work island there rested a miniature village under plexi-glass. The Counties as it would be when finished; endless curving culs de sac and puzzlingly abrupt roads. Essex Place, Sussex Court, Westchester Turn, Devon Drive, Kent Crossing. The Counties was an expensive dream world. Acres and acres of giant houses rising up below sea level on a former strawberry field.

Pauline drove slowly through the subdivision, down streets whose names were quaintly scripted on black and white enameled signs. Several houses in each area were already complete. Sod had been laid in the front yards.

"They're all garage," said Arthur as she stopped the car before a Tudor show home on Sussex Court.

They stepped from the car and looked. Yes, indeed. Garages on lots the municipality called zero-clearance. This meant the houses bullied their way to the perimeter of their shrunken lot lines and that the front yards were mostly driveway. The vast expanses of paved driveway led to double and triple garages. The houses, though enormous, seemed incidentally attached to their garages.

"Want to go inside?" Pauline asked.

"Definitely," he said, tucking his arms behind him to show that she was in charge. Lead on, his stance said.

They pushed open the exquisitely lacquered front door and were stunned, shrunken, by the immensity of the entry hall.

A tiled foyer, the realtor told them proudly when she appeared, stocking feet padding neatly across the vast and shining expanse. She swept her arms before her like the magician's assistant, indicating the trick they were to admire.

Arthur bent down and removed his walking shoes, setting them neatly on a square of carpet set out for this purpose. Pauline did the same. In stocking feet, but in it now, they soldiered on.

"Thirty five hundred square feet plus the bonus room," said the steely-eyed realtor.

A small radio played quietly on the glass kitchen table and there was a soft book open to a cross word puzzle lying there. The woman's shoes, black patent pumps, were visible beneath the table, a curious, intimate spectacle at odds with the brusque and businesslike bravado with which, in spite of her naked feet, she swept them through the downstairs rooms. They padded after her.

There was nothing for Arthur to reach out and pat here. No nifty, solid cabinetry called out to him.

Later, traveling home with the flat boxes containing Arthur's bookcases lashed to the roof of the Toyota, they laughed.

"She must have wondered about us!" said Arthur. "Traipsing after her like that. Neither of us saying a word."

They were enjoying a spontaneous hilarity, a release from the pent-up intimacy enforced on them by this outing. They'd been looking at houses. Furniture shopping! Walked about together in stocking feet! Had eaten hamburgers dripping in mayonnaise. It was absurd. But lovely.

"Oh, I know," Pauline laughed. "Her reeling off the square footage and us following her like we'd just arrived from another planet!"

She shook her head, imagining how the two of them had looked.

"That's where Richard's sister lives," she said as they crossed Cambie Road. She pointed toward a sea of rooftops punctuated by tall and gently trembling birch and ash trees.

"The Glens" was surrounded by a concrete wall stamped to resemble sandstone blocks. It ran on seemingly to the horizon, but in fact only to the next intersection. There was an imposing black gate surmounted by a discreet plaque bearing the name and the address written out in words. Like a formal wedding invitation. "The Glens," it read. "One thousand and twenty six Cambie Road."

"What do you think?" she asked as they slowed with the traffic, which even now, at two in the afternoon, was thickening with rush hour jitters. They were alongside The Glens.

"Ahh. I don't know. Arthur said. "I don't know what to make of these new subdivisions. I wonder, are we trying to make them soulless? I get the feeling, it's like bread now. You know? How we seem to take everything out. The nourishment? And then we try to add it back in. With vitamins and so on."

He was complicit in it, he knew. He watched The Glens as they inched past, tiptoeing toward the entry ramp of the freeway that would take them back to the city. It was getting late.

Pauline looked at her watch. "Do you mind if we stop to get Madeline before? I could probably get you home and then get there …"

"Nonsense," said Arthur. "Do what is most convenient. The most expedient. I have nothing but time."

⌘ ⌘ ⌘

"Mom and Mr. Dean came to get me," Madeline said importantly when Richard stepped through the kitchen door.

She was at her little desk playing with the tins Pauline had brought her from the afternoon's expedition. She held the largest aloft, turning it this way and that.

"See what Mummy got me at Ikea? They're for crayons and stick-ers." She shook the pastel tin, wanting him to admire it. Crayons rattled inside.

"You're a lucky duck," he said crouching down beside the little desk. "Give us a kiss."

Richard was happy today. He had been recounting his luck. Not counting his blessings exactly. But telling himself that all was well. Look. I have a business, which is doing quite well. I have a comfortable home. My child is beautiful. My wife had sex with me last night. What could be wrong in my life?

"How was your day, Hon?" he asked and leaned to kiss Pauline's cheek.

"Good," she said. "Interesting,"

She was chopping pepper strips and stalks of celery, pushing the minced green bits toward onion which lay neatly diced and glistening on the edge of the cutting board. Her eyes had stopped watering, but there were smudges of mascara below her lashes; black, mute evidence of the grief caused by the mischievous molecules of the lowly onion.

"Put on your reading glasses when you chop an onion," she had once been directed by Ellen who never cooked. "That stops the spray or fumes or whatever it is from getting in your eyes.

"I also read," Ellen had continued on that summer afternoon, sip-ping wine at the counter and watching Pauline prepare dinner. "That you should wear your glasses when you open the oven. So your mascara doesn't melt from the heat."

Pauline carried the cutting board to the stove and carefully scraped the diced vegetables into the pot. It sputtered and sent up a hot scent that reminded the brain of many things. Chili on a Sunday night? Hot dogs grilling at a booth at the fair? Soup? Exotic things to come.

Southern chefs called it the holy trinity, this chemistry of sauteeing onion, celery and green pepper. That part of the brain which processed scent without your permission, simply accepted the benevolence of the smell and went to get its knife and fork.

"*I am a lucky guy,*" thought Richard.

"I'm going up to change," he said pulling at the tie which hung loosely at his neck. He went into the hall carrying his briefcase, still tugging at the tie.

"Smells great, Paul," he called from the hallway, one foot already on the stair.

The scent was even out there, spreading its homey tentacles throughout the house, assuring the occupants that all was well.

Pauline hadn't a clue what she was making.

⌘　⌘　⌘

Arthur was steaming a salmon fillet. There was brown rice in a small white dish with a glass lid, ready to go into the microwave. He had cooked it the day before and now parceled out a portion for his dinner that needed only reheating.

In the microwave he had placed a package of frozen creamed spinach, now turning quickly from a bright green cube into a seductive little pile of nourishment. He liked to sprinkle garlic salt on it and wolf the entire package. It was a solitary vice, which he pretended not to indulge in by ladling the vegetable out in small portions which forced him to return time and again to the counter. Oh, it was good. Like grown-up baby food, the leaves soft but somehow still tensile and bound up with a creamy, salty sauce which held just a hint of the exotic.

Nutmeg.

Now, there was a spice. He liked to buy them whole and grate fresh bits of it across a Christmas egg nog. Or mix it with shreds of Swiss cheese and melt the whole mess on a piece of French bread, pulling it, brown and nutty from the broiler to eat with a knife and fork.

⌘　⌘　⌘

Pauline dumped a large tin of tomatoes in the food processor and whirred it to a crimson puree. She added it to the pot then dropped garlic in the food processor and added that too. Then olive oil and a spoonful of dried basil. Ah. It was to be a marinara sauce of sorts. She filled a second large pot with water for the pasta and set it to boil. There was broccoli to steam now, cheese to grate.

"Meringues?" said Richard when they had finished the pasta. "See how lucky I am?" he asked the record keeper in his heart. There was delight and something like pride in his voice. Meringues. For me. Imagine.

She had surrounded them with Grace's peaches and topped them with vanilla yogurt. A cool and golden bliss on a plate. The deceptive chewiness of the meringues gave way to the tart sweet thrill of the yogurt, its acid nicely balancing the sugar syrup of the canned peaches.

"Yuck," said Madeline who was eating her peaches with a coconut cookie. "I don't like those white things."

"English Bakery," said Richard. "Mmmmm."

⌘ ⌘ ⌘

CHAPTER TEN

She was at her desk creating an outline for the newsletter. On the desk were her scribbled notes from the visit to The Counties and a steno pad with notes from What To Where. She was decoding the fashion-speak of her interview with Debora Kee.

The little room was mostly dark, the only light cast by the screen of the computer and by a small angular desk lamp whose arm she had craned away from her so that the light fell on a small gathering of objects she kept there. A stone from the river's edge in Cedar Mills, a gilded picture frame fashioned from popsicle sticks by Maddie during kindergarten, a miniature statue of Rodin's Thinker, a wooden bookmark which smelled faintly of sandalwood.

Richard knocked softly at the partly open door and entered carrying her green striped mug.

"Brought you coffee," he said offering the cup, holding it so that the handle faced toward her.

"Thank you," she said without turning.

"How was your journey to deepest Richmond?"

She closed the file and turned. The ancient secretary's chair groaned on its swivel, a startling sound in the enclosed, still space.

She wanted to weep for him as he stood there offering coffee, his large face earnest and open above the ratty green sweatshirt, his flat blond hair wisping out in small tufts as the day grew late.

She took the cup from him and he sat down on the arm of the little sofa.

"I'm not staying," said his posture. *"Not trying to invade."*

But he was. What he really wanted to know, was why on earth she had taken an elderly gent with her.

"You say this Arthur Dean, is just staying for the year?" He leaned back against the wall, one leg angled across the other knee so that the ankle rested there and his foot bounced easily back and forth. Casual. A lucky guy at ease in his home.

She sipped at the coffee and sketched Arthur for him. A friend of friends of the Shepperds. Retired. Builder. Widower. Nice. Amusing.

"I'd like to meet him. Sounds like a nice guy."

She was surprised by the little thrill of alarm which zinged through her.

"He's my friend," her heart wanted to say. *"Mine."* *"Oh, grow up!"* cried the grown-up knitting socks by the fireplace someplace deep in her civilized brain.

"Ummhmm," she said. "I thought I'd invite him to dinner one night. Maybe have the Poulos over too. So he could meet them."

"Work?" He nodded toward the computer.

"Notes for my newsletter for the clothing store. The one on fourth? I want to get this interview typed up, then I can start on the brochure I told you about. For the new development."

"She paying you any better?"

Pauline set her cup down and swiveled the chair toward the computer screen. She was counting to ten.

"The same," she said. "The same. The same."

She pulled papers toward her and began to align the edges, tapping them on the rim of the desk. Her back was to him.

"Your time is worth more, Pauline," he said, standing to escape the chill which was seeping into the room although the window was closed, the blinds snugly drawn.

"Well." He leaned to kiss the top of her head. "I'm not trying to tell you your business. But you should negotiate better."

This is what you should do. You are foolish for not doing it. Or cowardly. Or temperamental. Or plain ignorant?

Richard left, drawing the door shut behind him. He was not quite the same lucky guy who had made the coffee and brought it as an offering. His life looked not quite as sweet as it had just moments before when he had mounted the stairs, bearing his wife's favorite green cup. How had things changed so swiftly? How had he begun so happily - whistling even, as he fiddled with the stupid coffee maker - and ended so poorly?

He needed to turn this around. Walk through the steps.

"I brought her coffee. I offered her advice. Which she misinterpreted, somehow." Richard told himself as he went down the stairs. "Besides which, I'm obviously saying that her work is worth more money. How am I wrong here?"

At the bottom step, he stopped suddenly. Cat poop.

"Figures," he told himself. "Pauline!" he called up the stairs.

⌘ ⌘ ⌘

The shower stopped and she heard him come down the stairs. She tossed the soiled paper towel and newspapers into a green garbage bag and set it on the deck then washed her hands at the kitchen sink. She went to the fridge and poured two glasses of white wine and went through to the living room.

Richard sat in the gold chair beside the fireplace rubbing his wet hair with a pink bath towel. He wore only the grey sweatpants, his long legs stretched out before him. Water beaded in small globes on the pale hairs of his bare chest and trickled downward raining little pinpoints of darkness onto the upholstery. His bare feet, balanced on the edge of the coffee table, were crossed at the ankle. Pink and new looking from the shower they wagged slowly back and forth. She saw the high instep which never quite met the floor, never quite felt the inside of his shoe. The overarching arch which made him leave comic imprints in sand and on tiles when his feet were wet. A fragile, untouched part of him.

She handed him the wine glass and crossed to the sofa, tucking herself into the far corner. She inhaled deeply and rubbed her still-damp hands together.

"Wouldn't it be nice to just stop all this?" She leaned forward. "Give up trying to be successful? Trying to get money. Be like everybody else? Trying to get a house in the suburbs?"

His arm fell and the pink towel dropped onto the hardwood. He swung his feet off the table and leaned forward, staring hard at her.

"Are you nuts?" He set the wineglass on the coffee table.

His eyes had narrowed, the brows pinching in toward the cleft above the small bump on the cartilage of his nose. A childhood hockey wound, the bump shone whitely when he was tired or angry. The corner of his mouth seemed to twitch, the lip drawn upwards.

"Then what?" He shook his head making a sort of spitting sound in his throat.

Suddenly he stood and grabbed up the towel from the floor, wringing it into a ball. He threw it hard against the sofa and it landed with an explosive thud on the cushion beside her. Stunned, she rose up a little as it hit and her hand flew involuntarily to her chest. As she slowly resettled the sound echoed in the quiet room, louder than fabric against fabric ought to sound.

She moved slightly away from the towel and regarded him. The glass in her hand trembled as she leaned forward to set in on the table.

"Christ, Pauline!" He seemed to pant. "You've hardly earned any money to speak of for nearly six years. We're drowning here."

She watched his bare chest rise and fall.

"You want to go live in a trailer park somewhere? You want to live in a shack out in Cedar and I'll go to work piling lumber for your old man?"

He jabbed at the air. Quick strokes, pointing first at her, then the floor.

"We don't have options." Enumerating. "I want to live. I want stuff. A nice house. I want Madeline to go to a good school. Live on a safe street."

He shook his head and held up a finger, pointing at her.

"And you know what? I don't care if you think my sister is an asshole. And her husband." He crossed the room in two strides and stood over her. Leaning down he grabbed up the pink towel. "I don't give a shit if you think that."

He went out the door with the towel hanging in his first like a limp flag.

She heard his bare feet stab the stairs. Heard the ancient noise which telegraphed fury, disgust. This is not to be borne, his feet seemed to say, taking him loudly away.

"For Christ's sake, Pauline," he yelled from the landing. "Grow up."

Above her, his bare feet splatted on the hardwood and then she heard the muffled sound as he crossed the carpeted floor of their bedroom. She pictured him throwing himself onto the bed, imagined him lying and staring unseeing at the dark window. He would have his elbows up, hands locked at the nape of his neck, his head cupped in his hands. Holding himself in the male posture which can as easily say "pissed off" as "just resting."

She picked up her wine glass and took a sip.

That went well.

Beside the gold chair, she saw a faint dark circle where the towel had lain.

Richard had invested heavily in the stock market during his career on Howe Street. One of the boys, he'd played fast and loose on the Vancouver Stock Exchange and seen it all slip away from them. They had lost the townhouse on the Fairview Slopes when Madeline was three months old and their savings soon after. He lived in fear now, a man shadowing himself, watching his steps. He knew what happened when you glanced away.

Heavily indebted now to his father and mother, he was obliged to accept their world view. And did. Money was the metaphor. The electroplating business was one which his father had acquired during his business career, not because Dick was smart or creative, but because he had begun with quite a lot of money and old-Vancouver connections. Dick's vague promises assured Richard that he was in effect, the owner of the business.

He lay on the bed in the rented duplex and looked at the dark window. For now he was like a man climbing a rock face. Each step was perilous, each forward movement required concentration and carefully placed pitons. He must, he felt, keep moving.

⌘ ⌘ ⌘

Arthur was assembling the book cases. He twirled the little wrench, snugged the final bolt into place and stood the second case upright.

They were firm enough, if a little pedestrian looking. He unwrapped the shelves and began to settle them on the little steel pins which would anchor the shelves which would hold his books. And the knickknacks which even now, were beginning to take shape in his imagination.

On his new desk he had lined up ten luminous chestnuts gathered from the sidewalk when he had gone out for his morning walk.

"I like to walk here," he'd told Greg on the telephone the previous evening. "I walk the two blocks to Granville, first thing." Then to forestall Greg's image of him as a wandering, nay doddering, retiree, he had added, "To get the paper."

Greg was perplexed by the addition of the desk and now bookcases as well, it seemed. What next? Was the old man planning to stay at the coast permanently? Was he going to drag all this stuff back home?

"He can afford it," Greg told his wife. "But it's pretty strange. He's got lots of furniture in the apartment downtown. Now he's gathering up more out there. Weird."

Arthur carried a carton over to the desk and set it down taking care not to scratch the rich finish or to disturb the contents of the box. He opened it and drew out Joan's picture of the tropical sunset, then Galen's baby picture and the one of Greg the toddler. Next, he lifted out the greyish photograph of five-year-old Joan standing before the screen door. He studied it a moment, then set it too on the desk top. He gathered up the chestnuts and set them one by one into a large and heavy marble cup. Then he began to unpack the cartons of books which stood beneath the window in Doris' dining room.

⌘ ⌘ ⌘

"It's a mortar," said Pauline. She held up the marble cup which Arthur had filled with the chestnuts. "You know, a mortar and pestle thing. For grinding spices?"

She had come to admire the new bookcases, taking a break from her morning's work on The Counties.

"Of course!" said Arthur. "Aren't you smart?"

"Well, my husband might ask you if I'm so smart, why am I not rich?" She set the marble mortar carefully on Arthur's desk top and stepped back to admire the bookcases again.

Another little pebble about Richard, Arthur wondered? Dropped into the still pond of their conversation much as the observation that her husband thought her "daft," had been dropped on the day they'd first had coffee together?

But Pauline left him no opening. "This looks fabulous," she said again, admiring the books in their new home.

He had positioned the bookcases on either side of the window, with the desk in between. This new arrangement filled the wall and did, in fact, make Doris' dining room look like a study. The desk needed a lamp.

"I see the joy of shopping, now," said Arthur who was on his knees on the floor. He had finished flattening the moving cartons which the books had come west in, and was bundling up the cardboard. He tied a knot in the slippery nylon cord.

"There." He straightened up brushing his hands on his khakis. "I'll put this out in the mud room, then make us a cuppa, shall I?"

He carried the cardboard through the kitchen. Pauline followed carrying the ball of nylon cord and the scissors.

"I kind of like this funny little room," she said, as they stepped into the mud room. "The windows are neat. And I love these little cupboards."

"Home of Doris' famous plastic bag collection," he laughed.

She handed him the ball of cord and the scissors and he tucked them into the cupboard which closed with its satisfying little snick.

They went into the kitchen.

Arthur stood at the ancient sink, washing his hands.

"What kind?" He nodded his head toward the row of gleaming tea tins. "I have quite a collection, now."

Almond, they decided, and Arthur dried his hands and set about filling Doris' aged electric kettle. It was curious to see his face elongated there on the shining curve of the kettle as he moved it from the sink to the mottled counter top. He watched his distorted image carefully plug in the soft and fraying cord.

It was like seeing yourself in the back of a spoon. It was the sensation which Richard had each day, looking down at the shining electroplated auto and marine parts on the floor of the factory. It was faintly disturbing. Menacing even. Like having a clown suddenly pop up in front of you. Not comic.

"Do you know, I haven't a cookie or a scone or anything," said Arthur when the kettle had boiled and he was setting the filled tea pot on the table.

"Well, then, let's have a smoke with our tea instead," said Pauline. "I've brought mine."

Arthur retrieved the tin ashtray from the mud room while she bent across the table and pushed up the window.

It was warm out, but it was the sharp and edgy warmth of late September. The earth was losing its heat and this was a fleeting warmth, recreated each morning and lost each night as the days grew shorter and darkness came, earlier and earlier. The sky was a hard blue and there was a fierce brightness to the day.

"It lasts until about the third week of October, if we're lucky," said Pauline. She bent to the light of Arthur's wooden match. "Then the rain settles in and you sort of tuck your head under your wing until March."

"I'll be Mother," said Arthur picking up the teapot.

She looked a question at him. *Pardon?*

"It means I'll pour the tea," he said. "You haven't heard the expression? That just shows how old I am."

The tea steamed in the tall white mugs and smoke drifted up from their cigarettes. They watched out the window. They could see Pauline's back deck; the yellowing geraniums, the scorched looking canvas of the patio umbrella, Madeline's doll stroller on the top step.

"Did I tell you that we have a new cat? A kitten. Madeline named it Mutter."

"She's a darling girl. She's quick," said Arthur. "What made her name the cat Mutter?

Pauline shrugged. "A sound association, I think."

He nodded.

"What will you say about The Counties?" he asked when a few moments had drifted out the window with the cigarette smoke and the steam from their cooling tea.

"Oh, I'm going on and on about charm," said Pauline. "Style over substance."

"Such huge houses," said Arthur. "Could you live there? At The Counties?"

"No," she said, shaking her head. "No, I couldn't. I keep racking my brain to see if it's a kind of reverse snobbism. I can't decide. But, no, I don't think I could."

"The grandness of the houses?"

"No," she said slowly. "It's the endless sameness of the neighbor-hoods. I can't explain it, but it makes me tired just to look at those new suburbs. Physically. Like I want to lay my head down and fall asleep."

"Enervating," said Arthur.

"Exactly," she said. "But why is that? What is it?"

"Well, I've only just begun to think about things like that," Arthur admitted. He tapped the cigarette against the tin and the little ashtray bounced on the wooden table. "Don't forget that I built suburbs my whole life. The more houses you could get into a development the bet-ter. And don't forget too, that it wasn't that long ago that a house in the suburbs was an impossible dream for most people."

"Oh, I know." She sighed. Her elbow was on the table, her chin propped in her hand. "That's why I'm always thinking, well maybe it is just reverse snobbism on my part. You know the 'down on the suburbs' thing."

"Ummhmm," said Arthur. "But, I think what we react to, is not just the monotony of a place like The Counties or the one where your in-laws live - Glenmore?"

"The Glens."

"Right. I think what we react to is the lack of soul or feeling. And because that's a nebulous thing, not something you can quite define, then it's discounted in our society. Suspect."

Pauline nodded.

"But ..." Arthur stubbed his cigarette in the little tin ashtray and spoke slowly. "This is all new to me. I couldn't have thought those things to save my life, when I worked at building houses. Building suburbs. I just kind of hammered away."

Pauline looked at her watch.

"I should get back to work," she said, pushing back her chair. "Back to The Counties."

"You're not too enthusiastic about it?"

"Not very."

"But it's an interesting kind of work that you do," he said.

"In a way it is. Sometimes it's kind of fun." She carried her mug to the sink. "But as someone said about journalism or perhaps writing in general, it doesn't seem like fit work for a grownup."

"Ha. Interesting thought," said Arthur.

It was as though they were old friends now. Just like that. Following each other's thoughts down meandering trails, stopping quietly to admire the view as they turned new corners.

Even so, she felt revved up.

"I should get a real job though," she said. She accepted Arthur's mug and rinsed it too then dried her hands on the tea towel. "This was good when Maddie was little. At home all the time? But really, it doesn't pay very well. And there's certainly no future in it."

They went into the dining room. Pauline needed to get her purse. They needed to look once more at the bookcases, at the shining desk. This was the purpose of her visit, after all.

There was her purse, quite at home and incidentally harmonizing color-wise with Arthur's new desk and his chestnut collection. It was sitting on one of Doris' dining chairs which Arthur had brought down from the little front bedroom where it had been stashed among the domestic debris and storage cartons. It made a very nice desk chair since it had arms and a comfortably padded seat.

She wanted to stay. To curl up in Arthur's wing chair, perhaps fling a leg over the edge and really settle in. To hunker down. Hibernate. Wait things out.

She picked up the purse with a sigh. It was getting heavy. There was a steno pad in there now, folded up notices from school, too many lipsticks.

"What are you up to today?" she asked. She looked at her watch again. It was nearly noon.

"I'm off to do some errands on Granville," he said. "And I think I'll take the bus downtown. Maybe hit the library. Wander a bit."

⌘　⌘　⌘

Pauline stopped at the foot of the stair to lift the folded towel off the putty-colored carpet. It looked dry and clean. She went down the hall-way to the kitchen where the kitten was shut in, disgraced. She looked down at the plastic litter pan on the floor. There was a small lump in the corner of the greyish gravel and a fresh damp spot showing darkly.

"Good kitty!" she said and bent to scoop the cat from the bed Madeline had created from a cut-down carton brought home from Graces' house. It was lined with ragged doll blankets and smelled of fruit and warm fur.

"You're a good cat." She held the kitten to her cheek. It yawned then blinked and sat passively once more as she rubbed her face against its warmth.

She placed it back in its flannel nest and picked up the plastic litter box which sifted up a fine sheen of dust as she carried it to the basement stairwell. She tucked it in beside the kitchen broom and wedged a paint can against the door, holding it slightly ajar.

The cat appeared at the doorway.

"You go down there, Mutter. Poop down there," she said. "Hey, I don't think it's any fun, either. Don't look at me like that."

She washed her hands in the small bathroom beside the basement door and went down the hall.

"I'm the one who gets in trouble when you misbehave," she called out from the stairs. "I can get into enough doo-doo all by myself."

The cat sprinted up the stairs behind her and settled itself in a corner of the little sofa in the office den. She turned on the desk lamp and took out her notes from the trip to The Counties. This was going to require more than simple effusiveness. She was going to have to dig deep.

"More cat poop," she said out loud.

The Counties was created with your family in mind. Think back to your fondest hopes for a life rich with meaning. For a home that both expresses and helps to create a sense of belonging for you, for your children. That will grow deeper as the years pass… You want a home which resonates, that expresses the way of life you're working hard to create. A home in The Counties is not simply a wonderful house, filled with little luxuries and creative conveniences, but a true home, part of a real neighborhood. Here, you will find a sense of place.

She eyed the computer screen.

Like putting toxic waste in someone else's backyard..

Where had the soaring feeling gone? The sense that she was pulling out of the orbit of the ordinary?

⌘ ⌘ ⌘

"Leslie and Uncle Tink want us to come for dinner," said Madeline when Richard came through the door. "Auntie Catherine left a message for me!"

Pauline had listened earlier in the day, while Catherine talked to the answering machine, her words spooling up on magnetic tape on the kitchen counter. It was a curious, guilty pleasure, like eavesdropping. She had listened, eating her tuna fish sandwich, while Richard's only sister enjoyed the other guilty pleasure of listening to herself be magnanimous. She might have thought to herself how pleasant her voice sounded. Like being on the radio. A dubious modern pleasure, Pauline thought, hearing ourselves speak into the ether like Narcissus peering into the pool.

They were invited to The Glens on Friday evening. Tomorrow night. Dick and Daphne would of course be in attendance.

"Is this a council of some sort?" Pauline asked.

"Just a family get together, I imagine," Richard's voice was tight. "What do you mean council?"

"I have the feeling that something is up."

"Bah. Catherine just likes to have us over."

"No, she doesn't."

"You're being strange."

⌘ ⌘ ⌘

CHAPTER ELEVEN

"**M**y in-laws want us to move to a house out there."

They sat on the front step, their bottoms growing chilled, a bit numb from the cool concrete of Edward Sheppard's ugly porch.

"Richmond?"

"Ummhmm. They want to give us money for a down payment."

Leaves had begun to fall heavily from the chestnut trees, following the downward progression of the nuts, so that now the walks and lawns up and down the street looked wild, as though they were reverting to silent forest floor. Footsteps grew muffled and even cars sounded blurred and indistinct, their rough engine noises softened and smoothed by this curious blanketing.

In the heat of summer, the canopy of the enormous trees held off some of the heat, creating smaller and cooler environments beneath their benign branches. Now, as the weather turned, their leaves carpeted the ground, laying soft benevolence there. Around and around, up and down.

Arthur was raking up the leaves, creating neat piles like little teepees across the Sheppard's yard and across Isobel's side too.

He had been thinking of the yard in Edmonton. His and Joan's. It had been a vast expanse of manicured lawn, its only salvation, the small ravine, a crevice really, which ran along the eastern perimeter. There, things were denser, there there had been texture. They had left it to grow wild. But why then, had they flattened the yard, punctuated it only with two severe pines? Low maintenance.

Arthur had been thinking these things as he pulled the heavy metal rake slowly across the leaves, gathering up the chestnuts too, and their spiked, split outer shells which lay like tiny ruptured porcupines, miniature hedgehogs scuttling through the leaves.

What a business man has set himself, he thought. Trying to impose order on all this apparent randomness.

"Will you do it?" he asked.

"I don't know that I have a choice."

"But aren't there always options? Different possibilities?"

He was, of course, thinking about Joan. How he had built her a house in the suburbs and set her there, behind the wide expanse of lawn. The pointed trees.

Pauline was thinking about the dinner at Catherine and Tink's on Friday night. She and Richard had spent the rest of the weekend in a polite and formal family configuration, taking Madeline to the market on Granville Island on Saturday morning, watching TV together on Sunday night.

"Dad wants to make the down payment a simple transfer of funds out of the company. Make it easy for us. You don't get that," said Richard on Sunday night when they were tidying the kitchen after Madeline had been tucked into the little white bed.

"What do you see us doing?" He had shut the door of the dishwasher with a restrained sort of vengeance which suggested he wanted to slam it. Like pulling his punches. Perhaps he wanted to turn around and kick at it with his heel as well. "Renting this place from the Poulos for the rest of our lives?" He snorted. "Be serious."

They were noncombatants again. Silent, aggrieved, wounded, they had embarked on another ordinary week. The third week of October.

Pauline wanted to shake her head, to think straight. If she did not want a house in the suburbs, then what did she want? To pay rent to Theo and Cossie Poulos for the rest of their lives?

"I have a feeling there's a silver bullet with my name on it," she said to Arthur. "Or maybe it's more like a golden cage?"

She shifted on the step and drew her light nylon jacket across her chest, hugging it to her. She watched leaves drift onto the pale grass.

"I don't know. I have no ideas about what we might do instead. But it feels like doom to me."

Arthur still held the rake. He bounced the handle in a meditative way, passing it back and forth between his hands.

"Are you a list maker?" he asked finally.

"Sometimes." She turned to him and smiled. "Why?"

"Perhaps you could do one of those benefits and drawbacks, kind of lists? Figure out what is good and what is bad about moving to the suburbs."

She could do this cost-accounting thing. But if she did it, - because it was a linear process, one that relied on the rational and the fixed, - why she would start packing tomorrow. For how could she account for the wisps, the reasons without reasons that were binding her up, paralyzing her. Of course they should move to a nice house on a nice street, where Madeline could ride her bike.

Richard would be ten minutes from the factory and she would get a real job. Become a commuter. She would drive the Toyota down Burrard Street in the morning and in the evening, passing fourteenth avenue, perhaps waving at Theo and Cossie. Saluting Arthur's ghost. What else was on offer?

She knew she would go. That they would get a nice house. Not, perhaps as nice as Catherine and Tink's. But in time, who knew?

So, was her purse of no moment? Had it meant nothing? Truly, what else was on offer? She had spent too long dallying without offering a different way of being, of living their lives. And that being the case, they were only in line for money and debt and for things. For small moments of pleasure and satisfaction. Perhaps another baby. Madeline's continued growth and nurturance. One day a graduation ceremony, then a wedding.

She and Richard would grow older, buy things, become pleased with their lives. Perhaps a life behind a stamped concrete wall. They would prosper and occasionally know moments when they heard curious sounds in the trees (would they be planted fully grown, like the ones outside Catherine's exquisitely draped windows?) at the foot of their paved driveway. But they would only turn in their sleep, softly unaware of voices. Perhaps they would have a pool.

"I'm going to take a watercolor class," said Arthur when they had been silent for too long.

"Are you? What an interesting thing to do,"

"I think it will be," he said. He stood up. Stretched.

"I'm keeping you," said Pauline, getting up from the concrete and dusting the seat of her jeans. She picked up her purse. "Sorry, I just meant to go for a stroll. Get some fresh air." She looked at her watch.

"You're not keeping me," he said. "I wish I had something brilliant to offer."

She went down the walkway with a little wave. Arthur, leaning meditatively on the rake, watched her go.

Early on, when they had first met, she and Richard had been half in love with the erotic image of themselves. The stock broker and the copywriter. They had seen themselves reflected nicely in the faces of friends and been pleased with what they saw. This was what they had been looking for at the far edges of their adolescent selves. Someone who completes me and with whom I can continue the ego's dance.

Even until the birth of Madeline, they had enjoyed this sense of completion. Pauline had thought to continue work at Sidlum Associates with the baby tucked neatly in daycare. But she had come out of the hospital quite a different woman from the one who staggered into Maternity with one hand pressed fiercely against her hot and tearing back.

"Fuzzy thinking," she told herself during the first months postpartum. "I'll be all right."

But it wasn't fuzzy, sentimental thinking. Indeed it was crystalline, sharper than any thinking before. Even when Richard lost their savings and then their home and she had thought that at any minute her old self would return and take up where they'd left off - even then she did not.

She had watched with a new kind of peripheral vision, watching and waiting for something. Life looked different seen from the corner of your eye. You felt you might apprehend it, sneak up on the truth, if you didn't try to see it dead on. But time had passed, Madeline was at school now and Pauline was left, not with a new vision of a life she might have, but only with the knowledge of what she did not like, what did not fit. Like a petulant child, she sometimes had a furious urge to hit her head.

It was cool. An autumn day without color or light. She walked toward Granville Street, passing the fading greens of the lawn bowling courts, empty now in the greying light and the chill. She walked, thinking of nothing, her purse hanging neatly from her shoulder but whispering with each step as it brushed against the nylon of her jacket. Her hands felt cold and rough in her pockets.

There she was, nearly thirty-five, a medium looking woman in a black nylon jacket and blue jeans. A white turtleneck sweater and white runners protected her feet and warmed her chest. She was walking for fresh air, walking to be away from her desk, walking to think. Walking to walk. The movement of her legs settled finally into a rhythm and she became movement only.

She passed cars and crossed streets. She went up the gentle slope of the hill that led to Shaughnessy. She walked past houses built nearly a century past for railway executives, and she walked past immigrant men who moved with their heads down, eyes fixed on the task of blowing leaves off the lawns of those enormous houses. The leaf blowers hung on their backs like children's backpacks and the hoses roared at the leaves laying there behind broad gates and spiked black fences. She walked on sidewalks which had begun to undulate gently as the earth beneath them turned and pushed upward against their imposed flatness, their aging concrete symmetry. She walked through hushed domestic forests of giant trees and past alleys where wild blackberry bushes grieved in the fading light.

And what a foolish thought kept playing through her mind as she walked. That this density, this overlaid pavement and board and metal and glass, these houses and cars and the very roads and sidewalks were not truly here. She could see, even as she walked through these neighborhoods of fine old houses, the land as it once was. If she lifted her head, she would not see the tops of sky-seeking buildings crowded on the peninsula of downtown, but instead the sails of ancient, silent trees; masts of a forest not yet claimed and laid bare. If she walked as far as Arbutus Street, she would not see traffic and the seldom used railway tracks, but the damp and rolling coastal meadow of moss and fern it had once been.

While she walked, her purse making little hush-hush noises against her side, she did not think, which is what she believed she ought to do, what she needed to do. She could not make the list in her mind, although she wanted to. She did not clear her head and get serious about the next thing, although she meant to. She simply walked. And when she got home, she simply sat. She had accomplished nothing.

And yet her head *was* very clear. It felt transparent. But we do not like the idea of an empty head; of thoughts having flown. We are exasperated when our heads become empty bowls with only the air moving about in them. We want action, movement, plans, momentum. We wish to snag passing information and turn it to our ends, to our benefit. We want the main chance. There is no time, we tell ourselves, for emptiness. An empty head is a suspect thing. It has no utility. Thus prayer and silence become suspect. We play with the change in our pockets and shift from foot to foot. We want the meaning of things to be clear immediately.

The list-making part of her mind was worried indeed, but the part which had stared at the aspirin bottle three weeks ago (was it only three weeks?) until it became a soft blur of redness and whiteness - that part of her mind was sorting images, gathering strength.

She watched the message light on the answering machine. It was and then it was not. Off and on. Light and not light. Someone had left a message.

Pauline took the glass from beside the sink and crossed to the water cooler. She drank a glass of the cold water and then another and then pressed the button on the machine.

Pauline, she heard her sister say, *it's Dee. Dad is in the hospital. Not an accident. They think maybe an aneurysm. Or a stroke. I think it's pretty serious. Mom is there, at the hospital in Mission. Call me as soon as you can.*

⌘　⌘　⌘

CHAPTER TWELVE

Arthur had been to his watercolor class.

"We are all artists," said the woman who taught them. "I believe that."

That being the case, he was prepared to enter wholeheartedly into the thing. He would be an artist. He had been given a list of things to buy at the art supply store.

He could hear Greg groaning all the way from Edmonton. Would his father now cart home an easel, a beret, a small cache of paint pots?

The easel was easy. He built it in Edward Shepperd's basement. It was a simple thing fashioned from smooth pine lengths he carried home on the bus from a Kitsilano hardware store. A length of light aluminum chain and a hook and eye came home in a small plastic bag as well. In Edward's cave-like basement workshop, a place which made you hunch your shoulders although the ceiling was high enough to accommodate a man, Arthur found a square of plywood which he sanded and fastened to the tripod with small, flat screws.

He set it up in the living room, where the muted northern light came more easily now that the chestnut trees were bare, skeletal things. He liked the look of the easel there in front of the window, although it seemed rough and unfinished, the soft pine a little juvenile and raw looking in the same room with his beautiful lamp, the Indian rug, the walnut step table, his prized chairs.

He clipped dense rectangles of art paper to the plywood with a pair of clothespins which he took from the cupboard where Doris kept boxes of laundry soap and bottles of fabric softener. He would paint the Vancouver sky on this curious, porous paper which the teacher had directed them to buy. It was like playing with blotting paper, watching the color move as it wished across the dimples and whorls, stopped here and there by an errant fibre.

"It's fun!" he told Beryl on the phone.

"You'll find this interesting," she said. "The instructor in that psychology class I'm taking told us a fascinating thing recently. Think about native cultures. Where people had time for art, for painting and making things? Those times allowed their minds to process problems that we so often get stuck in." Her voice had grown excited. "Think about it. Three or four hours a day perhaps, spent creating. It allowed them to work any problems - psychic debris, the instructor calls it - it allowed them to work through this stuff. Without thinking it through. Fascinating, no?"

"Kind of left brain, right brain?"

"Like that," she said. "Sort of the value of play. Like children."

"Mmm hmm," said Arthur. "I see that."

He had begun to play. And to work too. He had volunteered his time at the community center art gallery where his class was held and was now committed to several afternoons each week of crating pictures, cleaning glass and cataloguing curiosities bequeathed to the gallery by dead patrons.

"I'm a general dogsbody," he told Beryl. "It's riveting."

Beryl laughed. "You have developed a remarkable ability to find the fascinating in just about anything. I envy you that."

And so time passed into the end of October. Just as Pauline had told him it would, the fine weather maintained a tenuous hold through the final days of the final week of the month until finally it gave up and went south.

Where was she?

He had seen her bundling Madeline into the car several times. They had waved and called out to each other. "Hello. How are you?"

But she was no longer on the back deck to water the geraniums which he saw had grown brown and broken, reduced to elemental shapes in their boxes. He didn't see her walking in the evening. It was too dark and cool now to sit on the front step with the evening paper while Madeline rode her bike before dinner as he had seen her do in the early fall.

He would not call. The day before Halloween, he walked to the Korean produce market on Granville Street and bought a spectacular bronze-colored potted mum. It was enormous, its green plastic pot covered over with festive looking gold foil. He left it on her step with a note.

Pauline - Just a little late autumn cheer. You were quite right about the weather and when it would turn! You might be interested to know I've done a little research on Burkeville, those wartime houses you pointed out. Happy Halloween. Cheers. Arthur.

The following evening there she was, looking pale and thinner he thought, in a navy pea coat with the collar upturned. Madeline, a wide yellow crepe paper flounce around her neck and a brown speckled beret on her head, stood beside her on the Shepperd's concrete stoop.

"Trick or Treat!" Pauline said when Arthur opened the door. She smiled. Her hair was drawn tightly back in a clasp and she wore no makeup.

"I'm a sun flower!" Madeline said. She skipped a little and turned to show him the green leggings and the green crepe paper skirt which were her stem and her leaves.

"So I see," he said. He crouched down so that their eyes were level.

"I like your costume very much," he said. "It's artistic." He held out a packet of gummy bears and a handful of hard candies wrapped in foil. Madeline opened her drawstring bag and he dropped the jellies in. He straightened and held the hard candies toward Pauline.

"Do children choke on these?" he asked. "I wasn't sure. They're the English ones with soft centers."

"Probably not the best idea," she said. She reached out and patted his hand, "Better just to give out the gummy bears, I think."

The feel of her warm hand as it gently tapped his open one caught him by surprise. It was soft electricity, connecting directly to his heart. He was ambushed, nearly frightened, like someone bumping unawares, into a cupboard door left hanging open. Tears sprang to his eyes

While women have learned to widen their eyes to hold in these unbidden tears, to dab discreetly at the inner corners where the incoherent and duplicitous tear ducts lie, most men have not. They do not have the practice.

He stood there in his soft flannel shirt, his worn corduroy trousers and the soft leather walking shoes. He would not cry. His hand folded around the candies and he covered it with the other, as though to hide them. He looked past her, as if searching for the trick or treaters whose shouts and laughter drifted toward them from Burrard Street. His damp eyes burned with cold.

He had carved a jack o lantern and set it out on Doris and Edward's cold, gray porch. He had replaced the porch light with a brighter bulb. They stood, momentarily unsure, caught in the curious light cast by the wavering candle in the pumpkin and the hard brilliance of the new overhead light. A small tableau vivant of vulnerability which lasted only an instant. Then Madeline turned away.

"Isobel's light's not on, Mommy," she said, starting down the awkward stairs. "We can't trick or treat there. Come on."

Pauline turned as though to follow her and then looked back.

"Do you stay up late?"

"Eleven or so." He turned the candies in his hand like worry beads.

"Will you make me a cup of tea later? After I've finished my rounds?"

Arthur smiled. "Of course," he said. "I'd like to."

They went down the walk, Madeline giddy and pulling at her mother's coat. "Hurry, hurry, up, mummy." She stopped at the sidewalk and called from the darkness, "Thank you!"

He waved and then simply stood there, brightly illuminated on the brutal stage of Edward Shepperd's porch. When his eyes felt unbearably dry and sharp, he went inside.

Later, when he was sure there would be no more children ringing the bell he stepped on to the porch and blew out the candle in the pumpkin. He breathed in the singular smell of scorched gourd, a scent at once both wet and dry, like singed hair caught up in the iron curling tongs his sister had set to heat on the wood stove, long ago. He settled the little carved lid carefully into the pumpkin turning it until the edges met and fit.

Did boys still come along at night after the little ones had gone home to bed, smashing these jack o lanterns that householders left out on their stoops? He would see. He left the porch light on.

He went inside and filled the electric kettle. The heavy, brown-betty tea pot was set out on the counter, and the white cups.

⌘　⌘　⌘

They were awkward at first.

"The living room?" he asked, when she had stepped into the hallway. "I have a fire going."

"Perfect," she said unbuttoning the pea coat and shivering a little with the chill which had followed her in. She rubbed her hands. "A fire will feel good."

He took the coat. It had been easier when the weather was warm, before they had needed to negotiate the formalities of hanging up coats and choosing where to sit so that they might be warm.

He had turned both chairs toward the fireplace. Their backs were to the hall, so that the chairs now looked like a pair of confidantes gathered there in the friendly light of his lamp, watching the fire.

He wanted her to sit in the wing chair and had moved his glasses and book to the far side of the little table, nearer to the club chair, so that she would not think she was taking his seat.

He went to get the tea.

When he had settled the tray on the walnut table between them, she smiled. "Shall I be Mother?"

"Yes. Do. I've made us Earl Gray. Do you like it?"

The tea was good and Arthur had built up a good fire. They were warm and cozy there, drinking tea by the fire with their backs to the door.

"Thank you for the flowers," she said, setting her cup on the enameled tray. "They're beautiful. That was thoughtful of you."

"Well, you're quite welcome," he said. "I'm getting a lot of pleasure from that little produce shop. The one you directed me to? The woman there is a Picasso of plants. A Vermeer of the vegetable."

"Your art class. I'd forgotten." She turned to regard the easel which stood bare. "How is that going? Any masterpieces underway?"

"I'm having fun playing with paints. Water colors," he said. "And I've begun helping out at the little gallery at the community center too."

"Madeline went to nursery school there."

"Ah."

Arthur knelt to the fire and added a small length of apple wood from the battered old pail he kept there. It wasn't an esthetic addition to the decor but it worked very well for lugging firewood from the garage. It felt right to have a bucket sitting there on the hearth, he thought. Homely and purposeful.

Pauline leaned forward and held her hands out to the heat.

"I haven't been around very much because my dad has been very sick," she said slowly. "I've been traveling back and forth to my folks place for the past couple of weeks."

"Oh, Pauline!" He settled back in the club chair and regarded her with a sympathetic frown. "I'm so sorry. Is it serious?"

"A stroke. We're very lucky. He's beginning to recover."

"I'm going to have a dinner party on the weekend," she said later when he was helping her with the pea coat. "I need a little comedy relief. Will you come? Friday evening?"

"I would love to come," Arthur said. "I'd like that very much."

"You can meet the Poulos and my friend Ellen," she said.

"And your husband."

"I forgot that," Pauline said. "You haven't met Richard. Of course."

⌘ ⌘ ⌘

Paul Davies, huge and powerful, had been felled like one of the enormous cedars which arrived daily at his mill. He had lain, inert and silent for nine days while Grace sat beside his hospital bed, knitting and rocking, enjoying the quiet which overlay the smooth murmur of the radio she had place near his head. Paul, she felt, might respond to the rope of sound laid there by the radio, and might follow it back, hand over hand, while she waited on the shore in her small cocoon of quiet. Thus they both had what they required while they waited for his circuits to stitch themselves back together. If they could.

They could and they did. But when he wakened, he wanted to be over there on the shore with Grace's quiet, not out there shivering on the island of noise and movement and furious seeking where he had lived always.

He fell down angry and loud and woke up quiet and pensive. He could speak, he could move his hands and his legs. When he saw the hard hat laying there on the night stand, next to the portable radio, he simply watched it for a moment and then turned away. He had poured himself elsewhere.

Where had he been? He didn't know. Had he known Grace was waiting there, knitting and rocking like the smooth clicking of a metronome? Perhaps that was the sound he had followed back. He could not say. He reached out and turned off the radio and smiled at Grace.

No neurological damage, said the neurologist. No motor impairment, said the physiotherapist.

"I'm fine," said Paul Davies.

⌘　⌘　⌘

"We went to the market and got lots of stuff for the dinner party," Madeline told Richard as he bent to unbuckle her seat belt and help her from the car.

He had seen them from the window - had been watching for them, really - and come outside to help. He seemed, these days to think Pauline might be an invalid. As though her father's queer journey had affected her health somehow.

The street was dark although it was only six o'clock, and it was shockingly cold beneath the shadows of the naked branches. They hurried inside with the bags, making several trips to carry in the flowers, the bread, the brown wrapped packets from the fish shop and the cheeses and fruits which had begun to soften and to release their perfumes during the short trip home in the warm car.

"Nice to get a spot out front," said Richard, pulling a last bag from the back seat. "I'm just up the street too. In front of Shepperds."

They were careful with each other. Things had shifted somehow as the seasons had turned.

November. November. A month which straddled the indoor and the outdoor part of life, that opened the door into the cave, that reminded them that all was not as it had seemed in the heat and gaiety of summer. Time for a dinner party. Time to light the candles and draw people to the table. A time to watch your back and to turn up your collar. It was not yet truly winter, nor golden autumn any longer. A liminal month; a place between waking and sleeping.

"Why is it so dark?" Madeline asked as Richard leaned to pull the curtains shut in the kitchen.

"We're going into winter time," he said. "The sun only stays for a little while in the daytime now. Until spring."

He tugged at the fabric so that it overlapped. He did this, he told himself, because the windows were ancient and single paned and let the cold drop on them, insinuating itself into the warmth of the kitchen. Causing utility bills to spike alarmingly. In truth, he did not like to see them reflected in the dark glass. They looked brittle and colorless there, like people in an old documentary film. Soundless and dull, they seemed to go grimly about the actions of feeding and tending. Closing the curtains gave them back to themselves somehow, gave them their dimensions, enclosed them in the familiar space of their kitchen.

He went to the kitchen door to close the slats of the small window blind. He could see late commuters following their headlights up Burrard Street, waiting for the traffic light near the ancient stone church on the corner. He shivered.

"Into winter time," he repeated.

"I'm going to draw a dark, winter picture," said Madeline climbing down from the chair. "At my desk."

⌘ ⌘ ⌘

Pauline was going to serve fish soup. Bouillabaisse. Cioppino. Whatever. She had cobbled together several recipes, throwing out the necessity of boiling fish heads and bones and keeping the garlicky, fennel and leek scented stuff. Canned broth and a fine thread of real saffron from the spice merchant at the market would bind it all together.

She would make aiiole, garlic mayonnaise, in the food processor, a moderately authentic touch which might serve to transport them all to a sunny table outdoors in the south of France. There was crusty bread from the market and several kinds of lettuce for a salad. A white triangle of soft cheese rested beneath a napkin on the pebbled counter top and a plum tart she had baked in the morning was cooling there.

It was warm in the kitchen. Mutter had tucked herself under Madeline's desk, rolled into a neat ball, her paws placed just so beneath her and her eyes tightly shut so that she appeared to be smiling as she drowsed there in the shadows.

It was raining, the drops bouncing up from the sidewalks and dripping endlessly from the downspout outside the kitchen window. Pauline heard the water sluicing into the little pile of river pebbles she and Madeline had placed beneath the spout. The sound, she thought, of someone very small walking across gravel.

She hummed as she filleted pieces of fish and washed lettuce. She moved easily, holding her good knife so that it rocked neatly in her hand and made small hollow sounds on the cutting board. She patted leaves of wet lettuce and rolled them in clean dish towels.

⌘ ⌘ ⌘

Arthur was painting.

Unlike Madeline, who knew instantly what she wished to have appear on her paper and created it there, fully fashioned as darkness or light, winter or spring, Arthur was having trouble.

Although he had water colors and he wanted to create the look and the feel of wetness, still he was stymied; caught somehow between the intention and the representation. The paper before him showed only a gray wash where he wanted clouds and fog and the dense shadow of moisture that they were wrapped up in; the smoky ether that he could see beneath the branches of the chestnut trees.

Why, he even felt damp! Although whether this was because of his artistic intent or because his Alberta bones and sinews were shivering there in the unfamiliar moisture, he could not say. He had a fire in the fireplace and Doris and Edward's ancient radiators were pinging softly, sending gentle currents of steam heated air through the house.

What color is this moisture, he wondered? How do you paint rain or fog? Madeline might use her felt crayons to draw dots tumbling earthward from a dark sky, and then create an image of herself in a yellow slicker with an umbrella opened over her head. See, it's raining, but the little girl isn't wet. Satisfactory. On to the next thing.

Arthur stared at the fire, trying to think how he might paint wetness.

We apprehended a thing, had a complete image of it, but on their way to the paper, the pictures and the words spilled away like a handful of sand separating out into its grains, its individual bits. It ceased to be the handful we began with in the instant of our transporting it. Some part of it slipped through our fingers; fell away. We were left with the 'not quite' of it, the shadow. The large image, complete, lay there in the mind while the hands and the brain, poor handmaidens, tried to convey it outward, manifest it in the world, but it was always and forever, incomplete, and we were left with longing.

That's nearly it, we say, blurring our focus so that the Impressionist painting presents us with a memory of sky and bright sun, clouds and shadowed faces. But not quite.

A matter of light, Arthur decided. He laid down the brush and crossed to his desk in the dining room. He removed the library books stacked there on the seat, and then carried Doris' dining chair - his desk chair - back to the window. He placed it in front of the broad window, near his rough easel, and sat facing the trees and the street. He would study water and light.

⌘　⌘　⌘

Paul Davies sat at the living room window in Cedar Mills, and watched the rain in his back yard. The house had been built backward on its lot, so that it presented its kitchen and back door to the road while the picture window and the seldom used front door opened out on to a sort of domesticated wildness. In effect, the back yard was the front yard and the front yard, the back.

Grace's cats were out there, hiding in the tree stump where Caroline and Pauline and Dee had played. The stump was broader than Grace's laundry stand and as tall as a man and had been hollowed on one side, an indentation large enough for a cat and kittens or a small child. It was nearly obscured by salmon berry bushes and wild morning glory vine and the curious little saplings which tried to grow up each year and were cut back by Grace in the fall.

Down the hill, across the highway, at the mill on the river, men in hard hats and quilted nylon vests moved with their heads down, quickly crossing the yard to stand out of the rain beneath the corrugated metal overhangs where endlessly orbiting saws and vast pointed blades, like guillotines, sent rough boards and roofing shakes down metal slides which grew cold and muddy as the day went on. Their breath came out in wet gray puffs and the cedar around them was stained by the steady rain until it was the color of fire.

Paul Davies watched the rain in his front yard and Grace talked on the phone with Connie, who was in the office down at the mill, watching the numbers of board feet and shake pallets pile up on her computer screen. Paul's flat lumber pencil and his hard hat were in the closed porch, on a shelf above his steel toed boots.

⌘ ⌘ ⌘

"Ugh. Still raining!" Ellen stamped into the hall, shaking her shoulders delicately. She shrugged out of the silk trench coat and handed it to Richard.

"Clive is parking the car," she said. "Poor sod." She handed Richard a bottle. "Not Chardonnay, but yummy. Needs the fridge."

She sailed past him to fix her wet hair in the small bathroom off the kitchen. Clive appeared a moment later and they introduced themselves heartily.

"Clive Cherry!"

"Richard Thorne!"

Richard took the beautiful beige coat which Clive handed him. Beads of rain, like small pellets, ran across the fine, smooth fabric and dripped on to the floor. Richard ran his thumb across the collar as he fitted the metal hanger into the shoulders. The coat was not wet. It was made of some costly material which repelled rain and let the wearer move comfortably through days and nights in which lesser mortals became drenched and chilled. He closed the closet and led Clive into the living room. They told each other how dreadful the city parking was.

Clive went directly to the hearth where the gas fire was humming quietly. Pauline had laid out an artichoke dip and small crackers on the coffee table and on the mantel near Clive's head, at eye level, there was a bowl of salted almonds. When Richard left the room to get his drink, - "Scotch rocks, thanks!" - Clive took a handful and stood there, quite at ease, shaking the salted nuts in his hand like dice and tossing them one at a time into his mouth. He surveyed the room, enjoying the warmth at his back.

They had not been expecting him.

Arthur arrived wearing a muted yellow woolen vest over a dark patterned shirt. He kept the tweed jacket on, brushing at the damp, rough wool and protesting he was fine, fine, when Pauline offered to hang it for him. It looked good with the grey flannel trousers he'd pressed on Doris' kitchen counter top and wearing it gave him a certain gravity he thought. A weight, which flapping about in shirt sleeves, somehow lacked. The dark tie he'd nearly worn was slung around the newel post at the bottom of Doris and Edward's stairs.

Richard settled the guests and fetched drinks while Pauline moved swiftly about in the dining room, making room for Clive. She pushed her place setting down the table and then set out silver and a plate for herself and an unpressed napkin which she furiously smoothed and folded.

She did all this in rapid controlled little movements while Ellen, blithely unaware, prattled at Madeline who sat at the kitchen counter, fresh from the bath and glowing cleanly in flannel pajamas and enormous woolly slippers.

"What if you'd been serving steak? Only had a certain number?" Richard hissed when Ellen had followed Madeline upstairs to see the cat.

"Never mind," said Pauline.

Richard couldn't let go.

"She didn't explain? Apologize?" He shook his head.

She sent him to the living room bearing Arthur's glass of wine.

When Madeline had been tucked in and cocktails were well in hand - Arthur deep in conversation with Cossie, Theo nodding his large gray head as Clive punctured the air with hand held opinions, and Ellen laughing loudly as she flirted with Richard - Pauline took a cigarette and a book of matches down from the cupboard over the stove and went out the back door.

The rain had stopped. Water still ran from the eavestroughs, rattling down the downspout, and there were puddles on the deck, but no drops fell on her as she stood in the dark smoking.

She wore her 'company for dinner' outfit, a black silk collarless shirt with fine, flat mother of pearl buttons, which she wore long and loose over narrow black wool trousers. She pulled at the front of the shirt and it billowed slightly in the chill air, cooling her.

She was girding her loins. Readying herself to play hostess, steadying her nerves after the scurrying business of setting a place for Clive.

She plucked at the shirt front again, running her thumbnail over one of the thin buttons. How easily Ellen moved through life. Unaware, confident in her place and sure that life was to be lived in the getting and the going.

She dropped the half smoked cigarette into the wet hedges beside the deck and went inside. In the small bathroom she washed her hands and rinsed her mouth, swishing a small knob of toothpaste between her teeth. She put on lipstick then kissed a tissue and dropped it in the wicker waste basket. Ellen had left the small hand towel on the counter and there was a bottle of hair spray there too. Pauline re-hung the towel and put the hair spray in the cupboard below the sink. She went through to the living room.

The room, often dim and too cool looking, was at its best on a night like this, animated by people and by the warmth and the light of the gas fire. The drapes were a nubby beige linen with fine black stripes, unlined, stitched up on Grace's portable from a bolt of remaindered fabric and hung on heavy length of wood doweling. In front of the drapes stood a pair of cane back chairs which had once sat on either side of Daphne's china cabinet. Lacquered black now and with their seats covered in left-over drape fabric, they were far better to look at than to sit in. Theo, returning from the kitchen with a fresh drink, drew one over to the coffee table and sat with it tipped back, his big arms balanced awkwardly on the narrow sides..

The large chair near the fireplace was covered in gold, a beautiful thing, trimmed with heavy olive and gold corded piping. Lovely to look at but poorly upholstered, the chair tended to push your head forward, causing you to crane your neck at an awkward angle. You were not inclined to sit there for long. Not like Arthur's wing chair, Pauline thought as she perched on the arm of the sofa and bent to listen to Cossie's story.

When they went in for dinner, she carried in one of the cane back chairs and placed it at her end of the table. Now they were seven.

Like Arthur trying to paint rain and fog and light, Pauline had been trying to capture something when she had set the table. Slightly off kilter now from her hasty resetting it still looked very pretty. Fat ivory candles had been brought in from the living room and set in a row down the table's middle. She had laid a square of beige linen at right angles across the long white table cloth, so that there were points at her end and at Richard's and the broad edges fell neatly before their guests. She had pressed damask napkins the color of fresh celery and set them in neat rectangles on each white plate. The balloon wineglasses gleamed in the candle light and there was a large potted ivy in the table's center, its tendrils laid out across the beige cloth. On the sideboard, an old oak dresser from Richard's bachelor days, she had set out the salad in one of her painted Italian fruit bowls from the kitchen. Beside it sat bottles of red and white wine and behind them, in a finely glazed yellow china pot, was the bronze chrysanthemum which Arthur had given her.

"Bouillabaisse!" Clive boomed, when she brought in the tureen of soup.

As quickly as it had come, whispering her name, pride was dispatched. Back to the kitchen. Pauline dipped her head, "Well, fish soup," she said. "A *sort* of bouillabaisse."

As Richard poured the wine and the basket of bread went around the table, she ladled the soup into the shallow soup plates stacked at her elbow, carefully scooping prawns, a large piece of bass, mussels, a smooth, white knuckle of crab meat into each one. The filled plates looked dense and rich as she handed them down the table. The steaming broth was the color of old brick. Flecks of parsley and tiny pearls of olive oil glistened on the surface. The fish pieces looked generous and thick in the bowls. An offering.

The purse had been trying to tell her something like this. Own the things you do, the thoughts you think, the very soup you make. This was what called out to us in the things which had meaning for us. The single rock we picked up from beside the river, the tree we were drawn to in a dark forest, the picture of a garden gate left standing ajar. Enter in, claim these things, wake up. Called by, drawn to and brought to - things. They resonated, had meaning, if we would but see; truly see for a moment.

Say, 'oh, for heaven's sake,' to the broken dish which caused you to weep and you have shut yourself away from some significant part, some truth. Weep not and you have shut your eyes to the real seeing of it.

More, more, we cry and wonder at never getting the satisfying sense of having finally grasped the thing.

Pauline had set her table, created her soup and turned away from it all at the instant when Clive cried "Bouillabaisse!"

A lucky break, we tell ourselves, when we have created some good and worthwhile thing. Afraid the success will just sit there on the curve of our world or be a shiny thing to show to others, we disown it or settle for its reflected light only. If only you knew how paltry this is, we say silently.

On to the next thing. But not in the way that Madeline still could, when she was well and truly finished with something. Here is my picture of winter, she said, expecting that it would be received, clipped to the fridge with a magnet or pinned to the bulletin board over her small desk. There's more where that came from. Where are my red shoes? She cried, needing them, and was glad when they appeared.

When the soup tureen was empty and they had eaten the salad and the cheese and the table was littered with bread crumbs, they moved back to the living room for the plum tart and coffee.

When Pauline pushed back the cane chair and stood, Arthur was quite suddenly at her side .

"I'll take that," he said grasping the chair at its arm and back. He carried it through to the living room and placed it near the fire.

Ellen appeared and settled into the cane chair with a sigh. "That was fabulous. I ate far too much.

"Dessert too!" she cried, as Pauline set the tart on the coffee table.

⌘ ⌘ ⌘

Because the rain had stopped, Arthur decided to walk around the block, to take the long way home; to circumnavigate the neighborhood, rather than simply walking across the dark, wet grass and up the steps to home.

He said good night to Theo and Cossie who had stepped out onto the porch with him. "Need to stretch my legs," he said.

He walked down the front path to the sidewalk where small pools of water reflected the streetlamps overhead and the lights of passing cars on Burrard Street. He stepped lightly between the puddles with a sort of tippy toe step as he walked toward the midnight traffic.

It was colder than he had expected. He turned up the collar of his tweed jacket and made fists in his pockets. He hunched into the chill of the satiny lining of the light coat, glad of the warmth of the woolen vest against his chest.

As unbidden as the original tears had been, here once again was the shiver of embarrassment which had assailed him off and on since Wednesday evening; since Halloween. These came in actual physical tremors, slight but real, which ran delicately up his spine and settled somewhere across the top of his shoulders, just below the nape of his neck.

Part of being happy, he had decided though, lay in investigating these delicate twitches of the soul. What did this mean?

He had been inventorying his feelings for Pauline. To whom did those sudden tears relate? To her or to him?

He had enjoyed himself. They had laughed loudly and eaten well and shared too much wine. He had been delighted by the Poulos; by their slow and serious ways and by their solemn recounting of the summer week, ten years ago when Edward Sheppard had ripped out all of his shrubs and bushes, laid down a truck load of pea gravel and torn the front porch off the house. Why? Theo and Cossie only shrugged. Who knew?

Ellen was a study, he thought, by turns seductive and critical. But fun, no doubt about that. Like the teenage boy who is allowed to get by on charm and sex appeal even with the old aunties and grandfathers. Some people lived a whole life that way, as Arthur knew.

"Just for the fun of it!" she had exclaimed at his answer when she'd asked what brought him to Vancouver for the year. "Imagine!"

He had feared she might be about to slap him on the knee.

"I think that's fabulous," she had said approvingly.

Clive had been interested in retirement investment issues, advising Arthur against putting too much faith in mutual funds.

"Over rated and over subscribed," Clive had said, chewing carefully on a piece of fish. A small bone, perhaps? A man like Clive was prudent and watchful. Storing things up and watching for insurgents. He had watched Ellen with hooded eyes.

Arthur turned at the far side of the park, walking along its uneven perimeter which had grown spongy and slippery in the rain. His walking shoes made slight squeaking noises as he tramped along on the wet grass. Across the park he could see the back of Pauline and Richard's duplex. The Poulos' side of the building was already in darkness. In Pauline's upstairs bathroom, a light burned, casting a faint pink light through the drawn blinds. Perhaps they left it on for Madeline?

Richard, Arthur reflected as he moved along, had been charming and gracious.

"I'm so glad to meet you," he told Arthur in the front hallway, placing his left hand over their clasped right ones as they shook hands. As one does with the elderly or the infirm.

Putting me in my place, wondered Arthur. Or being sincere?

At the middle of the block, he turned and started down the alley, aware even as he did so that it mightn't be wise to walk down an alley at half past midnight. But he had struck bargains with himself recently, about facing fears. It was well lighted after all and the park was a vast open space without trees or hedges. No bogey men could hide there, certainly.

He let himself in through the mud room door, pausing to lock it carefully and then to lock the kitchen door too when he stepped inside. He faced fears but he did not invite danger.

It was hot in the house. Stuffy. He was not yet familiar with the idiosyncrasies of the old steam radiators and often found himself too hot or too cold.

"Goldilocks," he said out loud as he moved through the living room, stopping to turn on his beautiful lamp.

In the front hall, he hung the tweed jacket on a hanger and bent to slip off the damp shoes.

"What's with me?" he said out loud, surprised suddenly to see the task he was at. "I just walked right through the house with my wet shoes on. Hmmph."

He placed them on the rubber boot mat in the dark hall and silently, in his sock feet, crossed back into the living room. It smelled faintly of last night's fire, a charcoal, wienie-roast smell from long ago summers.

He picked up "Rumours of Civilization" and turned off the light. He went upstairs in the dark.

⌘   ⌘   ⌘

CHAPTER THIRTEEN

"**Y**ou know how we were talking about suburbs a while back?" Arthur asked. "After we'd been to your project and we had seen Burkeville?"

They were walking toward Broadway, matching their steps to the rhythm of passing traffic on Burrard Street, an unconscious response to the surrounding sound, the medium in which they moved.

"Umm. Hmm," Pauline said. "I'm just now finishing that. The brochure for the Counties, if you can believe it."

"I was intrigued by it," he said. "By Burkeville, I mean. And I went down to the library a couple of weeks ago and looked through the newspaper files. The microfiche? It's very interesting. The whole wartime housing thing."

"Did you do build them?" Pauline asked. "Wartime houses? In Edmonton?"

"Well, I did, you know. For a while," he said. "But I'm ashamed to say I didn't really think about the thing too much. We just built them in a hurry. Made a decent buck and went on to the next thing."

"Not too unusual." She reached up and pulled her collar higher around her neck.

"No." Arthur said slowly. "I suppose not. The thing is though, there were people thinking about the whole social issue, at the time. Whether you could change society by the way people lived. Whether good cities and real neighborhoods could change people for the better. It's fascinating."

They walked in silence for a few moments, thinking about this.

"Meanwhile, Dick and Daphne are still lobbying to have us buy a house out in Richmond," said Pauline. "Maybe they're trying a little social engineering on us." She laughed.

"Make you into decent, householding citizens, as it were," he smiled over at her. They had reached Broadway, a curious Vancouver street which seemed to intersect the city's future and its past. Further on, where Granville crossed it on the crest of the hill, sat the Aristocrat, an aging coffee shop whose rounded, theatrical snout, window booths and pinstripes of aging neon, anchored it firmly in the 1930s.

Pauline looked down the street to where the Pitman Business College seemed forever poised - in its upstairs aerie over a candy shop - to churn out white gloved young ladies ready to pound the keys on the manual Olympia or Corona typewriter in your insurance office.

She found it a disorienting corner. The intersection gave swiftly down to the Granville Street Bridge and then on into the urgent newness of the downtown proper. If you followed Broadway all the way inland from this quaint intersection, you were led out through the industrial parks and suburbs of Burnaby until the street became the Lougheed Highway, an old road which hugged the bank of the Fraser River all the way out into the valley, to Cedar Mills and beyond. She could walk straight home from here.

Why were there not more collisions there on the corner, she wondered, where the past and the future waited at the traffic light, restless and impatient?

They were on a 'walk,' not simply strolling. Pauline wore her runners and a pair of nylon warmup pants. Arthur had on the walking shoes and his khakis. Under her nylon jacket, she wore a hooded sweatshirt and he had layered on several sweaters, ending with the aged fisherman knit which Joan had knit when they had been the fashion for suburban men.

"Left or right?" She pulled back the sleeve of her sweatshirt and looked at her watch. "I should get back within the half hour."

"Left," he said. "I've already marched down Granville today. First thing this morning."

"You're putting on the miles today." She turned to smile at him.

"I like to stroll up for the paper, in the morning," he said. "It starts the day."

He had been at the easel, still at work on carrying water to the page, when he had seen her from the window.

"Wanna come for a walk?" she had asked playfully when he stepped onto the porch.

Nailing jelly to the wall, he told her, would be easier than trying to paint fog. He accepted the invitation gladly.

Now, as they neared home, he was loathe to let her go. They stood beneath the bare chestnut trees.

"Coffee?" he asked. "Juice? Gatorade?"

"What the hell." She laughed and patted his arm. "This Monday morning's shot now, anyway."

They went inside.

She stood at the easel studying his work in progress while he went to make the coffee. There was green paint, still wet on the page, mixed into the wash of gray now and it had begun to suggest the rolling damp he was trying to capture.

"Green Jello, I wonder?" said Arthur nodding toward the easel as he set the enameled tray on the step table.

"No." She stepped back and squinted. "It looks good. Green and grey are pretty much what we see these days. It's hard to get hold of. You see that mist and you think that you can arrive at it. But when you get to where you thought it was, it's gone. Pretty hard to paint. Like an hallucination."

She walked over to the step table and picked up one of the cookies he had set out on Doris' cake plate.

He went back to the kitchen for the coffee pot and returned, holding a folded tea towel beneath it

"My sister calls these nice cookies." She held up the cookie. "Not neese."

"They are kind of nice, though," said Arthur. He filled the white mugs and set the pot on the folded towel on the tiled hearth.

He nodded toward the folded tea towel. "I'm getting paranoid about Doris' hardwood. The other night after your party? I marched right through here in wet shoes. I've repaired the damage I hope, with some of that wood cleanser. The vegetable stuff?"

"They look fine." She glanced down at the floors.

Like hers, they were tightly laid strips of oak, stained the color of weak tea and with beautifully detailed corners inset with diamonds of parquet work.

Arthur's British India rug of apple colors, reds, greens and wines, was a small island on the wood floor, bearing the chairs, the step table and the beautiful lamp.

They sat down, Pauline settling easily into the wing chair and Arthur turning sideways in the club chair.

"I should build a fire," he said. "That's a neat little gas fireplace you have. Good heat."

He was reminded of the dinner party.

"That was a great evening," he said. "Thank you again for inviting me."

"I'm glad you came."

He leaned to the lamp and pulled at the amber tassel. Instantly they were in small pool of golden light.

They sipped carefully at the hot coffee.

"I've filled them too full," he apologized.

"My mother-in-law insists on a half-full cup." She wrapped her hand around the white mug, enjoying the hard warmth of the china. "This is fine. It will cool."

Arthur stood suddenly and crossed to his desk.

"I wanted to show you this …"

He lifted books and set them aside; finally found the brown folder he was looking for.

"This quote I copied down from a speech that the president of CMHC made in the fifties. He was talking about ideas in vogue then. About how to build proper towns and cities? Listen to this."

He settled again in the club chair and picked up his reading glasses from the little table.

He read: *"Must we look forward to wholly conventional living in our North American cities? Lives all alike in standardized subdivisions? This is the ideal that seems to prevail among governments, builders and planners … If environment has any influence on character, the one we seem to be providing has severe limitations. It seems aimed at diminishing the individual."*

"That was a chap named Stuart Bates." He set the paper on the step table.

"Here, here," said Pauline. "Isn't that remarkable?"

"Well." He withdrew his glasses, folded them and set them aside. "And the really remarkable thing, I'm realizing as I go through this stuff, is that there was this kind of thought going on in a government corporation for heaven's sake." He shook his head. "I could just slap myself."

"What for?"

"Well, I feel like I was asleep, all those years. It feels like such a waste."

"Because?"

"Because I was building houses, but not really thinking about what I was doing," he said.

How to explain this retroactive sense of guilt? Or if not guilt, perhaps something more like anguish. Where were the bookcases in those houses, for instance? The porches?

"Well, in retrospect, you can think that. But at the time, you couldn't know those things." She set her cup on the tray. "You were doing a job. Providing a service?"

"Yes, but some people were thinking about these things," he said. "I was not."

"Okay," Pauline said slowly. "But we are different people at different times of our lives. Don't you think?"

"It's just frustrating to me. Old age, I guess."

She laughed. "You're not old," she said. "You're one of the youngest grown-ups I've ever met."

He leaned forward with his hands clasped together and looked at the empty fireplace.

"Well, thank you," he said. "That's a great compliment. Thank you very much."

"You're welcome."

"You don't mean childish, I hope," he said after a moment.

"No. I mean observant, willing to see new things."

"Ah."

They stared at the empty fireplace, sipping at the hot coffee, enjoying the comfort of the chairs, their leg muscles slowly coming to rest after the brisk walk. They were in their sock feet. Old friends in white athletic socks and messy walking clothes.

Pauline picked up another cookie. Thin, sugary, rectangles. They were packaged cookies all right, but they somehow looked rich and golden in the light from Arthur's lamp. She took a bite and chewed thoughtfully. A mouthful of snowy butter. Coconut, sugar and something dense which filled her mouth with a satisfying roundness, the cookies were rich and melting, like Christmas shortbread.

"You're interested in other people, but aware of yourself," she said after a moment. "Like Madeline. She's curious about why people do things and what they have to say. But she's satisfied with herself. For now."

"She's a happy girl," said Arthur, rising again from the chair. He walked over to the radiator beneath the window and felt the dull metal surface. Cold. "I don't seem to be able to regulate these things anymore," he said. "They're mysterious to me."

He turned the small black knob at the end of the radiator and listened a moment. Water gurgled and there was a clunking sound. Something would happen. He went back to the chair.

"Are you cold?"

"I've got my sweats on," she said. "I'm fine."

"Does she like school? Madeline?"

"She likes the drama of it I think," said Pauline

"The drama?"

"It's like theater for her. She's kind of starring in this little play. She rewrites it every day."

"Well," he said. "Isn't that wonderful?" He laughed. "A play and she's the star."

"Something like that."

He remembered Madeline's sunflower costume at Halloween.

"Does she dance and so on?" *Who knew what little girls did?*

"She takes ballet. It's not serious, though. They run about in pink leotards."

"Lovely," he said.

The coffee had cooled and Pauline finished hers with quick swallows. She stood up, checking her watch.

"I've got to get back to work," she said. "Get that bloody brochure out of my life. I've got a fashion thing to finish too." She stretched raising her arms over her head and clasping her hands. "That was a good walk."

They went out to the hallway.

"What are you up to this afternoon?" she asked as she bent to pick up her runners from the boot tray. "More painting?"

"I might taxi down to the market," he said. "Maybe I'll get reckless and buy a whole lobster or something. Your fish soup inspired me. It was delicious, by the way. I've actually been thinking about it for two days."

Arthur held open the door and she stepped out onto the concrete porch.

"I liked the garlic mayonnaise stuff." He took a deep breath of the damp air. "Is that French?"

"Aiiole. It's French, but I cheat. I just beat up some garlic in the food processor and add pepper flakes and olive oil to jarred mayonnaise."

"Is that so? Well, it was very clever."

"You could whip up the real thing, Arthur," she said. "Get yourself a pestle for that old mortar on your desk and pound up some garlic and lemon and olive oil, a few pepper flakes. Boom."

"Not likely," he laughed.

They said goodbye and he stood on the step a moment, watching her walk across the damp grass and up the broad wooden stairs. She stopped to reach into the mailbox and stood a moment on her porch, her head bent over envelopes and flyers. He drew back and shut the door. The house felt warmer now.

⌘　⌘　⌘

Richard had been mournful since Friday night. Clive, who managed large municipal pension funds and had a suite of offices downtown in the Bentall Building, had put on his beautiful beige coat and gone out the door with a little piece of Richard's heart.

The car, which Clive fetched while Ellen shivered prettily on the front porch in her silk trench coat, had been too much to bear. Sleek and gray, waiting in the middle of the dark, wet street, with head lights that rode only inches above the road and doors so low that Ellen bent nearly double to fold into its leather interior, it was a car from a dream. Low slung, mysterious, impenetrable.

"Seems like a nice guy," Richard had said as they carried wine glasses to kitchen, tidying up after the dinner party. "Too bad your friend is such a ditz she doesn't remember to tell you when she's bringing a date. Or to ask."

He was afraid. Afraid that he had failed in some large and complete way and was doomed now to struggle upstream. The evening had wakened in him the desire to make lists, to accomplish unnamed things and to get more. He went to bed with an icy heart, frozen by the realization that he was slipping, slipping behind in a race that he could not name, whose rules were unwritten and seemed understood by only a chosen few.

He dreamt of Clive's car on Saturday night and on Monday morning went to work with the frantic feeling that he was moving in an awful and terrible slowness when speed was what was needed.

"We need a budget," he told Pauline on Monday evening when Madeline had been tucked up in the little white bed. "We need to figure out our expenses."

⌘   ⌘   ⌘

Arthur waited in an upholstered booth in Quarter Past Moon. The restaurant was humid. A tropical island in a monsoon. Heated air rose up from the gas furnace laboring in the cellar and was moistened by the lunch hour diners; damp salesmen and secretaries and shopkeepers, whose coats steamed on brass hooks and whose furled umbrellas dripped quietly in a porcelain urn near the door. The uncurtained windows were filmed lightly with steam from the kitchen and by the condensation of a roomful of Friday afternoon conversation. With each opening of the door, a gust of November wind was borne in and with it more moisture.

Plates didn't slip from their hands, but the waiters felt clammy and unsure of their reach. They set salads and beaded water glasses carefully on the tables and turned with precision, hearing their rubber soles squeak on the softening floorboards. Diners rubbed their hands together discreetly and felt inclined to wipe the silverware with their napkins, unconsciously trying to dry things. Anything. Hairdos wilted and frizzed. Men patted the backs of their necks where the rain had run beneath their collars and the cashier at the front of the restaurant sniffed daintily at the tips of her damp fingers which had begun to stink of copper. Receipts and lunch checks had become limp and would not tear evenly.

Arthur had arrived early and so had a window booth from which to observe the whole great, wet scene, inside and out. Pauline arrived under cover of an anonymous, black umbrella and he watched her fold it and shake it neatly as she stepped into the shelter of the dark awning over the door.

"Now that's rain!" she said cheerfully, sliding into the booth across from him.

"You're a happy woman," Arthur said. "Does rain lift your spirits?"

"No, it doesn't. But I feel happy today." She rapped her knuckles on the smooth table top. "Knock wood."

The dark-eyed waiter arrived and sadly handed them each a damp menu card.

"Ellen thinks he wears false finger nails," she said from behind her menu when the waiter had gone.

"Imagine."

Arthur turned slightly in the booth and watched the waiter return bearing a water pitcher and two stemmed glasses which he gripped tightly at the base.

"I think she's right," he said when the water had been poured and the waiter had turned away to another table.

They ordered cheese toast and Italian bean soup, which seemed to buoy the waiter.

"Wonderful," he said and lowered his eyes dramatically. "It's perfect today."

Cheered by this, Arthur asked for a small carafe of red wine as well.

"It's Friday," he said when she raised her eyebrows.

As they ate the fragrant soup of small, white beans and delicately cut vegetables, Pauline told Arthur about her morning's work.

"It's a newsletter they send to their clients," she said. "They keep in the store as well. A promotional thing. I suppose the theory is that it makes everyone feel that they are very fashionable and in the know. Exclusive. Which, by the way, Margaret Mead thought was the bane of our existence. The idea of exclusivity."

She had spent the morning in Debora Kee's office, wielding a red pencil. Some Christmas fashions would not be arriving. They needed to mention a fashion show in January. A series of tiny frowns had creased Debora's smoothly made-up face as they dealt with these problems. There would be a few more minor changes, but the newsletter was substantially done.

"And you're happy because it's finished now?"

"I'm happy because it's finished." She sighed. "Absolutely."

"I like this little vase thing. Or cruet," Arthur said, picking up the wine carafe to refill her glass. "I like it when things are used for other purposes. I don't know why."

They smiled at each other.

She had phoned him the night before - Richard's racquet ball night - to invite him to lunch.

"I thought," she had said, "That you might be on your way to your art class tomorrow. It's not far from where I'll be. I think you might get a kick out of Quarter Past Moon, this little restaurant on fourth avenue."

There were certain things which vibrated or resonated, she thought. And we could not say, it's because of this or that; were even repelled should someone try to decode the pull of the thing or the place. Yet we seemed compelled to share these things with those to whom we were drawn. Then, in spite of ourselves, we slyly watched to see if the thing or the place plucked a chord for them too. A sort of test. The answer might lead us to believe we were in love, had found a soul mate. And when the test was failed, it was of course, the thing that broke the heart; caused you to tell yourself to be brave when the chosen friend or lover saw but did not see, the thing which caused the small hum in that fragile place at the base of the neck. The pinch of delight. You were forced to put away the hurt of this disappointment, and even attempted small murders against yourself, believing that the wordless telegram sent up the spine by the soul could not be deciphered and was therefore not real.

She was slyly watching Arthur. The anticipation of his reaction was one of the reasons she felt happy today. She was like the child who showed you the piece of broken glass or the curiously shaped stone. Don't say anything, cried the heart. Lest you say the wrong thing. Simply observe. And if it means nothing to you, then only turn away, perhaps having offered to touch the thing softly.

Arthur liked the restaurant.

Pauline's purse, sat damply beside her. Having it - a good purse - had given her a sense of style, of being current and she had enjoyed that. But it had also allowed her to smuggle a piece of magic into the everyday literal world. Unlike the rock or the curious little statue which you tucked onto a corner of your desk and laughed away with a dismissive flick of the wrist, she was able to carry the purse about with her.

People saw a good purse and admired it; even thought how chic the carrier of the good leather bag was, but it had an interior meaning for her only. It went about with her on her daily business, driving her car, meeting with real estate developers and sellers of fashionable clothes, but it hummed the whole time, drawing her deep into the mystery of her imagining. A delicate thing.

"Where are my red shoes?" Madeline cried. But they were more than red shoes and she would carry them about in her heart forever.

The purse had given form to that part of Pauline which insisted on being known, even in the literal, pushing, cool, end decade of the twentieth century. The part she felt she was meant to slap down and to anesthetize with sheer volume of consumer goods. Not that, cries the soul. Well, perhaps then, a bigger house or a better job.

Having let loose this part of her longing, concretized it with her purse, for heaven's sake - that sack, that magical tote which went about with a woman wherever she went - (a woman should probably be buried with her purse, Pauline has thought, complete with ratty tissues and faded lipsticks, for did she ever leave the house without it?) - she now had a touchstone, a goad.

When the soup was finished and the mournful waiter had cleared away the plates, they remained a few moments with the crusts of cheese bread and dregs of red wine in their glasses, content in the dampness and the dim light of Quarter Past Moon.

"What time is your class?" Pauline asked.

"One forty five." Arthur turned back the cuff on his tartan wool shirt and looked at his watch. "I should get going."

"I'll drive you. I've got to get some groceries. I can drop you on my way."

Arthur had an anonymous Vancouver umbrella too, dripping in the porcelain urn. They went out the door, into the rain, hunching into their coats and pushing up their black bumbershoots. They flowed into the water ballet of scurrying pedestrians and late-back-to-work shop keepers.

"How is your father?" Arthur asked when they had tucked them-selves into the Toyota.

⌘ ⌘ ⌘

Paul was quite well. Like the recovered psychiatric patient who the therapist pronounces "weller than well," he was up and about, but no longer the man he once was.

He wanted to know about his grandchildren, applauded the marvel-ous flavor of the peaches, which were in fact no different from peaches Grace had canned each year, forever. And he was concerned about the lives of his daughters.

"Are they happy?" he asked Grace.

"I like the color of this sofa," he announced. And: "Isn't it pretty, the way the laundry stand has turned silver in the rain?"

Grace was puzzled, although he was only acting in the outer world, as the man she had always know him to be. Still, it was disconcerting to find him out there. With her, as it were. With everyone.

But had things gone down hill, down the hill? He had gone back to the mill, surprised to find that so many good and kindly souls worked for him. All these good men, he thought. Dutifully carrying, cutting and packing wood. Driving forklifts through the yard and drinking coffee from home, packed in tall silver thermoses. Taking their money home.

He listened carefully when Connie explained the accounting and dispersal methods on the computer screen. She reminded him to put on his hard hat when he went into the yard and she watched him pat the chest pocket where the flat lumber pencil sat.

And the wood!

"Doesn't that smell wonderful?" he asked, inhaling a huge lungful of the scent thrown up by the saws.

Caroline phoned Pauline and asked, "What gives with Dad? I hope Connie's watching things, because he's just drifting along."

The oldest sister, Caroline, had inherited Paul's furious drive and tendency to count things. Seeing him jettison this method of attack had left her nervous, as though he had reneged on an unwritten pact. What am I supposed to do now, was her unasked question.

"You'd better keep an eye on him," she cautioned Grace, her soft-hearted mother. "Have you thought about asking the doctor to send him to a psychologist?"

⌘ ⌘ ⌘

"Actually, he's very well," Pauline said. "A little fragile still. But he's a much mellower man than he was before he had this thing."

"Intimations of mortality?"

They were at the community center, an arid, modern building adrift on a featureless plot of land. It was in a sort of gully, ceded to the community by a builder who got his name on a plaque in the lobby and the right to build an eighteen storey building across the street in a formerly low rise neighborhood.

She stopped the car in the loading zone, near the wide concrete apron which led up to the steps and the tall glass doors. They watched a moment as mothers hustled preschoolers from the building, shepparding them down the stairs and across the wet parking lot. Nap time, she thought, remembering Madeline's preschool years here.

A young father stepped through the doors, holding a pre-schooler by the hand and wearing an infant in a carrier on his back.

"I don't know whether it's intimations of mortality," she said, watching the man descend the steep concrete stairs. He moved carefully, his right shoulder stooped awkwardly to hold the hand of the little boy while balancing the weight of the baby on his back. "He's become sort of a sensitive, new-age guy, though. And if you'd known my father before, you'd find it almost incomprehensible. My sister thinks we should have his head read."

Arthur laughed. "Poor man."

He opened the car door and stepped out, then reached into the back seat for the umbrella and his art papers which were shrouded in plastic.

"Doris' handy-dandy bag collection," he said, holding up the parcel. "I may have them all used up by the time she gets back."

Pauline smiled and nodded. "See. Old Doris isn't so daffy. She stored them for a purpose. We just didn't know what it was."

They laughed and said good by. Pauline drove slowly through the parking lot where mothers buckled children into car seats. The young father had opened a black umbrella over his little family and they moved slowly down the sidewalk, beneath its solemn shelter.

She watched their progress in her rear view mirror, until they were only a black dot moving across the flat expanse of the damp playing field.

⌘　⌘　⌘

CHAPTER FOURTEEN

Pauline looked up from her book.

"I'm going to get a job," she said. "Spilled Inc. is looking for a staff writer. I'm going to apply."

Richard looked up from the newspaper and took off the little half glasses he had begun to carry about with him.

They were in the living room waiting for Dick and Daphne and Catherine and Tink to arrive for dinner. It was Sunday afternoon and still raining. Stranded inside all weekend, they had been forced to accommodate themselves to hours which seemed to stretch and droop in the wetness.

She had cleaned basement shelves in the morning and dragged up bags of outgrown clothes and forgotten junk for the thrift shop. Richard had fixed rickety curtain rods in their bedroom and re-glued Madeline's rocking chair.

There was a roast in the oven now, a mound of sliced mushrooms on the cutting board and potatoes and carrots peeled and sitting in pots of water at the back of the stove.

Madeline had been taken to a matinee downtown by Kristen and her parents, hearty souls who seemed invigorated by the prospect of Volvo-ing through the deluge to fetch up at a family film.

Pauline stood up and stretched. She had been sprawled uncomfortably on the green sofa, too far from the fireplace to feel any radiant warmth yet too chilled to go in search of the soft afghan blanket which, in the winter, she kept folded across the sofa's broad arm. She had been reading a British spy novel.

"Why didn't you tell me before?" Richard asked. He squared the newspaper and set it beside him on the floor. He sat forward in the gold chair, alert.

"I didn't really know." She folded back the corner of a page and set the thick novel on the coffee table. "Hadn't really decided until now."

She crossed to the window and looked out at the black trees. "We might as well take the money from the company and start looking for a house, too. Tell Dick we've decided to do it."

"Well. But the job isn't in the bag, is it?"

"No."

"But, anyway, it's a good idea," he said. "You're not worried about Mad, anymore? You'll have to find some kind of after-school program or something."

"Yes."

Richard stood and went to the fireplace. Couching down on the hearth he turned the small lever that controlled the flame. The flames leapt higher and the gentle hum of the automatic fan began. A small domestic movement, but now his back was to her and he remained hunched there staring into the fire.

Pauline turned back to the window. The Volvo drew up and stopped in the street. She watched as Kristen's mother stepped out and opened the back door of the car for Madeline, who rolled out in the backward way of small children. Pauline thought of the physiology of the movement as she went toward the door. She rolled her arms slightly, trying to feel her way through this curious difference between the adult passenger and the child passenger. The adult stepped decorously out, first legs, then bum, then fully upright, while the child unfolded immediately, from sitting to standing. In the car, out of the car, the child accepted the next thing. Closer to the ground, she thought.

She opened the door and stepped onto the porch. When Kristen's mother turned to watch Madeline cross the road Pauline waved and called out her thanks.

The woman waved and smiled, then folded herself smoothly back into the shining, wet Volvo, which pulled away as Madeline ran up the walk.

"Kristen has a baby brother!" she cried. "We got to sit in the back where his safety seat is. I gave him his cookies!"

"Well, aren't you the one," said Pauline pulling the heavy wooden door shut behind them.

Madeline's eyes shone with pleasure. Her smooth blond hair had darkened in places from the rain and seemed stringy, as though she had perspired heavily. Pauline pictured her squirming hotly in an itchy theater seat, a box of popcorn clutched in her lap. She smiled and leaned into her daughter, inhaling the child scent of her and the foreign smells which now clung to her. Not home, not school, these were smells of a larger world. Madeline's world was enlarging, would grow larger still. She would be enrolled in some brisk and purposeful after school group at the community center or at some mother's home. Her world would grow larger, pulling her further out of Pauline's orbit.

Pauline hugged her and kissed the damp and sweaty hair as she tugged off the rubbery rain coat. Freed from the coat and then from the little blue and brown rain shoes, Madeline darted into the living room and flung herself at Richard who had settled back into the chair.

"They have a baby brother!" she said fitting herself into his lap. She reached down to tug at the socks which drooped, shapeless and damp, at her ankles. "I fed him!"

"Well, lucky duck," he said, tucking her into his arm. "How was the movie?"

Pauline hung up the little rain coat and set the boots on the mat, then went down the hall. In the kitchen she opened the oven and inhaled the sharp, dark scent of the roast. Crouching down, she prodded at the brown, smoky packet sizzling there, turning and lifting it with the long handled fork, vaguely repelled by the pleasure of this. Meat. She closed the oven.

She was slicing green beans at the sink when she heard Dick and Daphne arrive and a moment later the trills and muffled booming from them which announced that Tink and Catherine had arrived too. She went through the dining room to the living room. She had closed the kitchen door at the end of the hall, so that her mother-in-law and Catherine would not automatically come searching for her there. She reproached herself for this even as she moved toward the living room. But she did not like them in her kitchen, and felt crowded and alarmed when they came to help. They needed to be pinned to the sofa with a glass of wine, a dish of salted cashews between them.

"I went to a movie with my friend and her baby!" she heard Madeline announce.

They fluttered in the hallway a moment longer hanging up coats and putting away umbrellas. In the living room, Pauline bent to turn down the flame of the gas fireplace and straightened as Dick came into the room, booming,

"Darling girl!"

Tink crossed the room to her and kissed the air near her ear, saying, "Gorgeous as always."

He was short and firm, a man whose bulk lay in curiously broad shoulders. A precise, small man, he seemed to invade others' space with a kind of fierce confidence. He wanted something, it seemed to Pauline. Behind the rimless glasses, his eyes were measuring, given to "meaningful" looks.

She stepped away from him, nearly ducking, to hug her mother-in-law briefly and to peck at Catherine's cool, pink cheek.

A runner who gave the illusion of height, Richard's sister was a small, thin woman with pared down angles and tightly controlled movements. Her eyes moved quickly, inventorying the room and Pauline's clothes. Nothing new? Good.

"Madeline's upset with us for not bringing Leslie," she said, moving into the room. "Didn't you tell her she wasn't coming?"

"I did," said Pauline. "But Madeline lives in hope that what she wants to happen, will happen. You know."

But Madeline had recovered nicely and was showing Daphne the cat which had grown substantially in the seven or eight weeks it had lived with them. It now looked adolescent and thin; its legs dangling limply as Madeline carried it proudly among them.

"Mutter's sisters live in the tree in Grandma Grace's yard," she said, presenting the cat to Daphne.

"Lucky Grace," said Daphne, raising her eyebrows but reaching gamely for the scrawny cat which Madeline held out to her.

"You need to feed her more," said Catherine, folding herself precisely into the corner of the green sofa. "She's very thin. Cats should be round."

Madeline looked puzzled.

"She eats lots." She turned to Pauline, alarmed. "Doesn't she?"

What a lot of energy these people took. Pauline felt she was holding up something heavy.

"Mutter's just going through a stage." She placed her hand on her daughter's small shoulder. "She's like a skinny teenager. She eats lots of food."

The cat which had been standing on Daphne's unwelcoming lap, jumped delicately to the floor and padded out of the room, its ringed tail high in the air. Daphne smoothed her dark skirt and brushed at invisible cat hair. Her bracelets tinkled lightly with the movement, like small bells announcing her disapproval.

Pauline went back to the kitchen where she found Richard pouring drinks. There was white wine for the women, club soda for Tink and a short crystal glass bearing two inches of scotch for Dick.

"They are a pain in the ass, aren't they?" he said looking down at the glasses. He reached for a lemon from the fruit bowl near the fridge and then opened the drawer below. He lifted out a small knife. Running his thumb absently across the curved blade he looked over at her and frowned. "They really are."

Carefully, he sectioned a narrow, yellow crescent of peel from the lemon and dropped it into his father's drink. He looked at her again as he lifted the tray of glasses.

She placed the dish of salted cashews on the tray and smiled,

"Yes they are," she said. "In fact, they're nuts."

He leaned across the tray which he held awkwardly up near his chest and kissed her cheek. "I do love you."

"Well, look at the competition."

"Hah."

He went out the swinging door and she turned to the stove, settling the pots on their burners and turning up the heat.

⌘ ⌘ ⌘

Dick nodded and made a quick jabbing movement with his knife, pointing at the roast on its platter in the center of the table.

"Delicious beef," he said, chewing thoughtfully. He gave Pauline a serious look. "Top cabin."

"I don't usually eat beef, any more," said Tink slowly. "As you know. But this really is very good, Pauline. I'm enjoying it."

"You're a wild man tonight, Tink," Richard said. "Red wine and red meat. Whew."

A humorless man, Tink was nevertheless prepared to be jocular at times.

"I'm a crazy guy," he said cutting at the small slice of meat on his plate with an exaggerated sweeping movement.

Catherine watched him with a measuring sort of gaze. *"No, you're not,"* said her eyes.

Madeline, who was sitting at Richard's side looked up at him and announced,

"I like vegetables. See. You should eat more Dad. More carrots and even green beans."

She was carefully cutting the green beans into sections, having recently begun to refuse help with this. Dinner was lengthy this way and her food was eaten cold, but she was a good eater. They all agreed.

"She's like me," announced Catherine. "When I was little. Remember Mother? Richard really didn't eat veggies much, but I always liked them. Even cauliflower and turnips."

Pauline looked up, feeling an apprehension that presented itself as tiny pinpricks at her temples.

She is not like you. This had happened before when Catherine had observed that Madeline liked books as she had done as a child, or that Madeline's hair swept up in a sort of cow lick, like hers when she was small.

This was ancient, atavistic stuff, Pauline knew. The mother knows the child is hers, belongs quite irrevocably to her, but the father's family is ever measuring, saying no, not like us, or yes, this child belongs to us. And we'll take her too. The mother, on some level, feels her children can be taken by force, by the other side, as in ancient stories, fairy tales, myths. The child is more mine than yours, thinks the mother. If I want to call your attention to some trait that marks her as belonging to you people, I will. But, she is mine.

Madeline looked fragile there, between her father and grandfather, her small blond head bent to the task of dicing her vegetables. The knife and fork seemed impossibly large and awkward in her small hands, although Pauline was careful always, to set a salad fork for her and a small knife.

They passed the platter up and down the table. Seconds of the roast and an extra spoonful of green beans were asked for; the tiny saucer of horseradish mixed with sour cream was handed around several times.

The gravy was pronounced delicious. The mushrooms were a nice treat. Did Pauline cook them with wine? Yes.

They spoke of Leslie's violin lessons and Madeline's ballet. Tink talked about the boat and Daphne explained how she over-wintered the pansies which bloomed through Christmas on the south side of her Kerrisdale porch. An unremarkable family dinner. An ordinary Sunday gathering.

"By the way Richard," said Dick, leaning in to the table, past Madeline's bowed head. "Good news. Those Japanese fellows probably do want to buy us."

Richard's head came up sharply.

"What?" he said, alarm and surprise in his voice. "Since when?"

Slowly he set down his fork and knife, placing them carefully together on an angle; lining them up at the side of the plate; taking exquisite care not to 'rowboat' them,

His half-eaten meal looked suddenly quite finished, the mashed potatoes congealed and stiff looking under the gravy; the pink beef, cold and messy and scrappy. He pushed the plate away with his forearm and picked up his wine glass. He took a large mouthful and swallowed slowly.

"You've spoken with them recently?" he said evenly. He did not look at his father. He twirled the stem of the heavy glass, then set it down and pushed it away too. "Why wasn't I told?"

Tink and Catherine had grown silent. Pauline turned away from Daphne's description of her morning and Daphne turned toward her husband with an uneasy smile. Madeline's small fork scraped against the plate and muted Sunday evening radio jazz seemed, for a moment, suddenly loud in the room.

"Well, I talked with their fellow on Friday," Dick said mildly. He continued to cut the beef on his plate and then scooped at a small puddle of horse radish with the point of his knife "Didn't think you were that interested."

"Daa-ad," said Richard, disbelief in the drawn out cadence, a double syllable of dismay. "When? When are they wanting to buy? And you've made an agreement? Jesus."

He pushed back his chair with a sudden, jerking movement and shoved the green napkin down on the table.

Madeline's head came up. She looked around the table, at the silent adults.

Dick looked puzzled. "Well, soon, I think," he said. He sat with his knife and fork poised, his wrists resting on the edge of the table. His napkin was tucked in his collar.

Richard stood and gathered his plate and the nearly empty wine glass. He went to the swinging door in long strides and shouldered through it. It swung once and stopped, making a dull sweeping noise that was like the sound of air escaping. It echoed in the quiet room, the sound replaying in their ears; an exhausted sigh above the sound of the radio.

After a moment Pauline reached across the table for the empty gravy boat. "I'll get more gravy."

As she stood, Daphne leaned forward to ask Madeline about the movie while Catherine and Tink bent silently to their food. A look passed between them which Pauline saw as she moved toward the swinging door. Dick continued to eat.

In the kitchen she filled a measuring cup with gravy from the speckled, blue roasting pan, which sat cooling on the cutting board. She placed the cup in the microwave and padded in the time.

Richard stood at the window, looking out at the dark yard. His long arms hung loosely at his sides and his hands slowly flexed and unflexed, opening and closing in empty fists. She stood a moment at the microwave, watching him, then crossed the room behind him as he reached up and began to tug at the curtains. They saw themselves there, reflected in the cool, flat blackness of the glass.

When he had closed the curtains and overlapped them he stood staring at the green patterned fabric. Pauline put her arms around his back, reaching awkwardly beneath his elbows. She rested her cheek against his back and felt the heat through the cotton of his shirt, the fragile thump of his heart vibrating against her breasts. Lub dub. Lub dub. Lub dub.

"They really are a pain in the ass," she whispered.

Small sounds of eating and of Daphne's trilling voice came from the other side of the swinging door. The microwave pinged.

"Go ahead," he said. "I'm fine. I'll come back to the table in a minute."

She went to the microwave and poured the steaming gravy into the gravy boat. What had looked rich and delicious as it was passed around the table now looked thick and greyish. Gelatinous. She carried it through to the dining room and set it before Dick who looked up at her and beamed.

"Darling girl," he said, reaching for the little flowered jug. "Hot gravy!

CHAPTER FIFTEEN

"My father-in-law is an idiot," Pauline said.

"Many are."

They were in Doris's kitchen. Outside wet snow flakes fell softly, settling gently on the narrow railing of the little back stoop and on the window sill, where they melted and ran into the little pool forming on the warped wood, the peeling paint. That, Arthur reflected, was where the heat went. Outside. The kitchen was comfortable this morning though. He had turned on the oven and left the door ajar, warming the small room.

"My mother used to do that on cold mornings." Pauline nodded toward the oven. "We used to hang our socks over the door to warm them up."

Arthur smiled. "What will Richard do now?"

"Maybe manage for the new owners," she said. "I don't know."

"And you? You're going to go to work for friends?"

He poured coffee for them.

"I'm hoping to." She poured cream into her mug and stirred. "These are nice." She held up the blue mug. "New?"

"Chinatown," he said. "They'll go with my dishes at home."

Home.

"You'll need two moving vans to take your stuff back to Alberta," she teased. "You're born to shop, as the say."

"I've actually been wondering if I'm becoming compulsive," he said. "It's like things call out to me, 'pick me, pick me.'"

They laughed. Home. Alberta. The words seemed like things, there in the room with them.

It was, she thought, strange how two people could acknowledge and yet not, something acute. What does it mean, the heart asked in alarm. Shush, said the civilized brain, moving smoothly on to some less painful thing. And yet the two brains or the two minds have on some level nodded to one another and commiserated on this turn of events. You'll go? Yes.

But the two coffee drinkers at Doris' table could not name the pain of this little exchange and it went underground.

"I've got to stop shopping though," said Arthur. "Greg thinks I'm getting dotty. Daft, as you would say."

"It's not really shopping though, is it?" said Pauline. "Finding little things that give you pleasure? Not what you'd call power shopping, at any rate." She picked up the coffee cup. "Now, Ellen, she's a pro."

"Well, it's her work too, isn't it?" said Arthur. "She's literally a pro. I mean she has to buy things, choose things, get the best price for people? Clients?"

"That's true," Pauline said. "But it's also what she does for fun. You should see her apartment. Townhouse actually. You'd swoon."

"Nice?"

Ellen's Kitsilano townhouse had been decorated by a well known interior designer whose taste was often on display in local magazines. It was lacquered, painted and papered in precious taste, with shining surfaces and texture underfoot. It was cunningly accessorized with ornaments and found objects. It was professionally cleaned and cared for from the shine on the lion's head door knocker to the greenery which changed with the seasons and was set out in exquisite terra cotta boxes on wrought iron ledges at the windows.

"Not really nice," said Pauline. "Perfect. It's perfect. Like a picture in a magazine."

"I think I prefer comfort to perfection," Arthur said. "You should see my apartment in Edmonton."

"Is it different from the house you lived in before?"

"Very," he said. "Joan and I had one of those perfect massive bungalows. A rancher really. With the huge picture window? When I built it, I suppose I thought it was wonderful. Moving up in the world, you know. What we could afford then, as the business became successful."

"And your apartment?"

"Old," he said. He rocked back on the wooden chair. "It's in a building that I remember seeing there, near the river when I was still a teenager. It's got the baseboards that come up just about to your shins? And coved arches between the rooms. Very traditional thirties stuff. Hardwood floors."

"That's what I like about these duplexes," Pauline said. "The hardwood and the doors between rooms and off the hallways. Stuff like that."

"Enclosure," said Arthur.

"I suppose." She set the blue mug down and absently traced her fingertips across the scarred surface of the old table. "That and human scale. Not like The Counties, for instance."

"Back to comfort," said Arthur.

"Back to comfort."

They finished their coffee and rose from the table and gathered up the blue cups, the coffee pot, the cream jug, the sugar bowl. They moved together in the small, warm kitchen, stepping carefully around the open oven door, opening the ancient fridge to tuck the cream inside, running the water in Doris' old sink to rinse the mugs. When it was all tidied and straightened away, the counters wiped and the chairs tucked back beneath the wooden table, they moved into the dining room.

"I'm off to redo my resume," Pauline said. "I have an appointment in the morning. Now I've got to pull tear sheets together, get a portfolio organized. Do some photocopying."

They stood beside Arthur's desk which was littered with notes written in his square, draftsman's hand and with slick, grayish photocopied pages from the library. Yellow sticky-notes fluttered from the pages of a stack of books at one corner of the desk and at the other corner, the chestnuts shone in the mortar. The framed photographs of Joan and Galen and Greg sat at the back.

"And what about the plan to buy a house in the suburbs?" Arthur asked.

"On hold, I suppose," she said. "Everything is up in the air now. With this thing with the factory. Richard's father. Who knows?"

She picked up the photo of Joan.

"Who is this?" she asked. "I've been meaning to ask you."

"My wife," Arthur said. "When she was about five. It was taken on the porch at her grandmother's old place in High River."

"Pretty little girl."

"Oh, she was a pretty woman. Very pretty."

"She died young?"

Pauline studied the photo.

"Sixty-three," Arthur said. "A heart attack. Seven years ago, now."

Pauline set the photo back on the desk and they walked through to the living room.

"You've finished your painting of mist," she said, crossing to the easel, where Arthur now had a shadowy pencil sketch of a house clipped to the plywood.

"It's this house," she said, surprised. She bent to the paper. "Were you sketching from across the road?"

"I took the easel out there," he said. "If you can believe it. To the sidewalk. It's very hard to capture things you know. I had no idea when I began that I would get so wrapped up in it"

"Were you artistic …?"

"When I was younger? No. I don't think so," he said. "But this instructor says we're all artists. Maybe she's right."

Arthur sat on the arm of the wing chair.

"Pauline?" he said, drawing her name out, making it a question. "I haven't known you so very long, but I feel as though we have become good friends somehow ..."

She looked up from the easel with the slightly stricken expression of someone about to hear some unbearable, intimate thing. Like someone about to hear the declaration of a love which they cannot return

"The picture of Joan," he began. "I keep it because it reminds me of something about her that I could not or at least did not, see, when she was alive." He spoke slowly. "It's more like a feeling I have. That I did not allow some part of her ... Or perhaps it's more that the times did not allow it."

He was not accustomed in his life, to saying what he most deeply felt, but this too was part of his new courage. Life did not go on forever. You had to swing around and look closely at the thing that was following you. One must, he realized, say and do the good thing. He rose from his uncomfortable perch on the arm and sat heavily into the wing chair.

"I want to tell you this," he said. "If you have time."

"I have time." She crossed the carpet and sat down on the edge of the cushion of the club chair.

She looked around the room. In the dull morning light it looked temporary, unfinished. There were only the chairs and the little step table on the worn rug, after all, and over near the window, Arthur's makeshift easel and the paints. A cup of grey and murky water sat on an old step stool he'd brought up from Edward's workroom. The walls were bare, the hearth empty, the room dim and still.

Arthur reached up and pulled the tassel on his lamp. The black and gold shade creaked a little as it expanded and they were illuminated in the warm light.

Pauline inhaled deeply and sat back. There was a sharp scent of paint in the room and, because Arthur had not cleaned the grate, the edgy, burnt, charcoal smell of old fires.

His face was hidden by the wing of the chair beside her. She could see his corded hands folded in his lap, the fingers twined; the khaki of his trousers; one sweatered sleeve angled against the arm of the chair. His old-fashioned wristwatch with its expanding bracelet of dulled silver diagonals, shone, reflecting the lamplight

"I think Joan meant to live a very different life," he said. He looked straight ahead, at the smooth, lacquered brick of the fireplace. "I think she meant to live a kind of bohemian life." He stopped.

"Not bohemian. No. What am I trying to say?" His hands worked in his lap, trying to pin down the words for him. "A different kind of life. She liked books. She liked the little house we lived in downtown. She was … Well, this is what I think now …I think she was just coming into herself. Happy with the boys - Galen was just a little baby - and happy with an idea of the future. How she saw her life? This is just what I think, mind you."

He stopped again. They could hear the fridge and the clock on the old stove murmuring in the kitchen and the sounds of traffic on Burrard Street. The steam radiator clunked suddenly in the stillness and he turned toward it.

"Are you cold?"

"I'm fine," she said. "It's warm in here."

He sat back and folded his hands together once more, settling them loosely in his lap.

"Then Galen died."

She had known this in a factual way, but hearing it now - Then Galen died. Then the baby died - made her eyes burn. There was lemon on her tongue. Water sprang up in the back of her mouth and she tried to swallow but there was a hard roundness in her throat.

All the un-cried tears in the world. A fragment from something she had read long ago.

"When he died. When the baby died, I did what men do. I tried to fix things. I thought…Well I probably didn't consciously think this … But

I thought, if I could create a new life for Joan ... remove her from the pain. I thought that all would be well. But now, I think I made her live a life she did not want."

He sighed. "And of course, she didn't have the strength to resist. Who could? I built her a modern house in a nice, new suburb. And then we scarcely talked about Galen. About what we'd lost."

He leaned forward and looked at her, then sat back again. His voice was very soft.

"You see, I don't think we had the words."

Pauline strained forward to hear him.

"People talk now," he said. "But we didn't even have the words."

She expected to look over and see him transformed, made old somehow, by the telling of this. Instead he leaned his head forward, peeking around the wing of the green chair, and smiled at her.

"Stories, eh?" he said lightly. "We all have stories."

"The reason I'm telling you this." He settled back. "The reason I'm telling you this about Joan and about our life, is that I think there is a lesson there."

He laughed.

"I know better than to try and fix your life for you - that's certainly a lesson this old man has learned. But I feel as though you are perhaps going to do the kind of thing that Joan did. That you might accept that there are no other ways to live? Even if your heart or your soul - whatever you want to call it - even if that tells you something different. So..." he raised his hands, palm up, his shoulders in a kind of shrug. "So that's why I told you about Joan."

She brought her hands together, like someone about to play eensie-weensie spider. The fingertips balanced against each other and she squeezed them between her knees. She closed her eyes.

"Why does it seem like this is a board game? Life is a board game? You know, you might make a right move and you might make a wrong move. If you are not good at strategy, well then you lose."

"I didn't tell you this to make you sad," he said. "I do think though, that we're obliged, in this life, to share … to share stories. Particularly if they can help."

Pauline's purse had been leaning against the club chair. She picked it up and settled it in her lap. For a moment she felt like her mother, felt her hands fold across the top of the bag in an expectant way, ready for something. How, she wondered do we do this? How do we feel 'like' someone with whom we share genetic material, since we do not, in fact know how they feel?

Yet, the serenity which Grace seemed to possess, settled on Pauline as she sat there, 'like' her mother.

An old photograph could cast a very long shadow. The solemn gray and white faces of Theodores and Isobels and Henrys and Kathleens. The pinned up hair, the wide, flat hair bows, the vests and ties and smocked dresses. Faces of small children who had been and gone, who grew old and saw dreams become smoke or ash. And we, we could only picture their pasts in black and white. But the images called out. Warnings and signposts. Joan's little picture called out a warning to Pauline. It spoke to Arthur, told him to mind the days, to not misplace time. Serene and happy in a dappled sunlit day, long ago, there she stood, forever on the porch, forever in front of the screen door. Was she coming in or going out?

⌘ ⌘ ⌘

"Hi Pauline. It's Mom. Your Dad would like to see everybody. Could you bring Richard and Maddie and come out for the weekend? Or maybe just dinner? Call me back and let me know, dear."

Paul Davies smelled cedar now in the enclosed porch, in his pick up truck, in the very sheets in his bed. It seemed that it must be stuck in his nostrils, tiny molecules of the stuff clinging to the hairs in his nose, mixed in there with the mucous.

Grace smelled like peaches and Tide, sometimes like Noxema skin cream or the almond scented hand lotion she kept on the little shelf above the sink. He wanted to stay near her and breathe her in, get away from the smell of cedar.

"I thought you liked it," said Grace, when he complained about being dogged by the smell of the mill. He had begun to leave his work boots outside and his quilted vest too. He asks her to launder his worn flannel work shirts again. The ceaseless late-November rain and sleet made matters worse.

"I do. I do like the smell of it," he said. "But it won't go away. I breathe in, there it is. I breathe out. It's still there. I just want to not smell it sometimes. Like I used to."

Caroline had no children and smelled like expensive perfume. He inhaled deeply when she stepped through the back door on Friday night. Dee had a baby and smelled like spit-up milk and Ivory Snow. He stayed near her and sniffed at the baby's head for a long time. He had begun to wash his hands too often.

"You're a nice clean Grandpa," said Dee with a small frown as she handed him the baby.

Their father, one of those men more comfortable at the kitchen table, than in the living room, had set up a sort of camp near the living room window now. He had the big chair from the sofa suite pulled up by the glass and a little milking stool with a needlework cover which he used as a foot stool, set before it. At his elbow, he had the old demi lune table from the spare room, piled high with magazines.

Caroline raised her eyebrows when she saw what he was reading. Old Chatelaine magazines and back issues of Life, were stacked there, next to his coffee cup.

"He's reading those?" she asked her mother, arching her brows dramatically.

"I think he just leafs through the pages," said Grace. "He's watching out the window. He gets a charge out of watching the cats out there. And the yard, I guess."

"I brought Mutter to see you!" cried Madeline when Grace opened the kitchen door to her.

Pauline stepped into the kitchen behind Madeline. "It's an eminently adaptable cat," she said. "Portable too." She carried the empty picnic basket and the pan of dusty cat litter out to the closed porch.

Madeline darted through the house with the cat and returned empty-handed with a report,

"Grandpa likes the way Mutter smells. He says she smells warm."

There was a pleasant uproar in the kitchen as they crowded in. Caroline, still in her black suit, but with stocking feet, was at the kitchen table, on a chair at the far end, from which she could see into the living room where Paul sat in his chair, holding the baby.

Dee, in her young mother's uniform of black leggings and a baggy tweed cardigan over a turtleneck sweater, was at the sink, next to Grace, peeling carrots. Grace, wearing grey pleated trousers and a turquoise shirt had rolled back her sleeves and was washing an enormous cabbage.

"Lasagna," said Richard, inhaling deeply, as he stepped into the warm kitchen. "Hello, ladies."

He bent to kiss Grace's cheek and then Dee's.

"Wet hands," Dee smiled and turned her face to him, offering up her cheek. "How are you, Rich?"

He set the bottle of wine on the counter and crossed the room to Caroline. "Hello, Cee."

"Don't call me that," she said, as she always did.

It was their jokey, constant greeting. He called her Cee, in reference to Dee. Pauline had never cared to be called Pee and he had mostly resisted. A family of girls, they had never grown accustomed to 'boy humour,' and often found Richard's jokiness faintly jarring and inappropriate. He knew this, yet found it to be like a stutter or a purpose tremor of the hand. The more he consciously tried to avoid this flip, foolish manner around them, the worse it got. Often, he simply retreated to the closed porch or even down to the mill. He liked the smell there and found it soothing to be away from the female force of Grace's kitchen.

"How's tricks?" he asked Caroline, pulling out the chair across from her.

She hadn't offered up a cheek to be kissed and her black, padded shoulders did not invite a brotherly pat. She had a large glass of wine on the table beside her and although she looked like someone who would have an ashtray there too and cigarettes and a good lighter, she did not smoke. She sat erect, with a manicured hand around the stem of the wine glass.

Caroline was a heavier, rounder version of Pauline, but her brown hair was colored an expensive shade of blonde and her dark eyes were heavily made up. She looked 'done' in contrast to Pauline and Dee who looked more diffuse and unfocused, beside their older sister. Domestic.

Pauline returned from the porch and stopped to hug her mother and sister at the sink. She crossed to the table and bent to kiss Caroline's cheek.

"Carolina-rhymes-with," she said, inhaling her sister's perfume. "You smell delicious. And expensive. Very chic."

"I'm going to go say hi to your dad," said Richard rising.

He hooked his brown leather jacket on the back of the wooden chair as Pauline settled into it.

In the living room Paul sat in the big chair with Madeline and the baby tucked into his lap and the cat at his feet.

When dinner was over Paul and Richard went out to the covered porch to set up the little cot and fold out the sleeping couch.

"All set," Richard said, stepping into the kitchen. "We're going to take a little walk."

"It's cold out, Paul," Grace protested as Paul came into the room.

He waved this away as he bent to remove his house slippers. "Grace."

This meant, "My good woman," or "For heaven's sake."

Grace was silenced, but watched to see that he put on his heavy down jacket and the red, woolen ball cap with the mill's logo across the peak.

"Put the flaps down."

"Grace." He went out the door.

Richard followed, pulling the door shut with a little shrug and an apologetic smile at his mother-in-law.

Madeline came in from the covered porch where she had been play-ing in Grace's toy box and protested that she should go as well, but sub-sided when Dee told her that she could help bathe the baby.

Caroline had changed into sweat pants and a short gray sweatshirt and now looked more like one of them, less foreign. She even wore a pair of her mother's fuzzy mule slippers which flapped as she shuffled about the kitchen, clearing dishes. Her hair was tucked behind her ears and her lipstick had worn off during dinner.

"Use some gloves," Grace said, bending down and reaching into the cupboard beneath the sink. "You'll wreck your nails."

"I don't care Mom," said Caroline. "Never mind." She reached into the sinkful of soapy water and began to scrub at the aging glass casserole dish which their mother used for lasagna and for the mystery mixtures of frugal, long ago childhood meals.

Grace went off to fetch towels for the baby and Caroline and Pauline were left at the kitchen sink with the pots and pans.

"They aren't running a night shift are they?" Caroline asked. "The mill's not that busy?"

"I don't think so." Pauline snapped out one of Grace's carefully folded dish towels. "Male bonding. Dad and Richard just have to get out of here sometimes when we all pile in."

Caroline handed over the lasagna pan and Pauline took it, grasping it with the tea towel.

"How many times have we washed and dried this wretched thing?"

"Lots," Caroline said, reaching for a pot from beside the sink. "Dad seem strange to you?"

"Different."

"But weird different? Or just different?"

"I kind of like him like this," said Pauline. She smiled at their reflec-tions in the window over the sink, then laughed. "He never asked us all to come for a sleep over before for no reason."

"Yippee," said Caroline. "A pajama party."

"Don't be grouchy."

"Well, what if he's losing it?" Caroline asked. She inspected the large pot in her hands then held it under the faucet, rinsing off the suds. "Then what will we do?" She handed the shining pot to Pauline.

"I don't think he's losing it," Pauline said, slowly polishing the pot with the damp towel. "I think he's just switched gears. Changed his mind. He hasn't lost it."

They finished the pots and pans and wiped up the counters. They spoke of general things. Of work - Caroline was a claims adjuster for a large commercial underwriter, a woman accustomed to telling corporations that they would have to settle for less. And love. Caroline was off men for now, having been divorced for two years from Dan and convinced that love was a curious, old-fashioned notion - in spite of her parents' devotion.

"Which brings us back to Dad," she said, pouring them each a glass of white wine. "He just accepts that Mother will be there, whatever he does."

"Well, you can't get mad about that, Caroline," said Pauline accepting the glass.

The wine which had been sitting on the counter since dinner was tepid and looked unappetizing. Caroline had poured it into kitchen glasses because Grace had only six wine glasses which they had used at dinner. They were now all in the dishwasher and Caroline was cross about that too.

"Didn't we buy her some for Christmas?" She glanced around the kitchen as though stemware might appear. "Where the hell does she stash stuff?"

Pauline carried the milk glasses of wine to the kitchen table while Caroline took down Grace's hand lotion from the little shelf. She squirted some into her palms and began to massage her hands.

"You look like Mom, doing that," Pauline smiled.

"Right," Caroline snorted.

"Scrabble?" said Dee, coming in from the hallway. She crossed to Caroline at the sink, holding out her hands for a squirt of the lotion. "Mom's helping Maddie with her jammies."

Madeline appeared in her flannel pajamas and climbed into Pauline's lap, wanting to be babied. She had seen the tender concern that James enjoyed during his bath and the subsequent drying and diapering.

"I helped wash him," she said. "And helped with his toys too."

Pauline rocked her a little and patted her hair. "You are a helper," she said gathering up the legs and arms which dangled over her lap. Madeline didn't really fit there any longer and the realization of this subdued them both.

"You two go ahead," she said. "Maddie and I will go help Mom make up the beds. I'll tuck Maddie in."

She rose unsteadily, still holding the gangling Madeline, who did not protest, and carried her down the hall to the spare room.

"You in the porch, I think," said Grace when Pauline appeared in the doorway of the little room.

She tucked pillows into smooth white slips, snapping out the linen and holding the pillows beneath her chin in a characteristic movement which Pauline and her sisters did not realize they had adopted.

"I've put Dee and the baby in the bedroom. I think Caroline in here and you and Richard on the Winnipeg couch and Maddie on the little cot. It's still nice and warm in the porch."

"Can I do anything?" Pauline shifted Madeline to her hip. Madeline's arms were wound tightly around her neck, her head tucked awkwardly against her mother's collar bone.

Grace waved her away and she carried Madeline out to the porch where the little cot had been made up, the white sheets turned back against a dark blue quilt. Grace had been in and rolled down the bamboo matchstick blinds, so that the little room was snug and faintly tropical looking in the light from the old standing lamp.

Added on by Paul and his brother Clark, when the girls were young, the porch had been intended by Grace as a summer playroom and cloakroom or mud room. Winterized over the years, with insulation batts tucked in between the rough studs, the short walls beneath the windows covered over in smooth tongue and groove cedar planks, it had become a sort of family room. Double glazed, removable windows were brought up from the basement each fall to replace the screens. As teenagers they had sprawled there together on hot summer nights or enjoyed solitary bouts of reading while the rest of the family slept.

Mutter's picnic basket sat on the old wooden kitchen table that Grace had moved to the porch years before, and where they had often sat to do homework. An old fashioned thing, the table had a single drawer at one side meant for cutlery but filled now with crayons and odd pencils and pens, spools of thread from times when Grace set up the little sewing machine there to hem something or to make curtains. Pauline and Caroline had hidden unwanted bread crusts in the drawer twenty-five years ago, when the table sat in the kitchen.

She tucked Madeline into the little cot and settled the cat, who had been following them, at her feet.

"Leave the light on," Madeline said as Pauline turned to leave. "And tell Dad to come and kiss me too."

"Ask, Dad," Pauline said automatically. "You *ask* people to do things. Not tell."

She blew Madeline a final kiss from the doorway and stepped into the hall. She could hear her sisters in the kitchen, laughing.

They had set letter tiles for her in the little tray and there was ice in her glass. The lamp over the table had been pulled down on its retractable cord, and shone brightly down on the game board. The two women at the table were cast into shadow and the kitchen was dark around them.

"Looks like a poker game," she said, pulling out the chair where they had set her place.

"I know," said Dee looking up. "And it feels like Christmas. I feel like we should have a plate of disgusting stuff on the table … fruitcake and fudge and junk."

"Mom probably has some disgusting stuff if you really want some," said Caroline as she reached a handful of tiles across the table and began to lay them out on the board.

"Denizen!" said Dee, impressed. "She's used my 'zen' to make denizen. That's very cool, Caroline."

"Clever." Pauline studied her sisters a moment as Caroline wrote down her score on the little pad near her drink and Dee's eyes swept the board, looking for a good opening.

"It is like Christmas," she said, after a moment. "That same piled in feeling. Weird."

She lifted the milk glass and sipped her wine. Australian Chardonnay, Caroline's favorite, watered down by the ice, but still oak-y tasting. She was reminded of Ellen and her disdain for this wine, which might be more pose than actual preference. A way to define herself. Everyone drinks Chardonnay these days - not me.

"Did I tell you that Ellen is seeing someone?"

"No way," Dee said. "Who?"

Caroline looked up, interested. "Hope he's got money," she said. She tucked the pencil neatly at the edge of the little notepad. "Or Ellen will eat him up."

"He has," Pauline said.

"Who's got money?" asked Grace, coming in from the living room carrying coffee cups and desert plates.

"Ellen's new beau," said Pauline.

"Well, that's good." Grace opened the dishwasher and began to rearrange things, fitting the coffee cups and the plates in, turning the dirty dinner plates so that they faced the spray arm.

They discussed Ellen and her penchant for the good life and were launched on the subject of Clive's car when Richard and Paul stamped in the door, bringing with them a dampness and chill which clung to their coats. Richard shivered at the doorway in the leather jacket and his light running shoes.

"City kid," said Paul. But it was said with affection and as he said it he reached out an arm in the puffy down jacket and pulled Richard toward him into a quick and awkward hug.

The women at the table exchanged glances as Paul turned away to hang his big jacket on a peg beside the door.

"Clive's car?" Richard asked as he bent to remove his runners. "It's a beaut. Tres expensive."

They cleared the board and began a new game which Pauline joined. Richard took a can of beer from the fridge and drew a chair toward the table, hooking it over with his sock foot. He sat astride it cowboy style and sipped at the beer, watching them while Grace and Paul took the tea pot and cups with them into the living room.

"Like Christmas," Richard said when they had been silent for a while.

⌘ ⌘ ⌘

"Do you feel like we're waiting for the other shoe to drop?" Pauline said.

They were trying to get comfortable on the Winnipeg couch, an ancient fold down sofa which Grace covered with quilts and a foam pad when she needed extra sleeping space. Richard had propped pillows against the window sill above the bed and sat awkwardly, reading one of the old Life magazines from Paul's stash in the living room.

He looked up. "Your dad?" he said, peering over his reading glasses.

"Yes. Do you feel like something is going to happen?"

"Nah. He's just had a late mid-life crisis. Or correction. Whatever you want to call it."

He removed the glasses and folded them, then tucked them into the little step table with the magazine. He began to fluff the pillows, beating at them with gentle karate chops and punching in the ends. He stopped suddenly and sniffed at the pillow cases. They smelled like summer, like sheets hung out to dry in June. Like fresh ironing laid out on the kitchen table in Kerrisdale, long ago.

For a moment he was Richard Junior, on his way somewhere on a summer day. And Daphne was still the mother, standing at the ironing board with her iron, forever, in the cool dimness of their kitchen. On a summer day. He felt a quick, fierce longing for that slim, young mother; for the tinkle of her new, silver bracelets as her bare, tanned arm moved back and forth across hot, starched cotton.

"That's what I told Caroline tonight, when we were doing the pots." She yawned.. "But I'm not so sure."

"Don't worry," he said absently. He reached up and turned out the light in the old floor lamp and the porch became black and silent. They heard Madeline snoring gently across the room.

"Spoons," Pauline said and tucked her back against him.

He put an arm over her and pulled up the old quilt folding it beneath her chin. It had grown cold in the porch and they fell asleep, shivering slightly in the damp.

⌘　⌘　⌘

"Walkies," said Caroline as she entered the kitchen.

She was dressed in the sweatshirt and sweat pants again, with a ragged turtleneck beneath the shirt and heavy, white cotton socks on with her running shoes.

"You look fetching," said Dee who was feeding the baby at the kitchen table. She had a towel over her shoulder and the long-handled infant spoon in her hand. The baby sat curved in her lap like a pink comma, his mouth open like a bird. He flapped his limbs in protest as the full spoon hovered there, above his head.

"These are serious walking togs, Deedles," Caroline said taking a cup from the dishwasher. "Have you got coffee?"

"No. I have to wait 'til his nibs here has finished his mush."

Caroline poured coffee and sat down at the end of the table. "That takes a lot of time." She pointed at the baby with her mug. "Is it fun?"

"Fun?" Dee filled the spoon again, tapping it on the rim of the little bowl so that white gluey pablum drooled back into the dish.

"Interesting question." She inserted the spoon in James' mouth and then dabbed at his face with the end of the towel. "Fun. Hmm."

"I fed a baby," said Madeline as she came slowly into the kitchen. She still wore the flannel pajamas and looked like a baby herself, her eyes round and blinking in the morning light. "Kristen has a baby and we went to the movies with him."

She poked gently at James for a moment, making him laugh, then sat down beside Dee.

The baby turned his face from the spoon and smiled up at Madeline. White cereal bubbled from the corners of his pink mouth and Madeline laughed as Dee wiped him with the towel.

"He's finished now." She began to untie the bib as the baby squirmed in her lap.

She looked up at Caroline. "Get Maddie some cereal, okay?"

This had not occurred to Caroline and she startled, acutely aware, suddenly, of how little tuned in she was to the needs of others. She got up quickly and crossed to the counter where she pulled at cupboards looking for cereal and sugar. She felt a kind of foolish ineptness. How had she not been aware of this next step? A child appeared, you fed it.

She found the yellow cereal box and poured some into a small dish. Too small. When she added milk, the cereal flowed onto the counter. With a rising sort of panic, she took a larger bowl from the dishwasher and transferred the mess to it. Finally she set it before Madeline.

"Do you want sugar?"

"Mummy doesn't put sugar on cereal." Madeline looked down at the enormous dish where brown circles floated in too much milk. She looked up at her aunt expectantly. "I need a spoon, please."

"Ah." Caroline turned back to the counter.

Madeline looked at the large table spoon she handed her and then reluctantly began to eat, holding it in an awkward fist and sipping cautiously from the too-wide bowl of the utensil.

Dee tucked the baby into his plastic seat and set him on the floor then poured herself coffee and returned to the table. She watched her sister a moment.

"You don't need to look so stricken," she said, reaching out to pat Caroline's hand.

Caroline smiled. "Why don't you put Mr. Messy in his stroller and come for a walk with me?"

"Me too," said Madeline, getting down from her chair. "I'll come too. I'll get dressed."

Pauline came into the kitchen in her flowered robe. "Me too."

She dressed quickly, pulling on faded jeans, and the creamy, purl-stitch pullover that Grace had knit for her while she rocked at Paul's bedside. She took her black nylon jacket from the peg at the back door, shrugged into it and went out to the car for Richard's commuter mug.

"Dee must have made the coffee," she said as she snapped the lid down on the mug. "It doesn't look like Grace's."

Madeline appeared wearing a skirt and was sent back for jeans.

"A hat too!" Pauline called as they went out the door.

They unfolded the stroller from Dee's van and settled the baby in, pulling blankets up around him while their breath puffed out in wispy clouds and they stamped their feet a little on the damp and uneven lawn. Across the road, the blackberry bushes rose up like gigantic, dark cabbage roses; the morning fog steaming upward from the riverbank poured over them like scalded milk, erasing their brambles, their distinctness.

Pauline stared into the mist. *Something strange, some knew thing was wanted. The bushes might be giant black roses. The fog might stay forever. They might stand here on their parents' lumpy driveway through eternity, still waiting for the school bus.*

"He'll probably go right to sleep," said Dee as she tucked the baby's hands beneath the blanket. "It's nap time."

"Not for me," said Madeline. She had changed into red corduroys and her dark green jacket. She bounced up and down with pleasure, clapping her hands.

"Grandma gave me mittens." She pulled at Pauline's jacket and held up her hands for them to admire. They were hand knit, like mittens from the Dick and Jane reader.

"See," she said, stretching her arms up and turning her striped fists, flexing her woolly hands. "She has lots in the porch."

Pauline looked down and took the soft, mittened hand in hers.

They had decided to walk around the Belt Line, a road which encircled Cedar Mills, looping into the gentle hills behind the village and reaching as far east as the first dairy farms. A three mile walk they knew very well, having biked it and walked it all the years of their childhood.

Caroline was taking a turn pushing the stroller when they crested the rise above the small dairy farm where they would begin the loop back. Pauline and Dee were swinging Madeline between them. Suddenly they all stopped.

"Good grief," Pauline said. "What is this?"

The farm was gone. In its place there were houses.

⌘ ⌘ ⌘

CHAPTER SIXTEEN

It was like turning the corner in a dream and finding your mother's face on the body of a stranger. Like finding your house was not where you'd left it. There might never have been a farm there. Verhoeven's dim and benevolent dairy cattle might never have plodded nose to tail through the meadows and down to the mottled barn - although that venerable building still stood, grey and solemn in the dim light.

The farm house, though, was gone. In its place stood two frame houses, tall and painted a summery yellow, with six over six sash windows trimmed in gleaming white. There were porches on both and around one there was a picket fence and a gate which stood incongruously ajar, opening onto nothing.

"How cute!" Caroline said and began to push the stroller forward. "Let's go look."

They saw where streets had been laid out, and back lanes. Flags of fluorescent orange survey tape fluttered from tiny pegs, driven into the damp, brown earth and here and there were piles of lumber and pointed roof trusses stacked like awkward pieces from a giant geometry set.

"Fun!" Madeline tugged at Pauline and Dee's hands, trying to hurry them forward to this mirage, down the hill to this toy village set there in the little dell below them. "Come on," she urged. "Look at the little, tiny houses."

"They're ordinary houses, Maddie," Dee said gently, as they set off again, moving down toward the graveled road. "They look tiny from here, because we're far away. That's called perspective."

The houses grew bigger as they approached and when a man in a suit stepped out the door of the fenced yellow house, Madeline stopped, stricken.

"It's a real house."

The moment of charmed, misperception had flown.

"A big house."

The rules of the world had not been momentarily suspended. Perspective.

Pauline read her daughter's small, alert face as disappointment replaced confusion. Finally, Madeline made a little awning with her mittened hand, shielding her eyes from the weak sunlight. Curiosity drew her on.

They went forward down the gentle hill and were soon walking down the newly bladed but unevenly graveled roadway which overlay the old farm driveway.

How many times had the three of them walked down this drive, or ridden their bikes, delivering newspapers to the Verhoovens, stopping to pat the damp noses of the cows, to shiver to the thrill of a lick from a tongue which felt like soft, moist concrete? But this?

The man in the suit watched their progress as they wound slowly toward him, their progress slowed by the bumping of James' poor stroller over the potholes and the randomly laid gravel on the utility road.

⌘   ⌘   ⌘

Grace was pulling grocery bags from the back seat of her car.

"We saw little houses!" Madeline cried as she raced down the driveway toward her. "They weren't really little." She danced a little, pleased to be bearing strange news, fully recovered from the moment when she stepped through the looking glass and saw a miniature world. Perspective. "They were real houses. At a farm."

"Is that so?" said Grace. She straightened and closed the door of the car, bumping it with her hip. She watched her daughters come toward her. Pauline carried the baby and Dee pushed the empty stroller. Caroline was reading something she held up close to her face.

Did they need glasses, now, Grace wondered. Had they grown so old?

Richard was in the front yard, cutting neat lengths of apple wood for Paul, who stacked it by the armload against the side of the porch. He wore one of Paul's checked woolen work shirts and an old quilted vest. There were gray leather work gloves on his hands and he gripped the wood and the saw in an easy way which Paul watched from the corner of his eye as he stooped to gather another armload of the fragrant wood.

"Different smell," he said as he stood up with the new armload. It came up to his chin and he bent his nose to it "Sort of fresh."

Richard nodded. He was enjoying not thinking, entrained in the tug of his muscles as he pushed the saw back and forth, back and forth, through the pale wood.

"You didn't tell us that Verhoeven's farm was being turned into a housing development, Mom."

Pauline and Grace moved between the counter and the fridge, unpacking groceries.

"Didn't I?"

Grace held up a large bottle of white wine. "Will this do? It's Italian." She picked up the brochure from the counter.

"FarmGate," she said looking down at the glossy, yellow folder. "That's a curious name for a subdivision. It says there's to be seventy-five houses. Imagine."

"They're cute," Pauline said. "Very traditional."

"Verhoeven's got a lot of money for the land," said Grace. "I know that. But who is going to want to live out there?"

"Commuters," said Pauline, closing the fridge. "People who work in the city or in one of the suburbs."

"What a long drive. Your dad and I used to think it was an ordeal to drive into Vancouver for business. Or to get you girls new clothes." She shook her head. "I can't imagine."

"Neo-traditional architecture," the realtor told them. "It's what they call 'new urbanism.' The idea is to lay out the streets and so on, like an old town or city neighborhood. Close together and with back lanes and garages."

There would be an old fashioned corner store, he said.

"It's a fake idea," Dee said, as they looped home, following the Belt Line down past the café and service station. "It's a suburb out in the middle of nowhere. A pretend neighborhood without a city or a town. It reminds me of that old Twilight Zone episode where the perfect little American town is actually in Russia. Or on Mars. Or something." She shivered. "I think it's creepy."

A school teacher, on maternity leave, Dee was a practical woman. Her school teacher husband reinforced her prosaic view of things and encouraged her to schedule James early so that he would be ready to move on to daycare as soon as her leave was up.

He had accompanied the school band on an out of town trip this weekend, a move he felt built credit with the principal.

Ross would agree with her. FarmGate was a foolish idea. Their suburban home in Abbotsford, across the river and further out in the Valley, would soon be mortgage free.

"How can you stand to pay rent?" Dee had asked during the Scrabble game. "The Poulos are paying off their mortgage with your money. Doesn't that drive you crazy?"

Pauline took the yellow FarmGate brochure out to the closed porch and tucked it in her duffel bag.

"Does Dad just want to beam at us?" Caroline asked Grace. "He doesn't want to talk to us about something? He's not worried or anything?"

"He just wanted to see you," said Grace. "He just likes to know how everyone is."

"Hmmph." Caroline put on her reading glasses and scanned the directions on the box in her hand. "This is different," she said. "You don't leave it on as long."

Grace sat at the kitchen table, her shoulders covered with an old, pink bath towel held at her throat with a wooden clothes peg. She pulled colored perm rods from an old plastic ice cream pail and separated them by size. They piled up on the table in neat stacks like pastel-colored chicken bones. Blue, pink, yellow.

"It's supposed to smell a lot better," she said.

"Cheaper?" said Caroline moving to stand behind her mother.

"A bit."

"Mother."

"When did you start wearing glasses?" Grace asked. She looked over her shoulder at Caroline.

Caroline picked up the comb. "They're just drugstore." She began to part Grace's hair. "Here, hold the sheet of directions while I start putting these small rods in."

⌘ ⌘ ⌘

When they had gone and the house was still and quiet, Grace combed out her hair again and snipped at the straggling bits, using her manicure scissors and the magnifying mirror Paul used for shaving. It was handsome hair, still shiny and thick, although quite silver now. She studied her face for a moment. Pauline was most like her, she decided. She took off her glasses and leaned in to the mirror.

Caroline had done a good job with the permanent, there were no frizzes, none of the old-lady poodle look that hairdressers often clapped on the heads of silver-haired women. This looked smooth and orderly, with rich waves and a nice lift away from the temples and up over the ears. She would be able to manage this.

"Stick some of those sponge rollers in, Mom," Caroline had advised. That's what she would do.

The bathroom was steamy and untidy. The wastebasket overflowed with baby wipes and wadded tissue. There was toothpaste spray on the mirror and puddled water behind the taps; a faint, greasy ring in the oval basin. Towels hung drying on the shower rod and the shower curtain was pulled unevenly back, neither open nor closed. Someone had left a pink throw-away shaver on the edge of the tub and the plastic lids and measuring cups that Madeline had played with in her bath were stacked unevenly on the back of the toilet. There was hair on the floor and the mat looked soiled and shabby.

"Tomorrow," she said to her reflection. She turned out the light and left, pulling the door shut behind her.

Paul was at the window, in his chair.

She stopped a moment near the fireplace and watched him. He had drawn the drapes and was simply sitting, his hands still and quiet in his lap, his feet on the little milk stool. The magazines were here and there about the room. The girls had looked at them during the weekend and Madeline had even taken the sewing scissors to some of them, creating a collage from old pictures and disjointed words, a work of art which Paul had admired and posted on the fridge door.

Not an old man, Grace thought. But a very different man from the one he'd been until this autumn. As though he had had a change of mind.

He became aware of her standing there, beside the fireplace, as we eventually do when we are being watched. Was it the energy of the ethereal body as some suggested, or did Grace sigh in a soft way, quite unaware that she had done so?

He turned and smiled. "I like your hair," he said. "It looks nice." And then, "I think we should sell the mill."

In September he might have said, "I'm going to sell the mill." If such a thought had crossed his mind. "We" was quite a different matter.

⌘　⌘　⌘

The realtor had waved them in, telling them to make themselves at home. He was going outside for a cigarette.

The front door was shining white enamel. Three squares of bevelled glass set at eye level ensured both illumination and privacy in the tidy front hallway. Dark, wide planks ran neatly back through the kitchen doorway and had been used on the stairs set on shining white risers in a staircase which rose up at a pleasing angle beside the front door. A pair of narrow French doors opened on to the small living room.

"Like a parlour," said Pauline as they moved into the room, their sock feet making small, formal sounds on the hardwood.

There was a fireplace with a wide, tiled hearth and a simple polished mantle, and looking on to the porch, the trio of six over six sash windows which had charmed them from the top of the little hill. Like the exterior, the walls inside shone like sunlight, a luminous soft yellow, banded by deep white baseboards and enamelled trim around the windows.

Off the kitchen Pauline found a mudroom with neat beadboard cupboards which rose to the ceiling. The little room wrapped the corner of the kitchen and was meant to hold the washing machine and the dryer in a little nook at the end of the right angle.

You could fold your laundry on a bench beneath a pair of the double hung six over sixes, looking out on your backyard. Imagine.

"Surprisingly warm out here," said Caroline, stepping out from the kitchen to where Pauline stood daydreaming.

"Ummhmm," she said absently. She opened one of the little cupboards and inhaled the aroma of fresh enamel. Had she expected Doris Sheppard's bag collection? She closed the door, listening for the small sound of the old fashioned spring-loaded locks. Snick.

"There's a bedroom upstairs like mine," cried Madeline, rushing into the kitchen. "Blue. Like mine!"

⌘   ⌘   ⌘

Though it was tucked away in her nylon duffel bag, stowed in the trunk of Richard's Audi, the yellow brochure beamed at her as they rode along in the Sunday evening traffic.

Madeline was asleep in the back seat with the cat curled up beside her and Richard was at the wheel. Although Pauline could not see the gain, they had crossed the river and taken the meandering country route which connected eventually to the freeway. Because she had grown up in Cedar Mills and it seemed a straight line to her, she always drove the old Lougheed Highway. This was a male way of travel, she thought. Driving long distances to connect with a freeway which would then necessitate circumnavigation of the city. Rather than simply following the old high-way from point A to point B.

"It's quicker, Pauline," Richard assured her as they drove East in order to go West. "Check your watch and see how long it takes. Compare it to how long it takes you usually."

"I don't really care that much," she said. "You're driving."

"That's not the point."

She relaxed when finally they swung up on to the freeway and headed toward the ocean.

"So." She stretched and yawned. "Did you have a nice time?"

"In fact I did," he said. She felt him smile in the dark. "Your old man is sure different, isn't he? I felt like I was his new best friend."

"He did seem rather fond of you this weekend. Maybe he's decided you're a nice boy after all." She laughed. "Even if you are from the city."

"I dazzled him by cutting up all that apple wood."

"Your arm will be aching tomorrow."

"That's okay." He checked his mirrors and pulled smoothly into the fast lane. "I actually feel pretty good."

Pauline thought about her father, this newly gentle man who had sat on the floor to help Madeline with glue and paper and who had listened to them talk about FarmGate without observing that Nathan Verhoeven was a phony arsehole. "It's a pretty piece of property," was all he had said. "Very pretty."

And on Saturday evening, he'd rocked the fussing James, telling Dee, "Go have your dinner. We can do this."

Caroline, she knew, would be on the phone to her tomorrow with new concerns about his sanity. Perhaps people could simply change, though. Grow tired of who they had been and simply change their minds. She thought about Arthur and his story of Joan.

When she wakened, Richard was nosing the aging Audi up against their back fence.

"Was I snoring?"

"No, but I think you were drooling." He leaned across to wipe at her lip with the back of his hand.

She had dreamt that doctors were pressing her ears against some solid thing, a sheet of aluminum or cold metal, telling her to learn to listen. Her ear felt numb where she had lain against the slippery car seat. Listen to what?

She unbuckled the seat belt and picked up her purse from the floor of the car. Her beautiful purse. It was soft and supple, still the color of toffee or burnt sugar icing, but where had the sweetness gone? The promise?

She patted the purse. *All will be well and all will be well and all manner of things shall be well. Julian of Norwich?*

Richard leaned in the back door of the car which creaked as it swung, announcing another small wound to the little Audi whose dashboard was now coffee-stained and cracked, its upholstery gray and dusty looking.

Inside the chilly house, Richard carried the sleeping Madeline up to her bed, while Pauline dragged in the bags and parcels. Grace had sent them home with a frozen banana loaf wrapped in foil and a small cardboard box of fragrant Delicious apples, sent down from the Okanagan Valley by her brother.

Pauline opened the lid of the picnic basket and the cat blinked and resettled itself, kneading delicately at the beach towel for a moment, then plopping down with a little purr that was like a thoughtful murmur.

"I need to be more like you."

She pulled dirty clothes from the nylon duffel bags and set aside Madeline's books, Richard's shaving kit. At the bottom of her bag, beneath the toiletries case, she found the yellow brochure. She tucked it in her purse and carried the purse to the foot of the stair, the place she stowed the miscellany of things that needed to go 'up.' In the kitchen again, she bundled the laundry and carried it to the basement with the duffel bags.

The washer and dryer were in a corner, pushed against the rough cement wall, beneath a small window. She smelled the familiar sour scent of unwashed clothes and of the dank, dark water which never quite drained cleanly away from the terrible open hole in the concrete floor. She tucked the dirty clothes into the plastic garbage can she used as a hamper and went quickly up the stairs. She heard the Poulos' teenagers in their basement TV room, arguing in incoherent words.

⌘　⌘　⌘

CHAPTER SEVENTEEN

"That's about all we did," Pauline said. "We ate. We walked. My sisters nattered. We played with the baby. We drank a little wine. Richard and my dad chopped up an orchard of firewood. Then we ate some more."

"But it was fun," Arthur said. "You had a good time."

They sat at the table in Pauline's kitchen, drinking late-morning coffee. She had sliced some of Grace's banana loaf and set it out on a green plate.

"Delicious," said Arthur helping himself to another slice. "Too often, people put in a lot of baking soda, I've noticed. It gives a funny taste. But your mother has the knack." He buttered the brown slice, smoothing the pale butter neatly across it, then broke off a small piece. He held it up, as though to inspect it in the light. "This is perfect."

Pauline laughed. "Who knew you were a connoisseur of the lowly banana loaf?"

"Multi-talented," said Arthur. "Speaking of which, these are wonderful paintings that your daughter does for you. This must be her blue period. Like Picasso."

He turned in the wooden chair to study Madeline's artwork above the little desk.

"She likes houses," he said. "This looks like a whole little town."

Children went through phases. Of people, of trees, of flowers and of houses. Trying to name and claim the world around them, nail it down. What a curiosity of the development of the human. As though the real were not real until it was rendered in art, until the child had used her hands and some tool - a crayon, a pencil, a stick - to decipher it. Play therapists knew this. That the child might need to render the trauma, the event, the break, the joy, there on paper, before they could utter it. Perhaps we never lost the need for this? We daydreamed on paper. We doodled, we drew daisies and whirlpools up the edge of the phone book while we chatted on the phone and we drew in the sand with a finger while staring out to sea.

"Speaking of houses," said Pauline. "We saw the most interesting place out near my parents'."

"I'd like to see that," Arthur said, when she had told him about FarmGate. "Is there a train out there?"

"Just the bus," she said. "It's not much to see yet, really. There's just the two houses. Let me get you the brochure."

She returned with the yellow folder and handed it to him. "It's interesting," she said. "But I think my Counties brochure is snazzier."

"But you liked the houses?" Arthur took the brochure she held out to him. "You liked the idea of the place?"

"Very much."

She had been daydreaming about the houses. Seeing herself there.

It was as though an individual life was a journey in a small row boat. We were launched on a mysterious lake, whose nether shores we could not see, and we were given oars and the certain knowledge that we must go forward. Like the solitary helmsman, we too sat backwards, propelling ourselves across the water, and like the helmsman, the solitary rower, we saw the present and the past slipping into our wake. We rowed from the known shore, slipping always further and further away from people and places, as they died, as children grew, or as we moved on to some new thing. And always, always, we were rowing further out as those familiar things receded in the distance and we kept moving, ever moving, out and across the mysterious lake, to that unknown shore.

She felt now that the present had been shaken loose, was fast becoming the past, even as she lived it. Yet she could not move. She was becalmed.

"Would you like to live there?"

"I'd like to live in a house like that," Pauline said. She pointed at the photo on the front flap of the folder. "Doesn't it look like the quintessential house?"

Did the heart of a domestic dimwit beat beneath her dissatisfied skin? With a pretty hearth to sweep and a sweet place to fold her laundry would she be as happy as a lark, content to shine and polish?

"It's not unlike the layout of these duplexes, really," Arthur said. He pointed to the diagram, which detailed the floor plan of the yellow houses.

There was the mudroom, the hallway, the broad kitchen with its neat little breakfast nook tucked into a bump-out where Pauline remembered a built-in booth and another trio of the six over six windows.

"Similar," she said. "I suppose it's classic."

"Any bookcases? The built-in ones?"

"Yes. In the living room and a little one on the landing. Where the staircase turns?"

"I like that." He looked at the brochure a moment longer, then folded it shut and set it on the table. "I must get on my way," he said. "I'm working today, at the gallery. Crating up some dreadful oil paintings."

He was content at the little gallery. There was work to do, there were people and events to watch and the sense of being of use. Simple things surely, and ones which had once escaped him. His new way, his new path, the one which had opened when he had begun to observe himself and decided to be happy, was steep but compelling.

Lydia Martin, for instance gave him great pleasure. The young arts director wore black cardigan sweaters and kept her auburn hair in a sort of spiked brush cut. Her hand-made earrings fell against a long, white neck which swung like an ostrich's as she struck poses and made pronouncements. Like an automatic weapon, her rapid fire speech tended to pin the unwary in place, to spray the gallery with the live ammunition of her opinions on everything from the placement of paintings to the scheduling of children's art classes.

"These are dreadful," she told Arthur, waving a long white hand at the oil paintings leaning against the wall in her crowded office at the back of the community center. She shivered delicately, "Crate them or burn them."

She hurtled around the gallery in a white heat of feeling, spending herself freely, exhilarated, Arthur thought, by the thrill of her taut emotions.

He crated pictures for her and took water color classes from her.

"Delicious!" she cried, when he brought in the picture of the bare chestnut trees rising from the mist. "This speaks!"

The class itself, brought him great pleasure, as did the time he spent in front of the easel at home. He enjoyed the very bus trip which carried him between the community center and Doris and Edward's house on fourteenth avenue.

And now Beryl was coming.

He had stumbled upon a truth when he set out walking along the small stream near his suburban house. While walking he had seen that a full and happy way of living required attention to detail, attention to silence and attention to the moment. The past was memory, the future was not knowable, there was only this foot and then that foot. But moving along and feeling the firmness or softness of the ground beneath the foot, the lullaby of the summer grass or the crunch of hardened snow as the foot moved roughly against it. There was only this instant and then the next one. Paradox was his companion. He had learned to create his life from this instant to the next, paying exquisite attention to the small spaces in between.

Pauline moved about her days, waiting to hear from Sidlum or Spilled Inc., desperate to know what to do with herself, how to make money.

Richard went to the factory, driving through cold rain and gray slush. The Japanese people were working on the deal, their lawyer would have news very soon. Dick blustered about the office or leaned over the high metal catwalk, watching the factory floor below him while the shipping clerks and foremen raised their eyebrows and regarded Richard with fear and sympathy.

Pauline and Richard decided they would not buy each other Christmas gifts. Then just before noon of the day before Christmas Eve, Willie Ottler called to say Spilled Inc. wanted to hire her for a three month contract. Could she start the day after New Years?

⌘ ⌘ ⌘

"But what about Madeline?" asked Daphne.

They were in Daphne's dark kitchen, peeling plastic wrap from cater-er's trays and laying out plates of tissue-thin salmon and rare beef; readying stuffed mushrooms for the oven.

Daphne wore a silk tent which fell to the floor, a caftan whose broad, dangling sleeves distracted her as she fussed over the trays and sheets of food. She pushed anxiously at the drooping fabric causing the bangle bracelets at her wrist to clank each time she moved forward.

"Who will look after her?" She turned a distracted face to Pauline. "If only you were in Richmond, she could be at school with Leslie. They have special after-school things."

Pauline looked up from the cutting board, where she was slicing a loaf of the dense rye bread which the English Bakery baked only at Christmas. She held the knife in mid air.

"Daphne, we can't afford a house out there," she said, her voice thin with exasperation. "And we certainly couldn't afford to put Madeline in Leslie's school, for heaven's sake." She shook her head.

"We're broke." She turned back to the bread and her hand trembled slightly as she drew the knife against the dark loaf. "And Dick is selling the factory. Richard is trying to figure out what to do next."

She drew a deep breath and set the knife on the counter. She reached for her glass of wine and took a sip.

"Karina, - Theo and Cossie's girl,- is going to pick her up from school and bring her home on the city bus," she said. "She'll stay with her until one of us gets home. Maddie's looking forward to it."

Daphne said nothing. She stood, fiddling at her silver bracelets. Her face, overheated and flushed, seemed to melt into the magenta stripes in the circus-colored caftan. She would have been nipping all day, fussing about food for her Christmas Eve gathering and worrying at Dick about mix and salted nuts and ice. Her hair had been recently done, pinned up in a painful looking series of rolls and twists which sat about her head like coiled steel wool. Her gray eyes darted beneath thin and drooping lids which had begun to resemble miniature sheets of school paper, striped in fine blue lines - aqua eye shadow melting in the heat of the kitchen

"She'll be fine." Pauline set down her glass and turned back to the cutting board. She began to lay the bread out on the platter, fanning it out next to the pink salmon.

"Who'll be fine?" asked Richard coming into the kitchen. He carried a wine glass by the stem. "Come out of the scullery, you two. Everyone thinks you've been banished."

He was a little high, flushed, like his mother and speaking quickly. He laughed. "Come on."

He held the kitchen door open and they heard the sounds of the party - Leslie and Madeline tumbling down the uncarpeted stairs to answer the doorbell, Dick laughing with the elderly neighbors, Marjorie Trimble warbling a complaint and Burl Ives singing Holly Jolly Christmas on the stereo.

"Let's party."

Pauline followed him out the door, carrying the platter of bread and salmon and Daphne turned back to the caterer's trays.

⌘ ⌘ ⌘

She went to work. She took the purse and the canvas briefcase, walked down fourteenth avenue on the second day of the year, and got on the bus. It was cold and still quite dark and the bus riders, newly risen from their beds and still dazed by the swift passage of the holidays, sat subdued and mostly silent, as the bus swung down the hill and on to the Granville Street bridge. Pauline was among them, but not certain if she was of them.

"I'm happy about this," she told herself.

She was given a little office, a space really, with a computer on a white lacquered desk and walls wrapped in some gray spongy substance which absorbed sound and made her voice stop before it reached her ears. She felt that to be contained by the upholstered walls was to be rendered in a sense, both deaf and mute. There was no echo, it was as though a traffic cop had his hand up, pushing back the air and the sound waves. There were no vibrations, good or bad. Later, when she spoke on the phone, her words seem to pile up there, at the mouthpiece and she held her breath to hear Richard's words on the end of the line.

It was silent in the cubicle and the small window above the desk did not open, although it offered a truncated view of the mountains, crisscrossed regularly by float planes which angled silently across her field of vision, then disappeared behind the black tower which rose up across the street. If she stood and looked down, there were silent cars two hundred feet below her. She was boxed in, shut up, hermetically sealed. The air she breathed had been circulating silently for years.

"Settled in?"

Willi Ottler stood in the doorway; a tall, pale man wearing a black turtleneck sweater and narrow, black jeans. A Norse or a Swede with rapid speech and quick, almost spastic movements, Willi Ottler was a commercial artist who perceived swiftly and could draw your foot without asking you to take off your shoes and socks. Spilled Inc. was his creative agency and he gathered up new clients the way a stock broker on a winning streak attracted lazy money.

In his arms he held a stack of glossy brochures and pamphlets. He crossed the room and set them on the yellow canvas folding chair in the corner of Pauline's new cubicle.

"These are the client's old stuff," he said, still standing. "Browse through them, see what you think."

His arm came up suddenly and he looked at his watch. "We're meeting in the conference room at eleven. We'll toss it around." He flipped his hand at her in a sort of wave and backed out, pulling the black, louvered door behind him.

Moving, moving. And yet silently. There was much going on in the offices of Spilled Inc., but it was going on quietly. She read through the brochures, hearing the pages turn with small, snapping sounds and when it was five to eleven she went down the carpeted hallway to the conference room.

Sandwiches were brought in at noon and coffee was poured by the receptionist. Later, she went back to her cubicle and at four thirty she turned off the computer and stacked the glossy pamphlets and brochures on the white desk. She caught the bus on Burrard Street and rode home with the brown purse on her lap, her ears filled with silence.

⌘ ⌘ ⌘

"We came home on the bus!" cried Madeline, flinging herself at Pauline's skirt. "Karina came to my school and we went on the bus. We saw the big kids!"

When Karina had gathered up her books and her things and gone next door, they sat down at the kitchen counter. Pauline felt oddly formal sitting there in her rented kitchen wearing a black wool skirt. A woman decked out in business clothes listening to her child. She looked down at her shoeless feet, her toes coyly hidden by the opaque blackness of pantyhose, and felt foreign, a visitor in her own kitchen. A stranger's hands lay there on the cool counter top, the nails trim and polished, newly returned from a day tapping the keys of a computer in a small office in a large downtown building. The hands went about the business of unpacking Madeline's backpack, sorting out the lunch kit and the new pages of printing and artwork, while Pauline watched. The hands pulled lettuce and carrots and peppers from the vegetable bin in the fridge and took them to the sink. They washed the vegetables and sliced them and grated them; they patted at pale slices of chicken breast and dipped them in bread crumbs.

When dinner was finished and cleared away, the hands wiped down the counters and folded the dishtowels over the oven door. They spun the dial on the dishwasher and turned out the small light over the sink. The hands carried the up things upstairs and they carried the dirty laundry to the dark basement. She watched them hold a tissue against her eyes in the pink bathroom and smear cold cream there to wipe off the mascara. They held Goodnight Moon and turned the pages, then pulled the white comforter up beneath Madeline's chin. They smoothed across Madeline's warm forehead and felt for the tender, invisible hair there.

"I don't think your hands are connected to your brain," her grade nine business teacher had told her. "You don't seem to get typing."

Yet here were those hands, clicking across a keyboard in a tall building downtown and carrying food from the fridge to the stove and to the table. Wiping down counters, folding laundry, brushing her daughter's hair. Holding the overhead bar on the bus going downtown. She told herself that this was fine, this is what people did. They cleaned, they went to work; they opened the front door with one hand and carried a bag of groceries with the other. When she passed Isobel in the dark one morning, she raised her hand and waved. Hands did that as well.

⌘　⌘　⌘

Arthur was using his to paint. And to hammer nails into crates for dreadful paintings.

"Creating coffins for the ugly little suckers," he told Pauline as they fell into step together on a Friday evening, in the third week of January.

She had just stepped down from the Granville Street bus as Arthur came out of the hardware store, carrying a new hammer in a plastic bag and a bottle wrapped in brown paper. He had been to the liquor store too.

"Come for a drink," he said as they neared home. He held up the wrapped bottle in invitation.

And, because it was Friday and a ballet day and Karina had taken Madeline there and Richard would pick her up, she did.

"A real drink," he said as they stepped onto the concrete porch. "Scotch. What do you think?"

"I think yes," she said.

They stepped into the dark house and Arthur's hand felt for the light switch in a familiar way. It knew its way around Doris and Edward's hallway now.

Pauline crossed into the living room while Arthur went down the hall to the kitchen to fix the drinks. He had developed the habit of laying a fire in the morning so that when he sat down in one of his chairs in the evening he had the feeling of being tended to. (Oh, look. The fire has been laid!) Following the same habit of self-care that sees some people put out a place mat and a cup and saucer before they went to bed. (Oh, look someone has set the breakfast table!) It required labor and forethought as any delight did, whether it was we ourselves who labored or not.

When they gathered themselves in the chairs in the honeyed light from the black and gold lamp, there lay before them the possibility of fire. Warmth and comfort and light.

"Shall I light it?" he asked, setting down the enameled tray and nodding back toward the fireplace. "Are you cold?"

"I'm not cold," Pauline said. "But a fire would be nice."

When the kindling had caught and there was a good heat, he laid several lengths of the apple wood across it and waited a moment, studying the ragged up and down flight of the flames. There. He had developed a relationship with this fireplace, felt friendly toward it, as though it were an aged car or a familiar door whose key had to be inserted in an intimate and secret way. Just so. He now knew just how much draft was wanted on a winter night. He sat down in the club chair and adjusted his pant legs, smoothing at the canvas-y fabric which felt hot from the fire..

"Cheers," he said, picking up the old-fashioned glass from the tray. "Tell me about working downtown."

"I'll give you the snapshot view," she said. "The image that keeps floating through my mind … Not really an image. Whatever. The picture I have, is of being the goofy white guy at a blues concert - someone who just doesn't get it. But, they keep snapping their fingers and trying to bee-bop?"

"You're the white guy?"

She took a sip of the drink and held the glass to the light. "Umm hmm. Yes."

"Anything redeeming about it?"

"Well, they're paying me well," she said. "And part of what's absurd, is that sometimes when I'm buzzing around there with the rest of them, I kind of like it. It's energizing. But twenty minutes later, I'm going, 'what does it mean?'"

He smiled.

"My sister always says I think too much. Perhaps she's right."

"What are you working on? What is it you're writing about?"

"You won't believe it," she said. "Kitchen cabinets. From Europe."

"For heaven's sake."

"It seems ridiculous. I won't go into the song and dance, but we have to create a whole whack of stuff for retailers and the print advertising and packaging," she lifted the glass. "Enough about my scintillating work. How is life?"

"Life is very good," he said. "Very good. Greg is still cross with me for not going out there for the holidays, but other than that all the t's are crossed and all the I's are dotted. Beryl and I have been acting like foreign tourists the past week, swanning around the town, having fancy lunches and marching through the galleries and so on. We went to UBC this week and toddled about."

"I can't wait until I'm retired," Pauline said. "Who has more fun than you guys?"

Arthur laughed.

"You know what? If I'd started doing these kinds of things when I was a much younger man, my life would have been very different."

"How so?"

He took a deep swallow of the drink and thought a moment.

"I would have been down in the basement of life, helping to sort the boxes, rather than upstairs, shifting the furniture about."

"No more Scotch for you," Pauline said.

Arthur smiled. He held his glass up near his chin, resting it on his chest, nearly propping his chin there on the cool roundness of the glass. He was slouched in the chair, angled out with his legs straight before him, his feet at the fire.

"What do you mean?" she asked.

"I mean we spend too much of our lives on the surface. We don't really see and do what there is to see and do. We don't ask enough questions …" He shifted in the chair and pulled himself upright. "Never mind. I'm going on."

"It's refreshing," she said. "Tell me more."

"I'm just nattering on. Pretending to be wise."

"No," she said. "No you aren't. And you are wise."

"You know what my wisdom consists of?" He shifted in the club chair, pulling himself upright and looked directly at her.

"I decided to be happy. Once I decided that, everything else followed along like a train. And I don't mean happy as in selfish, although that might be part of it. Greg probably thinks so. I mean happy in saying well yes this is me or no that isn't me. But it might be that you have to get to a certain age to do that. Maybe without age it is only selfishness. But I don't think so."

He set the glass on the little enameled tray on the walnut table and folded his hands in his lap. "And that's my wisdom."

"But it feels like we're just bundles of duties." Pauline sighed and held the glass to the light. "Once you take responsibility for a child or a relationship ... or work. Whatever. You're just doing the duties. The ones inherent in the situation."

"I haven't worked out all the wrinkles," he said and laughed. "I'm going to have another. A weak one. You?"

He rose from the chair and reached toward her glass.

"Very weak." She handed him the glass. "I don't want to be too happy. I've got dinner to make and laundry to do." She laughed "Listening to Maddie requires that you be on full alert, too."

Because she stretched out to Madeline, even, or perhaps especially when she was not with her, she was ever on alert. To think that her child was out there in a large building all day with people with whom she, Pauline, had only exchanged a very few words. To think of it closely, was to be knifed.

Little Madeline. Taught to hold her mother's hand when she crossed streets, to look for the hem of her mother's skirt in a grocery store aisle and then loosed in a bureaucratic structure in the care of strangers ... It was to be afraid. Very afraid.

So, humming just below her consciousness at all times was the thought of Madeline. She sometimes pictured them as climbers, tethered together on a cruel ascent, vertiginous and cold. The rock face they were ascending was unknowable. But they were tethered together, and she, The Mother, was up ahead, pulling gently on the rope or sometimes, below holding, pushing the fragile body of her child, upward. No one knew what lay at the top. Perhaps only mist and a cold, fierce wind. You could not tell your child more than this: Enjoy the climb, I've got you. And when you disappeared into the mist and your child was adult, left behind, she became the guide.

And maybe, like the battery-operated toy you can buy in expensive airport gift shops, the little creatures fall off at the top, glide back to the beginning and go 'round again. Who knows?

Arthur returned with the pale amber drinks. Ice clicked neatly in the glasses as he set the enamel tray on the step table.

"We should have some pretzels or something," he said. "Something to snack on. Would you like a cracker? Shall I open a tin of those airline nuts? I've got some left from Christmas."

"No," she said, taking up the drink from the tray. "No thank you. I'm fine. Sit down. You fret too much."

"Getting old, you see." He settled into the club chair and picked up his drink. "That's not actually true. This 'fretting' as you call it is another thing that came along with the decision to be happy. I didn't have a hospitable bone in my body before I started thinking about how to be happy. Didn't think about it, you know?

"But when I really began to think about what I liked, what I didn't like, well then I sort of tuned in to what others would enjoy too." He sipped at the whiskey. "So you see, it might be selfish in the beginning, but it opens you up too. You start thinking about what makes other people happy. And you kind of know, too. So you offer it out."

"Women offer it out," she said. "But I don't think it starts from an idea of what makes you happy as an individual. In fact I know it doesn't."

"Surely part of it is that, though? Realizing what gives comfort, what makes people happy?"

"Well, maybe it's simply that women don't often turn it back to themselves. Don't offer it to themselves? They know, or think they know what makes others happy. But they don't think - aren't encouraged to think, you know, 'what makes me happy?'"

"Well," Arthur said. "What makes you happy?"

"Do we have to define 'happy' first?"

"Voltaire," said Arthur. "Voltaire said something like, 'if you wish to argue with me, first you must define your terms.'"

"How *do* we define happiness?"

"Well, what gives pleasure, joy? Causes you to feel pleased or revved up. Content. You know. What engages your whole self."

"Okay." She set down the glass. "Let's see. Madeline makes me happy, gives me a charge. Certain music ..."

"I know something that makes you happy," Arthur said.

The light seemed to shiver a little. She wondered if she had had too much to drink.

"What do you know that makes me happy?" She sat up straighter in the wing chair.

"Houses," Arthur said.

A laugh burst from her and her hand flew to her mouth. Relief. A starburst of glamorous light, a hallelujah of delight. I am known.

"You're right," she said and there was pleasure in her voice. "How do you know that about me?"

"Remember when we went out to Richmond in September? When we first met? And you were driving along - wondering, I think, why you'd brought this old chap with you - when I asked you about Burkeville. And your whole attitude changed," Arthur smiled at her. "And it was like you thought, well if he likes houses, then we can be friends. Am I right?"

"Something like that. Yes."

"So. Houses make you happy. It's not just a passing, intellectual sort of interest. You like to think about them. Study them. Look at them. They engage your whole self." He drank off the rest of his watery drink and set down the glass. "I think we can increase our quota of happiness by sort of pouncing on those things and helping them grow. That's my theory, anyway. And that's what I now try to do in my life."

"See? I told you you were wise," she said. She looked at her watch. "Richard and Maddie will be home in a minute. Maybe already. I've got to get going."

In the hall, when she had gathered up her purse and the battered canvas briefcase, while Arthur was bouncing on his walking shoes and jingling the change in his pockets, she leaned forward and kissed his cheek.

"Thank you," she said and went out the door.

To be known. To be known. Not for the things we accomplished, for what we had gathered to us or for the light which shone upon us, but for the small things which delighted the soul; the ineffable, unspoken, often unacknowledged whispers of that which spoke only to us. Someone else had heard the sighing, too. And that was why sometimes a gift was only a gift, while "I thought of you when ...." could be something we gathered to the heart and carried with us forever. I am known.

"When you were little..." we told the child, "you always ..." and "you were such a good ..." and the child heard it with her heart. This sang a song, not for the ego, but for the soul. The child who heard it enough, told softly and with love, went into the world, able. I am known. The child who seldom heard it, hardened her heart and worried, always, 'Who knows me?" "Look at me," she cried. And it was never enough.

Arthur, rare individual, in a period of grace after the death of his wife, had come to know himself. And to know that he was known.

"It is spiritual," he had told Beryl. "But, it's not "The God" of my childhood. A bigger God. It sounds foolish, and I wouldn't say it to most people, but I feel blessed. I've been given something. Blessed is about the only word I can think of. Grace freely given."

Pauline went home, across the wet grass, holding her coat close around her and with the purse and the little canvas case clutched to her, but something else too. A secret.

Arthur carried the little tray to the kitchen. He rinsed the glasses and set them upside down in the draining rack, then changed his mind and reached for the dish towel which hung neatly on the oven door.

"Don't fuss," he said out loud. He dried and polished the short crystal glasses and set them on the gray counter. "There," he said. He wiped up the counters where ice had melted and pooled. He turned the lid on the bottle of Scotch and carried it through to the dining room where he had set up a small bar at the end of Doris' mahogany sideboard. "There," he said again. And then, "Music. That's what I need."

When he had the volume set on the little stereo and there was Mozart in all the corners of Doris and Edward's house, he went upstairs.

The house seemed big this evening. There was music everywhere, but he himself was too small to fill up the space. He crossed the bedroom in the dark and sat in the small upholstered chair near the window.

"God is with me, God is helping me, God is guiding me," he said. He pulled back the curtain and watched the street a moment, then closed his eyes and inhaled deeply, feeling the air far down in his chest, in his gut. On Burrard Street, homeward traffic beat a Friday night retreat to the suburbs. Arthur listened until he no longer heard it.

Twenty minutes passed. He opened his eyes and crossed the room to the little night table beside his bed. Joan's tropical picture sat there beneath the lamp. He saw it in the morning when he woke up and he saw it at night when he set down his book and leaned to turn out the light. He had learned the nuances of the picture now. When you tilted it one way, the sun shone on an azure, tropical ocean, and when the picture lay flat you saw a full moon reflecting on a dark sea, silhouetting the black palm and a far away island or promontory. It was a lesson in perspective. Not such a cheap thing after all.

He turned on the lamp.

⌘ ⌘ ⌘

CHAPTER EIGHTEEN

Madeline, still in her black dance leotard and pale pink tights, leapt against Pauline when she came in the door. "We got pizza!" She sailed down the hall turning awkward little pirouettes,

"Come and have some, Mom," she called. "Come on. We waited. There's mushrooms on one for you."

Richard sat at the table, the newspaper spread before him and a glass of red wine at his elbow. Madeline's back pack and her school papers lay on the counter with the pizza boxes. A milk carton stood open and there was a smudged-looking glass in front of Madeline's stool which was pushed back into the room. Pauline could see where milk had been spilt on the counter. A roll of paper towel lay unraveled nearby.

On the floor, near her little desk, lay Madeline's hooded coat. Pauline shivered as she bent to pick it up. It was cold in the house and she could smell the cat's litter box.

Richard looked up. He had not drawn the curtains and she could see the disarray of the room, multiplied there, behind him.

"Hi Paul. How's the working girl?"

"Hi," she said. "I'm fine. How are you. How was your day?"

Still holding the coat, she picked up the back pack and the papers and took them to Madeline's desk then carried the roll of paper towel to the spindle by the sink. She went down the hallway to hang the little green duffel coat on the ceramic goose head hook that Arthur had given Madeline for Christmas. Richard had fastened it just inside the hall closet at the right height for Madeline, but she had not yet developed the habit of hanging things on it.

In the kitchen, she put the pizza cartons in the oven and set the dial to warm then wiped down the counters and took three plates from the cupboard. She crossed to the table and leaned toward the curtains.

"I'll get it," said Richard. He folded the paper and stood. "I'll get it."

"I'm cold," said Madeline coming into the room carrying the cat. Pale cat fur clung to the black leotard and she shuffled awkwardly in the enormous woolly slippers.

"I don't think the furnace is working," Richard said as he turned back from the curtains. "We've been home for fifteen minutes and it still hasn't kicked in." He went toward the basement doorway. "I'll go down and check."

Pauline pulled vegetables from the fridge and began to peel carrots and to slice celery and peppers. Madeline climbed up on her stool to watch.

"What about dip? I like that sour kind you make."

"The pilot light's on," said Richard, coming up the stairs. "The fan is busted or something. We'll have to call that guy Theo uses."

Pauline put the plates and the vegetables on a tray and carried it into the living room. She turned on the gas fireplace and watched the flames for a moment while Madeline spread out her quilt on the wood floor.

"A picnic," she said, settling before the fire with the cat. "I can write it in my journal when I go back to school. That we had a picnic for supper. A picture too."

Richard came into the room carrying two glasses of wine. He held one toward Pauline. "Can't come until morning," he said as he folded himself onto the floor beside Madeline. "You'll have to sleep with

Mommy and Daddy." He hugged her to him and jiggled her small body in an exaggerated shiver. "Keep us warm. The house is going to get really cold in the night."

When they had finished eating Richard took Madeline upstairs. Pauline moved about in the chilly kitchen, scraping the yogurt dip into a plastic bowl and snapping down the lid; wrapping left-overs and flattening pizza cartons for the recycling box. Above her she heard Richard and Madeline laughing in the bathroom - she would be brushing her father's teeth, a great source of hilarity since she was very small.

She wondered, as she once again wiped the counters and put away food, if she had become so small minded that domestic disorder could cause her to panic. Fear seemed a foolish reaction to a cold house, spilled milk, a coat on the floor. Perhaps fear was the wrong word. On the other hand maybe she was only a baby-step away from one of those obsessive-compulsive disorders which caused you to wash your hands a hundred times and to drive home to check on the iron. She saw very clearly, the small leap one made across the fissure which separated a satisfaction with order and tidiness from panic.

We awaken to chaos and spend out lives trying to impose order. Who said that? Step on a crack, break your mother's back.

She turned out the kitchen light and went back to the living room as Richard came down the stairs.

"It is bloody cold up there." He went to the fireplace and stood rubbing his hands a moment, watching the fire. "Dick signed the contract today."

He was silhouetted there, his back to her in the dark room.

"Oh, Richard." She had been about to curl into the gold chair, but stood up quickly and went to the fireplace. "Why didn't you say?"

She placed a hand on his back, and immediately the movement felt foolish and awkward, as though they were buddies. She leaned into him, trying to pull him toward her.

"Don't, Paul." His hands were in his pockets and he did not look up from the flames.

She dropped her hand. "Shall I get us another glass of wine?"

"Why not?"

He was sitting on Madeline's old quilt when she returned. He looked up from the fire and patted the blanket beside him. "Sorry," he said. "Sympathy was going to make me feel worse."

She handed him the glass and sat down beside him on the faded baby blanket.

"Well."

"Cheers," he said and tapped her glass with his.

Like actors waiting for a cue, they sat in the unaccustomed silence of the furnace-less house, stranded on the little quilt, watching the false, measured flames of the gas fireplace.

A part of their lives had drawn very quickly to a close. This seemed the denouement of a makeshift chapter. It had been propped up by a false belief in Dick's benevolence or his good will; a benevolence which Richard had known did not truly exist, but which his boyish heart had yearned toward, had tried to wish into being, even as he had hated the shackles which had been fashioned for him by the shiny metal of the factory. He didn't have to worry about that anymore. Although Dick was willing to sell Richard's services, too, along with the business.

"You know how I feel?" He sipped at the wine. "I feel like a fool. And worse. I feel like a childish fool."

"You did what you had to do, Richard."

"No, I didn't. What I did was sleepwalk into a trap." He held the glass up to the firelight, turning it by the stem. "I know what my father is like. You know what he's like too. A greedy man. A bit thick. He doesn't think very well. Never could, really."

He held the glass to his mouth and took a large mouthful, swallowing slowly.

"I feel like I've been sleeping and I'm just waking up," he said. "Just waking up."

He looked over at her.

"You're afraid to say anything." He smiled. "It's okay, Paul. You can say 'Oh, Richard,' again."

He put out his arm and drew her to him. She leaned into him and kissed his cheek softly.

"I'm sorry," she said.

He set his glass on the hearth and took hers from her hand, then pulled her easily down beside him on the old quilt.

"Please don't feel sorry, for me," he said and kissed her. "Don't do that."

Their hands found the old places, the small of the back, the hollow of the neck. She drew her hand across the familiar roughness of his face, felt again the surprising softness of his neck, then down, pulling up the green sweatshirt.

I'm sorry, I'm sorry. I'm sorry for us.

After, they lay wrapped in the little blanket, naked, both cold and warm at once.

"That's a guilty pleasure," he said, smiling down at her. "The old sympathy screw?"

"Strange isn't it?" she said. "Now what?"

Now what indeed. She lay back and imagined a life going forward, filled with odd moments like this. Lying with her husband on a faded carpet in the cold living room before a fake fire which gave off neither real heat nor light but only an irritating noise.

She sat up suddenly. "I'm going to bed."

Richard stretched and patted the old crib quilt, as though to smooth a spot for her. Trying to gentle her back to where they'd been. "Lay down for a minute."

She bent and gathered up her skirt and sweater, then felt about blindly for her underwear. He looked foolish in the meager light, a large, naked man on a tattered baby blanket.

Repelled suddenly, she turned away from the startled, newly-wakened look in his eyes and a shiver traveled down her spine. It moved in instant tiny waves, leaving a pinpointed knot of muscle between her shoulders.

She had a momentary image of herself clutching the scattered clothing to her bosom and pointing to the door with a wavering finger, like the recently ravished heroine in a B movie.

There was some light thing she ought to say or do now to move them back to familiar territory. She pulled the bulky sweater over her head and stood. Richard had pulled the blanket over his shoulder, rolling himself into the worn, pastel fabric.

I'll have to wash it now. And what in God's name possessed us to do that on Madeline's baby blanket? It's obscene.

She gathered the rest of her clothes and went up the dark stairs feeling the heavy sweater scratch against her bra-less breasts as she moved. Cool air rushed against her bare legs. Behind her, the gas fire danced small ovals of light against the doorway of the darkened hall.

⌘　⌘　⌘

Arthur cleared away the last of his dinner dishes, moving between the wooden table and the old sink. He folded his place mat in thirds and wedged it neatly into the drawer along side the napkin which he had rolled smoothly and fitted into an enameled napkin ring whose clay-ish color reminded him of wet stones.

When he had settled the dishes beneath the suds in the deep sink, he wiped his hands on the dish towel and took his tweed jacket from the back of the wooden chair. A cigarette was in order.

He went out through the mudroom onto the back step, pulling the door shut behind him. He breathed in the cool air, then struck the kitchen match and lit up. Paradox, he smiled to himself, inhaling deeply.

When the cigarette was finished, he stepped into the dark yard and walked down the concrete path to Edward's garage. Working in the dark, he quickly filled the metal bucket with narrow sticks of firewood. He enjoyed the connection to the task at hand that was to be had by working without light, guided by touch only. This way the wood itself came as a kind of surprise when he was back in the house, kneeling before the fireplace.

There were too many bright lights in the world, he thought later as he settled into the wing chair and reached for the tassel of the gold lamp. Too much brightness.

⌘ ⌘ ⌘

Pauline stood in the hot shower until her skin reddened and the water began to cool, then gathered her clothes and stepped into the startling coolness of the dark hallway. Wrapped in a pink bath towel, she went quickly down the hall to the darkened bedroom. Madeline lay quietly in the large bed, a small mound in the duvet.

She pulled the old flannel nightie over her head and yanked it down, feeling the thin cotton catch and tug against her damp skin. This, she should get rid of. It was disgusting to continue to wash and fold something which no longer gave any sort of pleasure, barely gave warmth. She settled into the cool sheets, lifting the duvet to let some of the warmth generated by the sleeping Madeline move over her. She shivered and tucked herself in, pinning the duvet against her with her elbow and her foot..

She heard Richard moving about below her. She listened, wanting to feel sympathy and guilt for deserting him but feeling instead a confused fury which seemed to spill across her mind in images; wordless and filled with ice. She pulled the duvet up to her chin and listened in the dark to Madeline's calm and measured breathing. Stiff and wordlessly angry, she fell asleep.

She woke to pale gray light and looked over at the clock. Madeline would sleep for another hour and Richard would doze, drifting in and out of sleep as the room grew lighter. She lifted the duvet carefully and sat up.

She stood, flinching a little as her sleep-warmed feet touched the cool carpet, then poked one foot beneath the skirt of the bed, fishing for her slippers. She stooped and pulled them on, feeling her feet settle into the small grooves her toes had made and the indent where her heel had flattened the synthetic fluff. In spite of this familiarity the fuzzy slippers felt cold and foreign on her feet, like hand-me-downs or soiled cast-offs plucked gingerly from a bin in the goodwill store. She shuffled across the room for her robe and pulled it on, belting it tightly around her and turning up the collar.

The house was very still, as though the night's chill had cemented things in place. Crossing the room for her robe was like tip-toeing through an abandoned house. She pushed her hands deep into the pockets of the fuzzy robe as she went down the stairs.

Why did cold do this? Did we need warmth to animate things. Was that why we felt more alive in summer, why the tropics seemed to hold the promise of fuller lives than the ones we led?

She made coffee in the icy kitchen and carried her mug into the living room, her hand, cold and stiff, thrilling, nearly hurting from the sharp sting of heat through the china.

Richard had tidied up before going up to bed and the shadowy room looked orderly and serene. The wineglasses and the little blanket were gone and he had pulled the gold chair back to its place near the hearth. She set her cup on the wood mantel and bent to the gas fire, turning the flame to maximum then went back to the kitchen to make toast.

She had turned on the oven and left the door ajar, warming the chilled air. But cool breezes stirred against her hands as she reached for butter and jam or pulled out the drawer for a knife. The white countertops felt like marble. She held her hands over the toaster and waited.

When she had eaten her toast, and finished a second cup of coffee she filled Richard's black ceramic mug and carried it upstairs. Tucked under her arm she held the business section of the morning paper, still damp from the porch and pulpy-smelling.

He lay on his side, watching Madeline sleep.

Seeing her, he pulled himself upright and tucked a pillow against the headboard, then reached for the cup and the paper she held out.

"Thanks," he said accepting this mute apology with a small smile.

"You're welcome."

She crossed to the closet and stepped inside, pulling the cord for the overhead light and drawing the louvered door shut behind her. It was warmer there among the clothes as though Richard's tweed jackets and heavy sweaters generated heat.

She looked up, scanning the shelf above her for the gray sweatshirt and the soft leggings she liked to wear on weekend mornings. She tugged absently at the nightie, drawing her arms from the sleeves and ducking her head to peel the thin shift up and over. Still looking up, she wound the worn flannel into a ball and turned to tuck it in the wicker laundry hamper behind her. She lifted the lid then stopped and looked down. She unwound the cotton, so that it lay limp between her hands. Worn nearly to its fibres, its nap mostly washed away, it was not much more than a rag. She studied the thin fabric a moment, seeing the miniature rectangles of the weave; the warp and the woof of the threads clearly visible, as though she were looking through a magnifying glass. She drew her hands slowly over it.

When she felt the thin ridge where the seam ran, she grasped the fabric on either side and pulled. The flannel tore cleanly along the seam, sending up tiny particles of dust and cotton molecules. It ripped with a satisfying noise; the sound brisk and business-like and final, like breaking glass. The tear stopped where the seam met the intersecting seam of the sleeve, where the stitching was firmer, the seams doubled. She gripped it again, taking hold of another handful of the thin stuff and pulled hard, tearing away the whole sleeve. She flung it on the floor and in a swift, furious movement tore across the fabric so that she held the top and the bottom like separate limp flags in her hands.

Her breath rattled in her ears, amplified to a curious hollowness in the muffled womb of the closet. Richard turned a page of the newspaper and she heard it as a sharp snapping sound, clear but far, far away.

Clutching the fabric, her fists clenched against her breasts, she pulled again and again until she held only a damp length of it - a cuff or piece of collar - which would not tear, and there was a small drift of faded blue and white stripes at her feet.

She bent down, naked, crouched, nearly weeping and scrabbled at the floor, gathering up the ragged bits; raking at the threads with her fingers and using the side of her hand to sweep at the particles of cotton dust which powdered the dark carpet.

They kept a small plastic wastebasket in the closet; a place to toss the pins and tags and the static-y film from dry cleaning; the wrappers and thin rectangles of cardboard from pantyhose packages. She dropped the handfuls of flannel into it and stood up.

She found the soft leggings and pulled them on, then drew the sweatshirt over her head and pushed up the sleeves. Reaching up, she tugged at the light cord, then pushed at the louvered door, her moist hand slipping against the lever. She stepped into the bedroom, drawing deep breaths of cool air and blinking in the brightness.

Madeline slept on and Richard's coffee mug - still full, she saw - sent up a fine thread of steam. She rubbed her face. Surely she'd been gone a long time?

She crossed to the bureau and took up her brush. Tugging furiously at her hair, she yanked it back into a low pony tail. In the mirror her eyes looked pink; the lids puffy and swollen. Stunned. She twisted an elastic around the handful of hair and turned.

"What time does the furnace guy come?"

Richard looked up from the paper, squinting over his reading glasses to peer across at the clock.

"Should be any minute." He shook out the newspaper and smoothed it into a neat rectangle then bent to it again, studiously browsing the business pages for quotes on stocks they no longer owned.

She moved to the window and pulled back the curtains. The chestnut trees stood black and bare on the flattened winter grass of the boulevard, their knobby exposed roots fingering darkly toward the wet sidewalk.

A man wearing a dark woolen cap pulled low over his forehead swung a metal box from the back of a van parked near Arthur's walkway, then pushed at the van's sliding door with a booted foot. She watched him move carefully across the slippery roots, balancing himself against the weight of the shiny metal tool kit which pulled awkwardly against his left side. It was a childish movement - a personal challenge. He might have just walked up the little concrete path from the curb to the sidewalk.

"He's here."

"Throw me my sweats," Richard said. He dropped the paper to the floor and swung his legs from beneath the quilt. "I'll come right down."

"Me too," said Madeline coming instantly awake. She sat up and watched Richard tug at the sweatpants, folding the boxers he slept in into a sort of skirt and tucking them into the baggy jersey pants that Pauline handed him. His stomach sagged over the waistband and he patted it in an affectionate way as he reached for the green sweatshirt.

"Daddy's fat," she said.

"Hey!" he said. "You'll hurt my feelings."

⌘　⌘　⌘

Madeline emerged from the basement wearing the striped mittens and her hooded duffel coat. Beneath the coat, she wore red jersey sleepers. Her "baby pajamas." The enormous, fluffy slippers on her feet had slowed her progress up the basement stairs.

"It's fixed," she announced, a little breathless from the awkward climb. "The furnace man showed us the broken thing. A fan to blow the heat.

"Listen," she said, moving toward her desk. She pushed back the hood of her coat and tilted her head, straining to hear news from the heat vent beneath the little red table.

They heard the familiar rumble of the furnace and then the whoosh as air exhaled hotly through the pipes and vents. The house stopped holding its breath. Madeline took off her mittens and dropped them on the desk.

"See?" she said. "Fixed. You can turn off the stove now."

Pauline shut her book and stood. She had drawn a chair over to sit before the open oven, her stocking feet propped on the door. She closed it and turned off the stove then carried the chair back to the table.

"Hang it up Maddie," she said as Madeline dropped the hooded coat to the floor and pulled out her little chair. "Come on, hon. Go hang it on your goose hook."

The phone rang as Richard and the repair man arrived at the top of the stairs. The woolen cap was still snugged down low on the guy's forehead, making him look furtive, Pauline thought, like one of the perennial dimwit thieves in the Scrooge McDuck comic books.

Richard filled the doorway behind him, studying the bill or a warranty, the white square of paper held up near his nose. He looked messy and forlorn, squinting at the paper, his hair sprouting up, uncombed, his jaw whisker-pebbled and grayish.

Madeline bent to pick up the coat, her face pursed in a little scowl, but looking cute and comic too in the red sleepers which made Pauline think of logger's underwear -an old-fashioned union suit, complete with trap door at the rear.

These images stayed with her and she remembered them years afterward, when she recalled the moment she picked up the phone and learned that her father was dead.

"Pauline?" said Grace. *"Daddy died this morning, honey."*

⌘ ⌘ ⌘

CHAPTER NINETEEN

Had he died while she was flailing about in the closet shredding her nightie? Was he shedding his mortal coil, while she was shucking that unloved garment?

"He was getting up from the chair," Grace said. "He just fell back, I guess. I heard something, you know, and I thought, 'Well, he's tripped ...' But I listened for a minute - I was at the sink. Then I went over to the doorway. The little demi-lune was tipped over and he was kind of sideways in the chair."

She waved her hand toward the living room, indicating the empty chair, the bare semi-circle of the table where Paul had piled the old magazines.

Pauline and her sisters listened closely as their mother told the story once more, hearing it weave itself into history - becoming 'the morning that dad died.' They were subdued, like the small girls they once were, listening to their mother tell a piece of the family story. This is how it was.

Grace was at the kitchen table, near the window, where she had been much of the time for three days; since Saturday morning when she and Dolly Knecht from next door, had sat there holding hands, waiting for the ambulance.

"What a feeling that is," Grace said, rising from the table. "Waiting for the ambulance."

Faith, Grace's sister, shook her head sadly and put one hand to her throat in a protective way. She twisted the pearls at the neck of her dress and watched Grace. She too, had heard the story before.

Grace stood and crossed the room to the sink and took the hand lotion down from the little shelf. She poured some into her cupped palm and rubbed at it absently. Staring out the dark window she began the small familiar ritual, washing the lotion into her hands, stroking it gently across the fragile bones and corded veins of the backs and then scrubbing it along the palms and up the fingers, ending in a sort of fretful wringing motion, a final pat at the wrists. Pauline and her sisters watched her set the plunger bottle back on the shelf then rub the back of her left hand against her black skirt. Polishing her rings.

"I'm going to sleep," she said.

Faith rose from the table, tugging at her plum-colored dress, smoothing it down over her hips with soothing little pats. She replaced the kitchen chair, pushing it gently beneath the wooden table and silently followed her sister down the hall.

They cleaned the kitchen quietly, tearing lengths of plastic wrap and waxed paper to cover the squares and tarts and the cakes which still crowded Grace's normally clear countertops. They spoke in near-whispers, making a hushed business of whose tea towel had covered what dish and had to be returned and which neighbor had brought the patterned cake plate. They took down their mother's Tupperware for the noodle salads and the chicken casseroles and set them in the fridge and when that was full, took the containers out to the freezer which Grace kept in Paul's tool room at the end of the carport. Creating order out of chaos.

"What a ridiculous pile of food," they told each other, clucking.

⌘　⌘　⌘

"What will your mother do now?" Arthur fitted the lid into the fat, brown teapot and set it on the enameled tray. He had fanned slices of fruit bread across Doris' cake plate and set out a pair of her china cups and saucers, which he added to the tray.

Pauline followed him to the living room and slouched into the wing chair, drawing the footstool toward her, using her foot to hook it across the carpet. Arthur settled the tray on the step table, shifting aside folded newspapers and a pair of spiral notebooks. He picked up the little case which held his reading glasses and tucked it in the pocket of his woolen vest.

She lifted a slice from the plate and studied it as he folded himself into the club chair. "Chelsea Bread from the English Bakery?"

Arthur nodded and lifted the heavy pot.

"I love this stuff," she said. "I don't know why I don't buy it any more." She chewed a moment, tasting the little jells of fruit, smooth and mysterious - like jube-jubes in your bread - and feeling the miniature crunch of currants. "Richard and Madeline don't like it, I guess."

Arthur handed her the cup and saucer and then lifted his own. They sipped in silence.

"She's doing okay. We're convinced she was expecting this. In spite of the fact that the doctors said he was fine."

She set the cup and saucer on the little table and picked up another square of bread. "Who knows?"

They had been over this. Arthur had come to the funeral, riding out on the express bus and surprising her at the funeral home.

"I wanted to come," he had explained as they walked on the sea wall the week after the funeral. They had stopped to watch rain-booted toddlers puttering below them where the ocean poured ragged lines of dull gray foam onto the gravel beach. "I liked your dad.

"Remember at Christmas, how he told me about hand-splitting those roofing shakes with your mother? How they used to do that?"

They had continued their aimless walk, ambling slowly through Stanley Park in the sulky, late-winter rain. A hooky day, Pauline said, although Willi Ottler had told her take as much bereavement time as she wished. This underscored for Pauline the fact that she was on contract. An employee would have been on the meter, she knew.

Today, two weeks later, she had come home early and found a message from Arthur waiting on the machine.

"It's Arthur. Just checking in. I hope you're all well. Give me a call when you can. And please Pauline, let me know if there is anything I can do. Cheers."

"I'm just putting on the kettle," he said when she called. "Come over and join me."

"I hate February," she said, setting the tea cup on the tray. "It's an absurd month. It's not winter, it's not spring. It's even difficult to say and it has an extraneous letter that most people don't bother with."

"They'll be counting the crocuses in Victoria soon, I suppose," Arthur said. "So they can brag to the rest of the country."

"Umm hmm."

"I'm going to take the ferry over and check it out next week," he said. "Just for fun."

Pauline said nothing.

"So, your mother will stay in the house?"

"I'd say so," Pauline said. "She seems quite placid. Sort of going about her business."

"And the mill?" Arthur said. "Who will operate it?"

"Connie - his secretary, office-manager is running it for now. She and Mom actually. But they had been in the process of selling it, as it turns out."

"What will happen then?"

"Who knows? My Aunt Faith would like mother to go dancing on cruise ships with her. Maybe she will."

"Pauline," Arthur said. He smiled. "February may be hateful, but there's good news. It's also short. It will be over very soon."

She began to cry. Water-borne salt crystals stung the tender, wounded surface of her eyeballs. Moisture that did not soothe. Tears wept, of their own accord, from her eyes, and their falling caused an exquisite pain which radiated out from two points which she pictured as a pair of dull copper pennies - or electrodes - at the back of her skull. She was caught in a sort of feedback loop which encircled her head and would not be quelled or quieted. This orbiting sorrow had a life of its own, it seemed, quite separate from her

"I'm very tired of this," she said, leaning to her purse for a Kleenex. "It's exhausting."

She blotted her eyes with the tissue and wiped at the tip of her nose, then stared a moment at the wadded paper. "You have to make sure you're well-stocked with these things." She stretched her arms above her head and breathed deeply, pulling air down into her chest and blowing it out with a sigh.

"You can't leave the house without making sure you've got one of those little purse packs or grabbing a handful from the bathroom. I find balls of soggy Kleenex in all my pockets."

She was perplexed at her reaction to Paul's death. She had been surprised at the anger that insinuated itself into her grief. And was she grieving him or her? Or was she grieving the irrevocable closing of some door to her childhood? "Wait! Wait Dad!" had been on the tip of her swollen tongue these past weeks. *Wait 'til I ask you where you're going, what changed your mind.*

For that was how she saw her father's death. A decision. She sometimes pictured him yawning in the chair by the window and then rising - about to tell Grace that he's off. Then - falling back. Finished.

Wait.

She was angry, too, at herself because the grief felt like self-pity. This death of a parent had drawn her back to the childish self who sees everything in terms of self. How does this affect me? This sickened her. When this thought struck her, she vowed to grow up, to buck up, to get over it.

She was pissed off at death.

She was pissed off too, at the part of the human brain which poked and poked at this pain, the way the tongue will just keep rubbing against a molar, irritating a canker sore, hurting itself. And yet, surely we were not meant to just forget? Get on with things?

She and Margaret Gage had discussed this after the funeral.

Margaret - she of the perfect purse - had attended wearing a dark tweed suit and little black patent flats and dancers' black tights.

"We're not meant to get hold of this with our rational brain," said Margaret, old, nearly elderly now, but still very upright and keen, still in touch with life and death. "In spite of what the books say. You have to go down into it. I prefer swimming underwater as a metaphor, myself. I don't like to think of it as wallowing. But it's deep. Dark too."

Margaret lived by herself, in an apartment whose walls were covered in Degas ballerina prints and framed family photos. She still carried a good purse (black now, and shiny - not patent, but the deep color of expensive English licorice), never missed a dance recital, served on the library board and attended the Canadian Club on Wednesday evenings once a month. Still creating a life, still layering it into meaning.

"Your dad was so different the last time I saw him," she told Pauline. "He actually patted my arm and stood with me on the street corner. I hadn't seen him in such a long time."

"Everyone says that," Pauline said. "How different he was."

"Lighted up," said Margaret. "He was lit." She laughed. "That used to be an expression we used, you know. When someone was drunk. All lit up. Or 'he was really lit.'"

Pauline had driven away from Margaret's apartment with the feeling that she had been given something.

"You know what else is strange?" She turned to Arthur. "We humans actually plan to be sad. Or we prepare for it. I haven't worn mascara in nearly a month and I carry these bloody tissues around. When I go into a room, I actually look for the Kleenex box and when I lay down on the sofa I put a paper bag beside me to toss snotty tissues in."

She picked up her cup and tasted the cooling tea. It had grown bitter; sharp and astringent on her tongue. "I'm sick of it."

"What did your dad want you to do with your life?" Arthur said suddenly. "Was there some 'thing' he wanted for you? Try thinking about it, Pauline."

He rose from the club chair and picked up the tea pot.

"I'm going to get us some more hot water."

"Tea and sympathy from Doctor Arthur?"

He laughed and stopped at the dining room doorway. "Lots of it," he said, then turned serious. "But that's not all. I really believe there are messages for us in the events of our lives. It's up to us what we do with them. I think you know that too, but you fight it."

He went through to the kitchen.

She knew she was ricocheting between the linear rationalizing of her sorrow - her life in general - and the sentimentalizing and trivializing of it.

⌘   ⌘   ⌘

CHAPTER TWENTY

March marched in. February, as Arthur had said it would be, was short. Not sweet, but short nevertheless.

Grace would go on the first Alaska sailing in May. She and Faith had the tickets in hand.

Her contract with Willi Ottler would soon end.

The trustee had appointed a manager for the mill. Connie was teaching him about cedar.

The Japanese buyers of the electroplating plant (people who knew a thing or two about cedar and in fact revered it) had moved in their manager. Richard was teaching him about nothing, except perhaps, despair.

"First of April, I'm out of there," he said casually. "Time to move on to something else."

"You should be happy, Richard," said Ellen. Her tone was firm. "You've always hated it out there. Take the money and say thank you very much. Adios."

She swiveled neatly into the wrought iron chair and set a large platter precisely in the center of her glass and iron table. She rubbed her hands and sighed. "Elegant Edibles. Isn't it beautiful?"

It was beautiful. The catering company's most expensive seafood curry sat before them on a deep white oval platter. Four enormous pink prawns lay in the center, artfully curled together like miniature quadruplets asleep on a bed of fragrant gold. The platter was surrounded by tiny terra cotta plant pots filled with chopped fruits and nuts and chutneys. There was basamatti rice in a lidded copper bowl.

Ellen wore a sleeveless shift the flagrant red of a newly polished fire engine. A deceptively simple dress confected from weightless, finely woven tropical wool, it hung perfectly because it was cut to flatter and held up by an exquisitely engineered lining. It was a dress which melted over the wearer, embracing her. In the dressing room yesterday, even before she had wiggled her arms back to pull up the cunningly hidden zipper, the dress had whispered its satin secret - "You look fabulous."

The dress had not been lying. She did look fabulous. Buffed, cosseted, moneyed, capable, at the top of her game. She lifted the copper lid and began to scoop rice onto their plates using a small paddle made of polished teak. She passed the heated plates down the table, smiling pleasantly at each of them as she offered the dish. They helped themselves to the curry and passed the condiments in their little pots.

Then, smiling the coy smile of the kid who gets the highest mark on every test, Ellen announced:

"Clive and I are getting married."

"Congratulations!" Richard rose quickly, setting aside his napkin. "Well!"

He leaned across the table to shake Clive's hand then pushed back the chair and bent sideways to kiss Ellen's rosy cheek and pat her manicured hand.

Pauline went to her side, knowing Ellen expected it, and hugged her and kissed her cheek. "You!" she said.

Ellen shrugged prettily, lifting her bare shoulders into this embrace and smiled widely, presenting her small, white teeth in a precise and practiced way. A photographer had once told her to clamp her teeth together (having first licked them with a wet tongue) and then pull back her lips, a trick she had never forgotten

Pauline stepped to the side of the table and bent toward Clive who smelled like lavender and cloves to her, a mingling of scents which seemed not wholesome and sweet on this man, but sickly. She kissed his cheek, surprised by this aromatic information but unsure where it fit or what it meant.

"Congratulations!" she said and lightly patted his back.

Seated again, they solemnly raised their glasses. Clive went to the refrigerator for champagne - "Champers!" - and they toasted again.

The date was set. September.

There would be no bridesmaids. Ellen would like Madeline and a young Toronto niece to precede her up the aisle.

"I know why," said Pauline when they were in the Audi and on their way home. "She doesn't want anyone to look at another woman. Just her. That's Ellen."

"So?" Ellen would say. *"People like to be admired."*

Never mind that the bridesmaids had a symbolic role. Never mind that. This is my show and I mean to be the star. All eyes will be firmly on me.

A creature of her times, Ellen cared little (or would if she knew) that the wedding ceremony was not about her, that it was not created for the purpose of showboating. She and the groom wouldn't realize or care that they were meant to be "of" the ceremony, but that it was not about them. That the ceremony was for the village, for the community. Lacking the village or any connection to the truth of the tradition, they saw the wedding production as an occasion for self admiration and congratulation, for being on show. Didn't I look fabulous? Wasn't it beautiful?

"It's *my* day," the petulant bride will pout and wonder at the hollow feeling she is left with when the show is over. "Did you see the video?"

When the ceremony belonged, without question, to the community, people didn't know that they *knew* the purpose. But moderns didn't know that they didn't know. Thus, the wedding ceremony became strictly personal, another way to spotlight the magnificent separation of the self. And have you seen the Christmas celebration at *our* house?

"Don't tell Maddie, please," Pauline said to Richard. "It's too far away. She can't live that far ahead."

⌘ ⌘ ⌘

Her contract with Spilled Inc. was meant to end at the end of March. In the middle of the month Willi Ottler called her in to offer an extended contract. Another three months?

Pauline twirled a pen and watched Willi jerk open drawers in his desk, looking for the contract. Was that what they did now? Dangled contracts like carrots before the noses of workers? And yet, like many, it suited her. For now. She signed the contract and went back to her upholstered cubbyhole. There was still work to be done on the kitchen cabinet copy. Next they would be creating a catalogue and sales brochures for a sofa company.

"I'm peddling domesticity," she told Arthur.

They stood on the newly greening grass, admiring the enormous forsythia which had recently ignited in a fragile yellow fire in the Sheppard's front yard.

"I wanted to give you an armful of these things," he said. "I've even got some garden snipper things, I found in Doris' mud room. Secaturs, I think they're called."

He had cut himself a bundle of the yellow branches and set them on the hearth. He meant to paint them and was perfectly positioned at his window-front easel, to observe both the bush flowering on the greening lawn and the bouquet he'd set out in Doris' tall, pink art deco vase.

He was convinced that these branches - these sticks - with their little yellow blossoms, which ran like sunbeams up and down their twiggy brown-ness, had a sort of energy. There was some essence of spring there, which spoke to the soul, he thought.

The forsythia branches in front of the fireplace caused him to do a little comic double-take when he entered the room. They were so resolutely yellow, so insistent in their brave, thin, early-spring unfolding that he thought everyone's psyche - their very souls - would be helped by them. Tomorrow he would carry a large parcel of them to the community center, some for the gallery and some for the reception desk out front. The winter-weary would see them when they plodded past on their way to the final hours of some prosaic course they had signed up for in January's darkest hours. Joy!

"Just look at them!" he said and Pauline could not help but really look.

She put down her briefcase and looked closely. They were sublime. Just as Arthur said. Sunshine on a stick. Who knew?

They were the promise kept. Spring had returned, redemption was at hand. Halleluja.

⌘   ⌘   ⌘

Just before April Fool's Day surprised them all, the buyers of the Richmond factory announced that they could not let Richard go. They needed him to go to Tokyo. He must. It would be very pleasant! Just a few months. Please.

"Imagine!" said Daphne.

"Top cabin bunch," said Dick. "Top cabin."

⌘   ⌘   ⌘

At the airport, Madeline was cool and distant, watching Richard from behind a soft drink can. When he was gone, she flung herself against the door of the Toyota, flailing her arms and legs and weeping loudly. It was the first tantrum she had ever thrown and some part of Pauline watched in admiration, wishing that she too could rail and rant with her body, at the unfairness of things.

Her father, after all, was gone for good.

Eventually, they gathered themselves together in the parking arcade. Poor Madeline was spent and ruined from weeping and writhing, her flowered dress and the new, pale cardigan, creased and filthy.

Exhausted, Pauline hauled them both to a bench which had been bolted to the concrete wall of the car park and sat down on the cold cement, holding Madeline on her lap in the growing coolness of a late April evening, until it was dark.

Madeline fell asleep on the drive home, drawing shallow, little triple breaths which shuddered on her lips - the aftermath of the enormous storm which had blown her about, all tears, mucous and screams. Pauline could not bring herself to wake her from this deep and sorrowful sleep and so forced herself to haul the surprisingly heavy little body from the car in the back alley, through the back gate, along the concrete walk and up the stairs.

She balanced Madeline against one knee as she unlocked the kitchen door and they nearly collapsed into the dark room as the door swung in, startling the cat. She propped Madeline against the breakfast counter and kicked off her own shoes then staggered down the hall and up the carpeted stairs. The burden of the small body seemed to grow heavier and denser with each step. Finally, gently, she lowered Madeline onto the little white bed.

She took off the new patent dress shoes, carefully pulling the straps from the miniature buckles and then tugged gently at the sweaty white socks revealing the small, puffy feet which were red and injured-looking in the pink light of the little bedroom lamp. The new shoes had squeezed and pushed, pinching the toes. The fragile white bone that angled out at her arch was shockingly visible beneath the translucent tender skin and there was a pattern, an indentation in the still plump flesh where the skin had been bound in.

One at a time, Pauline raised the small feet to her lips and kissed them. They radiated a damp heat which rose up, mingling with the clean and innocent smell of baby sweat and the not-unpleasant scent of new leather shoes. She covered Madeline with the old baby quilt and turned off the little lamp.

Light shone in from Burrard Street and she could hear the cars passing. They moved through the lavender dark with the peculiar, nostalgic noise of traffic on a spring night

⌘　⌘　⌘

Arthur had begun to read library books about architecture, the histories of houses, the nature of domestic comfort and adornment. Decorating magazines caught his eye while he waited in line at the supermarket checkout and he turned to the homes section of the weekend paper with the eye of an anthropologist. He wondered if he was now trying to understand his work backwards, just as he had been trying to know Joan.

"They're called shelter magazines," he said, pointing to the stack of glossy monthlies on the little walnut step table. "*Shelter*. Isn't that wonderful?"

Pauline laughed. "You'll get addicted you know."

"I've thought of that," Arthur said. "My plan is to begin reading them at the library only. Not buying them. It's some curious twist of the human psyche that you can become addicted to the glossy pictures. Not even wanting to own the stuff *in* the pictures!"

"Well. What have you learned?"

"I've learned that I might want to build another house," he said. "Isn't that something?"

"For yourself, you mean," she said. "To live in?"

"I'm not even sure about that. Whether it would be for me to live in," he said. "I don't know."

They talked about Arthur's water colors and his work at the gallery and about Pauline's work.

"We're on to sofas now," she said. "Not literally. Although I have been out to the warehouse and flopped about on some of them. Test driving them." She laughed. "They are beautiful, though. Want me to get one for you wholesale?"

"Then Greg would have me committed," Arthur said with a rueful little smile.

They were light hearted. Bantering. Spring's returning warmth had loosened something. Even as the earth softened, so did their hearts. Although the April sky still shifted low and often gray, the blue came often enough and expanded the space above them so wide when it did, that the human heart could believe again that the sun was indeed always up there, behind the clouds.

They were drinking white wine, christening a pair of mismatched Venetian water goblets

"That's another good thing about spring," he said holding his glass toward the light of the brass lamp. "Garage sales on Saturday mornings."

"Here, here," said Pauline.

Madeline was at a sleep-over, her first. Pauline had delivered her to Kirsten's and upon returning to the empty house had asked the cat:

"Isn't this nice?"

But it wasn't. There was a peculiar volume to the house which felt like a long and ill fitting gown whose hem she kept trying to draw up and whose skirts seemed to droop and trail loosely about her. She couldn't fit into it or fill it up.

She had phoned Arthur.

"Arthur, you'll think I'm a pain, but do you feel like company? Or are you going out?"

⌘　⌘　⌘

"I can start using that as a wine bucket soon." He pointed with his foot toward the galvanized pail which he used for firewood. "Then I won't have to trot back and forth to the kitchen."

"You really have made this into your home." Pauline looked about her. "You've settled in and made it your own."

It was queer how little the room they sat in resembled the room it had been last spring when Doris and Edward were still there. The couches and end tables now slumbering in a storage place in Burnaby; the dull dining room table and the lamps; they might never have been here. And yet they would come back. Arthur was the temporary tenant. His things were in transit, settled here only temporarily and yet they were so very connected to him that they seemed always to have been here, in this room, set about in just this way.

The chairs, which still faced the fireplace, were occasionally moved about now that spring had come; pushed back a little to catch the sunlight which sometimes shone through the high dining room window; sometimes pulled nearer to the wooden easel at the broad living room window.

It was not that there was much furniture in the room. There was no sofa, only the chairs and the little step table on the worn rug and of course the stool and the easel at the window. But Arthur's desk and the cheap bookcases, just through the arch in the dining room, lent an air of permanence which reflected into the living room. The books and the papers, his small things tucked here and there. Pictures. The bottles of scotch and gin set out with glasses in a small wicker tray at the end of Doris' sideboard.

The pleasure of Arthur's life was manifest. Here was where he lived and moved and thought, where he carefully carried in his pail of firewood and made up small fires on the hearth.

Yet they were in transit.

Pauline and Richard had been tossing a light ball of discontent across the waves, via satellite telephone. He, in Asia, sent out the message that they must decide something. Soon they would have no real means of support. She caught the volley and lobbed it back with the agreement that this was true. The weight of this sphere ought to have pulled it from the ether somewhere over Hawaii, but seemed not to. This thing they were tossing back and forth remained hollow, like a ping pong ball landing with the lightest sound on either side of the Pacific before it was sent aloft again, bearing their unhappiness.

They should have a house, they should have real careers, they should be sailing neatly toward retirement, nearing the zenith of their grown-up years, readying for a comfortable downward ride of ease and merited western comfort. But all bets were off. They had missed a turn somewhere. They continued to hit the ball, volleying, resolving nothing.

"Have you eaten?" Arthur asked.

She set down her glass. Food seemed a very good idea. Her head had begun to ache from the wine.

"No. Let's walk down and have something at the little pizza place. What do you think?"

They gathered up their coats, which were light now. Unlined and easy to forget in the car or at the office now that the afternoons were warm, they were spring jackets, and picking them up, their very lightness, was a small cause for joy.

Pauline's navy wool blazer with the silver buttons was hunched on the newel post at the bottom of the stairs and Arthur's beige canvas golf jacket rested lightly on a hook inside the hall closet. It was easy to take them up and shrug into them and go out the door.

In the early dark, the chestnut trees shone, newly leafed and proud.

Her purse had softened since September. It fit more smoothly beneath her arm; the shoulder strap rode easily, cushioned on the shoulder pad of the blazer and her arm moved against it, polishing the leather as she walked. She felt it against her now as she had not through the winter when she had been insulated against it by the weight of her wool coat or by the slippery down-filled jacket she sometimes wore.

As she and Arthur went down the avenue she could feel its easy weight, the way it balanced at her side.

"Do you ever hear strange sounds in the street?" he asked, looking up into the trees.

"Sometimes."

⌘ ⌘ ⌘

CHAPTER TWENTY ONE

Madeline came first, a miniature bride wreathed in a white tulle gown which swung like a soft bell, billowing gently with each step. Below the hem, her movement revealed white kid leather shoes, smooth and delicate looking and tied up with velvet ribbons, like a ballerina's.

Behind her came Ellen's niece, a small duplicate copy, but with a shy, dark head bent intently over a bouquet of linen colored miniature roses which trembled against her sparrow chest.

Madeline sailed past looking straight ahead, bearing her bouquet at an awkward formal angle, elbows slightly bent, her wrists turned back so that the densely packed orb of flowers remained upright, their exquisite dermal purity, shining against the long white gown. She landed softly at the front of the church and turned to smile at Pauline, opening her mouth in a wide proud grin which displayed for all to see, the new black hole behind her pretty pink lips.

Tell her not to open her mouth, said Ellen when she learned of the lost tooth.

"Oh, for Christ's sake, Ellen," Pauline had said into the phone. "She's a little girl. They lose teeth. It's not a black eye."

So there she was, at the front of the church, smiling at Pauline and at Richard, temporarily returned from Japan once more and standing tall and resplendent in his bespoke suit from a Hong Kong tailor.

Richard's suit, perfectly cut and exquisitely fitted to his body which had settled somehow and grown plumper since his defection to Asia, was but one of the treasures he had been trying to use as a lure to draw Pauline back across the Pacific with him. The Japanese liked Richard and wanted him to stay.

But she would not succumb to this sartorial seduction. She was happy in Cedar Mills.

Arthur had built bookcases for her in the covered porch, fitting them snugly beneath the broad windows and trimming them with lengths of egg-and-dart carved molding. The old wooden kitchen table had become a spacious desk, its homely little drawer, former hiding place for childhood bread crusts, now held her pencils and pens and disks. Even with her computer and the angle arm lamp stationed in the center, there was plenty of room to spread out her notes and papers and books.

The faint scent of cedar moved through the room at night, when she worked at the computer or curled up on the little sofa to read.

"We have the house," she had told Richard. "It's ours. There are no strings."

Caroline had used her share of the proceeds from the sale of the mill to buy a townhouse near the water in New Westminster and Dee and her husband had paid off their mortgage. Pauline had the old house.

"You're running away, Pauline. You're hiding. It's ridiculous."

"No, Richard," she told him. "You are. You still need to impress your father and people like Clive Cherry and Ellen. It doesn't work. It can't. I don't want to do it. I won't."

Richard's fury at her refusal to follow him to Japan, was boundless.

But she had sailed through some sea and truly woken up. She had jettisoned her illusions about the provisional life that she and Richard had created; the perfectly acceptable life of on-goingness. Richard had told her that they could have more money, more things, more of the same in a different place and she had said no.

But she had said yes to herself. Yes, to answering the call of a deeper self, the one who simply would not shut up. Yes, to the self who said no, when Willi Ottler offered her a full-time position in the airless, downtown tower. She had packed up her briefcase, taken her purse - and left the building.

And she had said yes to casting out the net which might haul in the mystery of her life. She had indeed gone back to the place where she began and was learning to know it for the first time.

But the house was not the same place in which she had grown up. Grace had picked up her skirts, gone out and delicately shut the door on the old house. When she moved out, taking the boxes of photos and selling off the old furniture, the house became a canvas on which Pauline might paint the picture of the rest of her life.

But she was creating a home to which Richard might return when he had grown tired of his new suits and the expense account car. Tired of the foreign country to which he thought he had truly journeyed, but had not.

"I'll be here," she had told him.

And so she sat at the old table with her computer, her angled lamp and her small bits of stuff and at her back were the bookcases which Arthur built for her. Over the summer he had polished and sanded them, imagining the things that Pauline would place in them as the years went by; the books and the rocks and the plants. The collections of unimportant things.

She had begun to write articles for Our House, one of the shelter magazines which called out to Arthur and which one day, she had turned to, thinking, "I'll write about Burkeville." And, with the help of Arthur's notes, she did. And then she wrote about FarmGate. More assignments had followed and she had found, it seemed, her work.

Less glossy than some but not a learned journal, Our House aimed to cause people to think about their homes not as places to store the stuff they had gathered in that outward journey, but as places in which to create a self.

⌘ ⌘ ⌘

Clive waited at the altar and when the organist began the fateful music which would bear his glamorous bride toward him, Pauline saw him shoot the cuff of his brilliant shirt from beneath the white jacket, showing for just a shining moment, his beautiful watch; thin, elegant and expensive. She was sure she saw him check the time, but perhaps it was only nerves.

Gap-toothed and pleased, Madeline watched Ellen bear down on them in a gleaming, narrow tube of dense, ivory satin.

Across the street from the old church, on the other side of the park, out in the paved alleyway behind the quartet of duplexes on fourteenth avenue, Arthur watched the movers load the desk, the Ikea book cases, his rustic easel and his bedroom furniture.

Boxes lay piled all about in the hot September light. His rug, rolled into a tube and bound up with the nylon twine from Doris' mudroom cupboards, lay incongruously on the pavement. The movers would heave it in last; the beautiful muted island that had borne the wing chair and the club chair across the arc of the year.

The chairs too, were out in the alley, their cushions up-ended and untidy looking, their threads and the small wounds of their lives illuminated by the sharpness of the autumn light.

⌘ ⌘ ⌘

"Ladies and gentlemen," said the minister. "I give you Mr. and Mrs. Cherry."

⌘ ⌘ ⌘

In the curious moments of milling about near the church steps which happened after weddings, while the guests digested what they had just witnessed; when the men checked their watches to see if it was too early to head to the country club or the reception hall and the women admired each other's hats and touched the bridesmaid's gowns - in those few minutes out of time, Pauline stood with her back to the crowd, her hand vizored across her brow to deflect the late afternoon sunlight, and stared hard across Burrard Street like a sailor searching the horizon.

There finally, was Arthur. She watched as he walked around the moving van, pausing to bend over a box and then to absently lift the cushion of the club chair. He walked to the side of the truck and stopped near the rolled carpet, looking down. Using the toe of his walking shoe he lifted the end of the rug and let it drop. Then, hands in pockets, just as though he was simply looking around, he turned and looked out across the flat park. At her.

There was nothing left to do.

The week before he had ridden out on the express bus, carrying the black and gold lamp packed in a cardboard box and protected by wads of Doris' plastic bags that he had balled up and tucked around it as makeshift packing material. After dinner they had washed the dishes together at Grace's window and then, when Madeline had been tucked up in the white bed in Pauline's old room, they had simply sat for a time, once more drinking coffee beneath the light of the beautiful lamp.

When the taxi came to take him to the express bus, Pauline walked him to the back door. She held on tight and Arthur said, "I'll build you a house one day."

She kissed his cheek. "You already have."

THE END

⌘ ⌘ ⌘